"Are you h

"Just shaken
Just called th

"Good. Do you want me to look inside for you?"

"That's why I called you over here, isn't it?" she snapped. "I hope you didn't think I was just scared and wanted your lovely company."

Her brisk attitude rocked him back on the heels of his cowboy boots and he held up his palms as if speaking to a spooked horse. "No. Definitely didn't think that."

She squeezed her eyes shut, and when she opened them again, she finally met his stare head-on. "I'm sorry. That was uncalled for. I didn't know what else to do after I called the authorities. I figured..." A hint of desperation clung to her voice as it trailed off.

"You figured you'd call someone close by who owns a security company who might be able to help." He finished the sentence for her in a way that wouldn't ding her pride. Wouldn't let her know he understood she'd been desperate enough to reach out to him.

Dear Reader,

I decided to take a trip down memory lane the other day. When I look back at what the past few years have brought to me and my career, I'm astounded by all the changes. I realized the thing that led to so many wonderful turns, twists and forward momentum was my choice in saying yes to things that scare me. Yes to speaking in front of crowds. Yes to meeting new people. Yes to putting my introverted self out for the world to see.

I'm so happy, that once again, I said yes to something new and a little bit scary. For the very first time, I said yes to writing a romance novel set in the American West. I love to read Westerns but never thought about writing one. When the opportunity came around, I said, "Sure, why not?"

Because of that, I created a new world set in the fictional town of Cloud Valley, Wyoming. A world with handsome cowboys, tough-as-nails women and beautiful scenery. I had so much fun creating these dueling ranchers whose love of their land rivals the fierce love they find in each other.

I hope you enjoy Madden and Lily's story, and you find something to say yes to today.

With all my love,

Danielle M. Haas

WYOMING BODYGUARD

DANIELLE M. HAAS

ROMANTIC SUSPENSE

ISBN-13: 978-1-335-47154-3

Wyoming Bodyguard

Copyright © 2025 by Danielle M. Haas

For questions and comments about the quality of this book, please contact us at CustomerService@Harlequin.com.

TM and ® are trademarks of Harlequin Enterprises ULC.

 Harlequin Enterprises ULC
22 Adelaide St. West, 41st Floor
Toronto, Ontario M5H 4E3, Canada
www.Harlequin.com

Printed in Lithuania

Recycling programs for this product may not exist in your area.

MIX
Paper | Supporting responsible forestry
FSC® C021394

Danielle M. Haas resides in Ohio with her husband and two children. She earned a BA in political science many moons ago from Bowling Green State University but thought staying home with her two children and writing romance novels would be more fun than pursuing a career in politics. She spends her days chasing her kids around, loving up her dog and trying to find a spare minute to write about her favorite thing: love.

Books by Danielle M. Haas

Harlequin Romantic Suspense

Sunrise Security

Wyoming Bodyguard

Matched with Murder
Booked to Kill
Driven to Kill

Visit the Author Profile page at Harlequin.com.

To my husband, Scott Haas.
Thanks for always supporting and encouraging me.
You're the reason I know I can always move
whatever mountain is placed in front of me.

Chapter 1

Madden McKay scrubbed a palm over the scruff along his jawline and studied the information on his computer screen. The numbers made his head hurt, but he couldn't look away. Not until he figured out how to stretch the limited amount to pay the bills at Sunrise Security for another month.

An impossible feat if he couldn't drum up more work.

Pushing away from his cluttered desk, he blinked the barrage of rows and columns from his brain and stared out the lone window in his office. His view of Main Street showcased a cluster of mom-and-pop shops with colorful awnings stretched onto the sidewalk and hand-painted murals celebrating the town of Cloud Valley, Wyoming, on the storefront windows.

But it was the mountains in the distance that called to him. That made his blood hum, and he wished he could shut off the damn computer and enjoy the land that was a part of his soul.

Sighing, he pinched his nose and refocused on the computer screen. Working outside on the ranch where he grew up, the mountains his constant backdrop, wasn't an option anymore so no use daydreaming about what might have been. Especially when he had a struggling security business he needed to save.

Sunrise Security had given him purpose when he'd returned from The US Marine Corps a few years before, broken and with no direction. He couldn't let the business fail—couldn't let down his partner, Reid Sommers, who'd stood beside him month after month to make this new dream a reality.

A sharp knock on his open door lifted his head.

Reid stood in the doorway, arms crossed over his chest and concern in his narrowed gaze. His gray T-shirt matched the color of the walls. "How ya doing, boss?"

Madden rolled his eyes. "I told you not to call me that. We're partners. Evenly split in this whole mess." He picked up the pile of unpaid bills then let them fall back down.

Reid shrugged then crossed the room to sit in the single black bucket chair in front of the desk. "Not from where I sit. You've got a lot more to lose—a lot more invested."

"And most of the reason for our financial issues is my fault."

"Dude, you've poured your blood, sweat and tears into this place. Things will turn around. We've gotten a few more clients this past month."

Madden huffed out a frustrated breath. "Yeah, two ranchers who want us to install cameras on their property to catch cattle rustlers. We need more consistent work. Higher paying jobs. People in this town don't trust me to protect them—protect their property—and my bad reputation is taking you down with me."

Reid ran a hand thought his shaggy brown hair then leaned forward, resting his forearms on his knees. "We both knew it'd take time. We knew people here would hold some resentment after your father sold a parcel of land from McKay Ranch to developers. But maybe if people understood why he sold part of the land they'd be a little more forgiving."

"Not gonna happen." No one except him and his dad knew the full reason his dad had to off-load a big chunk of the ranch. Neither of them wanted those reasons to be public knowledge.

Reid frowned but nodded. "That's your choice and I respect it. But the fact remains, something's got to give."

Madden sighed and leaned back in his chair. "Whether folks around these parts like me or not, I know them. They're stubborn as hell, and in their eyes, selling family land to out-of-towners is an unforgivable sin. No matter the reason."

"You knew that before we decided to set up shop here. You were confident you could change minds. That you could show you care about Cloud Valley and what happens here—that you want to protect the folks you've known your whole life. We can still make that happen. We just have to figure out how."

Listening to Reid speak reminded him of his reason behind returning to his hometown despite the dirty looks and snide remarks. He had something to prove not only for himself, but for his dad and brother as well.

With a surge of determination, Madden rose to his feet and swiped his black cowboy hat from the coatrack shoved in the corner. "You're right, and moping around locked up in my office isn't going to help a damn thing. We need to show everyone we're a part of this community, and we ain't going anywhere."

Reid clapped his hands then rubbed them together before standing. "Hell yeah. That's what I've been waiting to hear. My boy's got some fight back in him. What's the plan?"

A quick glance at the clock ticking away on the wall showed him it was lunchtime. "We're heading to Tilly's Bar and Grill."

"Not sure what you plan to do at Tilly's to help drum up more work, but I'm down for a burger and fries."

"We're buying more than that today my friend." Madden slapped a hand on Reid's shoulder then strolled down the narrow hallway, which spilled out to the lobby.

Reid dipped into his own office, situated directly across from Madden's, then appeared with a tan cowboy hat covering his mop of hair.

Peggy Reynolds, the receptionist Madden had mostly inherited with the rental space, ate her packed lunch at the sitting area in the middle of the room. She'd laid her plastic containers on the coffee table in front of her, balancing a peeled clementine on her knee while reading one of the magazines usually splayed where her lunch now rested.

"Where are you boys off to? Got a hot new assignment?" Peggy popped off a wedge of her clementine and slid it into her mouth, smearing a bit of the pink lipstick that always painted her lips. She wore her gray hair straight and to her shoulders, her bifocals on the top of her head keeping the locks from spilling on her lightly wrinkled face.

"It's May in Wyoming," Madden said. "Everything we do is hot."

Peggy flicked a finger toward her desk, situated where it was the first thing a customer saw when they walked in the door. "Madden, Dax called and left a message. Not sure why that boy refuses to just call your cell, but so be it. I left the note by the phone."

"Thanks, Peg."

Irritated, he stalked past the potted Ficus and skirted around the metal filing cabinets beside Peggy's workstation. Her messy handwriting scrawled across a bright blue sticky note. "Pops wants you to come by for dinner tonight."

He fisted the note and tossed it into the trash can tucked under the desk. He'd call his dad later. A home-cooked meal was tempting enough to have him stop by the ranch after work, but the fact that Dax wouldn't just call him directly chapped his ass.

At some point, they had to bury the hatchet.

"We're heading to Tilly's," Reid said. "Madden's got a plan to win some good favor."

Peggy arched her brow, deepening the wrinkles along her forehead. "Is that so?"

Reid aimed a bright smile at Peggy. "Sure is. Want to join us?"

"Nah, you boys have fun. I've got plenty to keep me busy around here." She flipped the next page of a home decorating magazine, her sign the conversation was over.

"Things are pretty slow today," Madden said. "Why don't we all knock off early?"

"You don't have to tell me twice," Peggy said.

Madden couldn't help but grin at Reid then tilted his chin toward the front door. His grin widened at the golden letters scrawled across the glass. Money might be limited, business slow, but having something he created tightened his chest in a way nothing else ever had.

Not even the McKay Ranch.

Because Sunrise Security was *his* baby. His lifeline after an injury overseas stole the future he'd been raised for.

Madden stepped outside, and a wall of heat pulled him back to the moment. He filled his lungs with hot, dry air before turning toward Tilly's.

Reid fell into step beside him. "No matter how much time I spend here, I'll never get over how pretty this place is. The mountains looming on the horizon, the wide-open space on the other side of this charming ass town and the local women aren't bad to look at either." He dipped his chin in the opposite direction.

Madden followed Reid's eyeline and grimaced.

Lily Tremont walked along the sidewalk arm and arm with her father. Her hair was the color of unharvested wheat and tumbled down her back. It framed high cheekbones and sun-kissed skin. Her long legs matched the length of her dad's, and her sleeveless shirt showed off toned arms.

A part of him wanted to encourage his best friend to take a shot at the woman he'd known his whole life—their families' ranches side by side. But he wouldn't wish her icy demeaner on anyone.

"You don't want to bark up that tree, my friend. Trust me." Madden watched her disappear into Tilly's and bit back a groan. Walking into the tavern with her as a witness set him on edge.

"You sure? She's always friendly when I see her around town. Couldn't hurt to say hello."

The smirk lifting a corner of Reid's mouth told Madden his buddy had more in mind than a quick hello. Madden kicked a cluster of pebbles on the ground and a cloud of dust covered his cowboy boots. He shoved his hands in his pockets, aiming a tight smile at a duo of women who slid past them on their way to Cloud 9 Café. The smell of coffee permeated the air as they passed.

"Even before I enlisted, her nose was too high in the air to notice anything beyond herself."

A quick glance showed no traffic coming from either direction. He jogged to the other side of the street. Sweat dotted his hairline that had nothing to do with the blistering heat.

Reaching the old, weathered door, he pulled it open and stepped inside. The dark paneled walls and scarred floors swallowed the natural light. Neon signs buzzed, showcasing drinks offered at the bar. Square tables cluttered the interior of the room with booths lining one wall, interrupted by a stone hearth and giant fireplace.

Reid swept off his hat and led the way to the long bar stretched along the back wall. Madden followed, sandwiching his hat in his hands.

Chairs scraped against the floor as people swiveled to watch him walk through the lunch crowd. He met every gaze, lifting his lips at the side and nodding in greeting.

He approached Lily's table on the way to the bar. She narrowed her hard, blue eyes, her pouty red lips pressed in a tight line.

He widened his grin and shot her a quick wink. He might never win over Lily Tremont, but he wouldn't let her get under his skin. Wouldn't let her derail him from his mission, not today.

Because today was the first step in winning over his town and setting his business on the right path.

Reid made a beeline for two empty stools.

Madden settled beside him, greeting the middle-aged man to his left.

Eve Tilly, owner of the bar and grill, hurried out of the kitchen balancing four plates on a round tray. Her auburn hair was pulled back in a high ponytail, and her hazel eyes were friendly yet focused.

She acknowledged Madden with a nod then weaved through the tables to deliver the orders. She deposited the meals then approached him and Reid with a wide smile. "Afternoon. Don't see you much this time of day. You usually stop in when the place is empty, not busting at the seams. Must be hungry."

"More like thirsty," Reid said, snagging a menu and flipping it open.

Eve chuckled and fisted a hand on her hip. "Most people here are."

"Glad to hear it. I want to buy a round." Madden plucked his wallet from the back pocket of his jeans and tossed it on the bar.

"Seriously? During the lunch rush?" Eve bounced her gaze from Madden to Reid and back again.

"It's all part of the plan, darling." Reid slapped a hand on Madden's back. "After you get those drinks passed out, we'll take some food. But we don't want to overwhelm you. We can wait to make that order."

"Okay." Eve shook her head and huffed out a small laugh. "Hope you boys know what you're doing. No bulk discounts in my place."

Thankful he still had at least one friend in town, Madden lifted his palms, eyes wide. "Wouldn't dream of asking for one."

"Here we go," Eve said, letting out a long breath. She took three short steps to a triangle hanging from the ceiling and grabbed the metal stick she used to make the instrument sing. She banged the stick against the three sides of the triangle, the tinkling sound cutting into the noisy room and quieting everyone who understood the significance of the call. "All right ladies and gentlemen. Round on Madden McKay. Figure out what you want to drink and be quick about it."

A whoop of excitement and gratitude exploded, lifting Madden's spirits along with the cold beer Eve had slid into his hand.

Maybe this would work. Little by little, people would stop seeing him as the villain and start welcoming him—and his business—back into their folds.

The sun might have set on one dream years ago when his dad had been forced to sell their land, but it had risen on another.

And come hell or high water, he'd do whatever he could to keep this dream alive.

Whatever he could to make Sunrise Security a success.

Chapter 2

Disgust slid down Lily's throat along with her ice-cold cola. No way she'd pander to Madden McKay's sleazy attempts to redeem himself. Around these parts, selling the family land was practically a crime.

And when selling that land brought in developers who didn't respect traditions, it pissed off a lot of locals.

Her dad, Kevin Tremont, clicked his tongue before finishing the whiskey in his glass. "That boy's got a lot to learn if he thinks buying a few beers at the bar will make everyone forget what his family did. Damn shame."

She allowed herself one more look at the cocky cowboy before turning away and spearing the last tomato from her mostly eaten salad. She hated that she let Madden get to her—that the swirl of green in his smoky eyes had sucked her in for even one second before her wall went right back up. "Madden's always been the guy who thinks he can get away with murder. People always fell for his charm, even in high school."

Kevin leaned forward, his hefty middle smooshing against the side of the table, and patted her hand. "Glad my girl had enough sense to see through the bullshit. Those McKays can't be trusted. Ever."

Offering a weak smile, she finished her meal and wiped

her lips with a napkin. Madden and his family were responsible for bringing trouble to their doorstep, but now it was up to her to find a solution. It's been weeks since they'd had a guest stay at Tremont Ranch, and soon they wouldn't be able to afford to keep their doors open. "You're right to have warned me about Madden and his pa since I was a teenager. They've left us all hurting, and we really need to figure out how to stop the financial bleeding. We can't compete with that new hotel. They offer too many of the same amenities we do at half the price. I think we need to—"

Kevin picked up the bill the waitress had dropped off a few minutes before. "Don't you worry about all that. I've got a handle on things. Now be a dear and head on up to pay. I need to run to the restroom before we leave."

Lily tightened her jaw, plucked the bill from between her dad's fingers and sprang to her feet. Irritated, she skirted the cluster of tables as she made her way to the bar, where the old-fashioned cash register stood.

Eve Tilly wiped down the bar with a white rag and held up a finger before disappearing into the kitchen.

Sighing, Lily leaned against the scarred wood and counted enough cash to cover her tab and leave a nice tip.

"Hello, there, Ms. Tremont."

The unfamiliar voice had her turning toward the duo sitting at the bar. Madden's business partner smiled at her. She raised one eyebrow, waiting for the man with the quiet brown eyes and clean-shaven face to say more.

"Uh, I'm Reid Sommers, ma'am. We've met in passing a time or two." He extended a hand, his gaze fixed on her.

Madden snorted out a laugh. "Dude, I told you not to bother."

Refusing to acknowledge Madden, she finally fit her

palm in Reid's and gave a little shake before pulling away. "I remember. It's nice to see you again."

Reid's smile grew. "I noticed you didn't let us buy you a drink. Can we change that now?"

"No, thanks. My father and I have work to get back to. At our ranch. You know, the one that's been in our family for generations." She couldn't help aiming the cutting remark right where she knew it'd hurt Madden most.

His pride.

The sudden stiffening of Madden's shoulders gave her a tingle of satisfaction. The sting of the McKay Ranch being sold off might fade in some people's mind but never hers. The impact had caused a major hit in revenue for her own family. The developers had swept in and destroyed all the natural beauty, choosing instead to provide an almost theme park–styled destination for naive tourists.

Tourists who'd never understand what Wyoming was really all about. Camping under the stars, dinner cooked over the fire, or a magical horse ride through wooded trails with mountains their constant companion. All things Tremont Ranch offered.

All things slipping through her fingertips as her dude ranch's vacancies grew higher and higher.

Eve rushed back to the bar balancing two plates and placed them in front of customers before returning to the cash register. "Sorry about the wait, Lily. You know how it gets at lunch."

"No problem at all," Lily said, and handed over the cash. "Can you give the rest of that to Nellie?"

"Sure thing."

"Thanks. Have a great rest of your day." She aimed her most demure smile at Reid then met her dad at the front of the restaurant.

"Making friends?" Kevin asked as he pushed open the door, letting in the blinding sunlight.

She huffed out a humorless laugh then slid her sunglasses from the top of her head to cover her eyes. "Hardly."

Reid seemed harmless, but no way she'd let her guard down enough around him to learn more than what she already knew—he was Madden's partner, which meant she'd stay far away.

The door closed behind her, and she strolled beside her dad toward her truck. "Enough about Madden McKay. I wanted to have a nice meal with you and forget about our worries for a while. Not get bent out of shape about a man who doesn't matter."

"Honey, don't let anything get you all fired up. The ranch will be fine. I'll see to it. You just keep doing what you're doing—making sure things run smoothly. I've got the rest covered."

Her stomach dropped, and she swallowed the words she knew wouldn't matter a lick. At least not to her father, who never trusted her enough to really let her in on what was happening at the ranch.

But she wasn't an idiot. She didn't need to have access to their financial records to understand that Tremont Ranch was in trouble. She feared if something drastic didn't change, they'd be yet another casualty in the war waging between family ranches and hotshot developers looking to exploit the land for a quick buck.

The lone traffic light in town changed from red to green and a black truck shot forward, tires squealing as the tinted window rolled down. A ray of sunlight bounced off something sticking out of the passenger-side window.

Time slowed. Fear made her knees weak and her heart pound in her ears. Lily's father shoved her to the ground as the deafening sound of gunshots exploded into the afternoon.

Squeezing her eyes shut, she threw her hands over the back of her head. Pebbles dug into her forearms. Panicked screams filtered through the haze of confusion engulfing her. An engine roared, then an eerie silence settled into the air. Shaking, she opened her eyes and a different terror flooded through her system like a burst dam.

Her father lay sprawled on the ground, eyes closed, blood staining the sidewalk beneath him.

Scurrying to his side, she reached for his hand and screamed.

Madden tightened his grip on his glass before downing the rest of the cool, amber liquid. The bitter taste coated his tongue, matching the feelings simmering in his gut.

"She seemed nice enough to me," Reid said, picking up his beer and taking a sip then setting it back on the bar.

Eve chuckled. "If you're talking about Lily, she is nice. To everyone except Madden. Been that way a long time. Must stick in your craw she still won't swoon over you like all the girls used to."

Reid bumped his shoulder against Madden's. "Swoon, huh? I'd like to hear those stories sometime."

A blush stained Eve's cheeks, matching the color of her auburn hair. "Anytime, cowboy."

"Don't encourage him." Madden stretched to his feet and swiped his hat from the bar.

Bang!

The all-too-familiar sound of gunfire blasted through the bar, followed by the shattering of glass and shrieks of fear.

Bang! Bang!

Two more shots.

Madden's gut tightened, and he whirled toward the broken window, catching a glimpse of a black truck speeding around the corner. Harsh light streamed inside. Customers fell to the floor while outside people ran for cover.

And one piercing scream raised the hairs on the back of his neck.

Instinct kicking in, Madden sprinted toward the door and rushed outside. "Someone call 911. We need police here now."

"Police are on the way," someone yelled from behind him.

Lily sat on the sidewalk with her father's head cradled in her lap. Blood covered her hands and splattered her blue shirt. Tears streamed down her face, and the haunting scream that had drawn him outside continued to pour from her mouth.

"Lily. Lily, are you hurt?" Crouching beside her, he searched for signs of injury. "Lily!"

Her screams quieted and she blinked up at him. The fear in her eyes tore at his chest like talons. "He's shot. Dad's shot. There's so much blood."

Shock made her words choppy and faint, and her skin was almost as pale as the motionless man on the ground.

Madden wanted to reach for her, to comfort her any way he could, but he knew his touch wouldn't be welcomed. "Help's coming, okay?"

Hurried footsteps and panicked mumblings surrounded him, but he kept his focus on Lily.

Reid rushed to his side. "Truck's gone. People are scared, but sheriff's deputies are coming."

As if summoned by Reid's words, the sounds of a siren split the afternoon air. Neighbors and friends cluttered the sidewalk, concern drawing them to their own, one fallen and frail—another scared and paralyzed with fear.

Madden rose and turned his head to speak to Reid so no one else could hear. "Try to steer everyone away from Lily and her dad. Paramedics will need some space, but the deputies will also want to talk to anyone who saw the shooting."

Eve picked her way through broken glass and inhaled a shaky breath. "People can come inside Tilly's. It's a mess, but at least they can get out of the heat."

"Thanks, Eve. That's a great plan. I'll stay with Lily." He glanced down at the woman who drove him crazy, but her attention was locked on her father.

"I'll help you," Reid said to Eve.

Madden stood guard beside Lily while Reid and Eve ushered frightened witnesses into the bar. His body was rigid, nerves stretched tight, as the sirens wailed louder and louder. A deputy's cruiser finally arrived, followed by an ambulance.

Deputy Sanders, a seasoned officer who still played poker with Madden's dad once a week, climbed out of his patrol car and made a beeline for Madden. A quick glance down at Mr. Tremont tightened his jaw, and he snapped his fingers high in the air. "Medical help here now," he shouted toward the EMTs. "Gunshot victim."

Lily stayed frozen, tears continuing their twin tracks down her puffy face.

"Anyone else hurt?" Sanders asked Madden.

"Doesn't look like it."

Two paramedics jogged to the sidewalk, wheeling a gurney with medical equipment piled high. A middle-aged woman and younger man knelt beside Lily and her father, their hands moving between the injured man and the medical supplies they needed to help him.

"Ma'am," the woman with serious, hazel eyes and a tight frown said to Lily, "if you aren't hurt, I need you to move."

Lily shook her head. "I can't leave him. I'm all he has."

"We'll do everything we can to help him, but you have to step back and give us space."

Lily opened her mouth, but no words came out.

Madden understood her shock, her terror and distress. Witnessing someone you loved fighting for their life made it hard for the mind to move forward. To react.

Gently placing a hand on her shoulder, he crouched again beside her. "Lily, I know it's hard, but you need to let them do their job."

Her watery eyes locked on his and she nodded.

He hooked an arm around her waist and helped her to her feet. The feel of her body so close to his sent a shock wave through his system.

She leaned against him as if unable to stand on her own, her focus now fixed on the EMTs who loaded Mr. Tremont onto the gurney and rushed him into the back of the ambulance. "I want to go with him." Her breath hitched with each word.

The back door slammed shut, and the woman jogged to the front of the vehicle. "Meet us at the county hospital. We'll take good care of him. I promise."

Lily lunged forward as the woman jumped into the ambulance and took off down the road. "No!" she screamed. "I need my dad. He shouldn't be alone."

Keeping his arm firmly in place around her waist, Madden kept her from spilling onto the road. "He's not alone. I promise."

Her body trembled and she faced him, eyes swollen and

filled with grief. A sob shook her shoulders and she collapsed against him.

Madden held her tight and met Deputy Sanders's eyes above her head. "I'll drive her to the hospital. Reid and Eve have the witnesses inside Tilly's. Come find me for my statement, but there's not much to tell."

"I'm gonna need Ms. Tremont's statement, too. I'll swing by and see you both once I'm done here."

Madden nodded, grateful the old man wouldn't push Lily to talk right now.

"Okay," he said, steering her in the direction of his truck parked down the road. "We're going to go see your dad now. I'm going to drive you. Is that all right?"

Walking beside him, she reached for his hand and squeezed.

That was enough of an answer for him. He stood steady beside her, keeping her upright and stable, and helped her climb into his truck. He shut the door and ran around the front fender to the driver's side. He cast her one quick glance and his heart crumbled.

Throwing the truck into Drive, he shot off toward the hospital, reached for her hand and sent off a quick prayer that her father wouldn't die.

Chapter 3

Time crawled by slow as molasses while Lily sat in the waiting room, anxious for news about her father's condition. She shifted in a hard chair, clasping her hands in her lap and staring at the double doors that only medical staff could enter.

He was back there. In surgery. Fighting for his life.

Tears hovered at the corners of her eyes, but she kept them from falling. She couldn't fall apart again. Her dad needed her to be strong, because once he pulled through surgery—which he had to—she needed to be there for him. To help him regain his strength and put this entire mess in the rearview mirror.

The smell of old coffee and disinfectant turned her stomach. A few people loitered in the room, huddled in seats or propped against the wall waiting for their family or friends. But she couldn't get past her anxiety to focus on the other folks around her.

The doors leading outside whooshed open and let in a huff of hot air. The sound of heavy boots pricked her ears, and she found herself staring at Deputy Sanders. He offered a tired, sympathetic smile that made his full cheeks impossibly rounder.

Madden returned, a cup of coffee in his hands. "Did you find the shooter?"

She bounced her gaze from one man to the other and fought the haze of fear that hadn't left since she'd seen the gun in the truck window.

Deputy Sanders swept his cowboy hat from his head and settled into the chair beside her. "Sorry, but no. None of the witnesses were able to provide much. Lily, I know it's a tough time right now, but can you tell me what you remember?"

Drawing in a shuddering breath, she steeled her nerves as much as possible. "Dad and I walked outside after we finished our lunch. The traffic light changed, so we stopped, and a truck charged forward."

"Did you see what color the truck was? Make or model? License plate number?" Deputy Sanders asked.

"Um, black. Tinted windows. I can't remember any other details. The window lowered, and I saw a gun seconds before my dad shoved me to the ground. Then the gunshots rang out." Emotion lodged in her throat. She rubbed her fingers over the base of her neck as if to dislodge the building pressure, to breathe easier.

But nothing helped. Nothing stopped the screams echoing in her mind or the image of her father motionless and so damn pale on the sidewalk.

The lump in her throat grew. Her breath hitched higher until her lungs refused to take in more air. She squeezed her clasped hands tighter as her vision wobbled and the buzzing of the overhead lights morphed into panicked cries.

Madden appeared in front of her and gently placed his hands on top of hers. "Lily, you're safe. Take a few minutes. Look at me, okay? Focus on me while you catch your breath. Just inhale slowly then let it out."

She stared at the green in his eyes and mimicked his actions. She pulled in a large, steady breath through her nose then blew it back into the air. Her muscles relaxed. Her hands unclenched. The feel of his rough palms on her knuckles grounded her, centered her.

"You've got this," Madden whispered. "Take all the time you need."

She took a few more seconds to calm the frantic beat of her heart before continuing. "Dad pushed me out of the way. I was so scared, so confused, and when I finally looked around, I saw him on the ground. I started screaming. The rest is a little murky."

Deputy Sanders cleared his throat. "What about you, Madden?"

Madden stayed crouched in front of Lily with his hands wrapped around hers, but he shifted his attention to the deputy. "I was in Tilly's with Reid and Eve. I heard gunshots then the window shattered. I heard Lily screaming, people yelling. I ran outside and found Lily and Mr. Tremont. I stayed with them until you came."

"And the truck?"

"Already gone by the time I made it outside. I did notice a flash of black when it sped around the corner, but that's about it."

Deputy Sanders nodded. "Most everyone has the same story. Lily, is there anyone you know who'd want to hurt your father?"

She reared back her head as if slapped. "Are you serious?"

He nodded.

"Sir, you know my dad. He's never hurt a fly—never would. He doesn't have trouble with anyone. This has to be one of those freak accidents. Another random shooting where we were at the wrong place at the wrong time." Her voice caught as the whole horrible event played on repeat again in her mind.

"You may be right." On a heavy sigh, Deputy Sanders pushed to his feet. "I wish your dad luck, and if there's anything else you remember, give me a call."

Unable to speak, she nodded.

"You okay to get yourself home tonight?" the deputy asked.

"My truck's still in town, but it doesn't matter. I'll be here with Dad. He won't want to be alone."

"You'll need to get some rest," Madden said. "Not to mention a change of clothes. Toiletries. Once you're ready, I can drive you home to grab some things for both you and your dad. He'll probably want some personal items as well."

Madden might be right, but she'd have to be peeled off this chair and carted away before willingly leaving her father.

A wave of exhaustion slapped her on the face, and she leaned back in her chair. "My mind can't even go to what happens next. Right now, I just need to think about this surgery and Dad surviving."

"No problem. We'll wait and when you're ready, we'll figure it out."

"You're still a good kid, Madden," Deputy Sanders said. "Thanks for sticking with Lily through all this."

A sudden jolt of realization struck Lily like a bolt of lightning. Madden wasn't supporting her out of the goodness of his heart. He was using her tragedy as his next stop on the campaign trail to make himself look good.

Yanking back her hands, she jutted her chin and pressed her lips in a firm line. "I don't need Madden to sit with me.

I'm fine on my own, and when the time comes that I need to go home, I'll figure it out. Now if you'll excuse me."

She jumped to her feet so fast, Madden almost fell to the floor before righting himself and standing, a frown turning down his full lips.

She ignored the hurt in his eyes and confusion from the deputy, but she couldn't quite ignore the feeling of loneliness as she walked away, leaving behind the man who'd brought her nothing but comfort in one of the hardest times of her life.

But that comfort was an act. A farce. A way to manipulate people into forgetting the sins of his family. And no matter how she yearned for the sturdy touch of his hand, she refused to be used.

Especially by Madden McKay.

Anger boiled in Madden's gut as he stormed out of the hospital and drove to his father's ranch. He blasted the air conditioner, but the cold temperature did nothing to cool him. Damn it, he'd spent hours by Lily's side, supporting and comforting her while she waited in fear for news of her father. Her sudden change of attitude gave him whiplash.

Whatever. Not his problem. He'd acted out of kindness and compassion. An impulse to jump into a horrible situation and actually help. If she didn't want him around, fine. He'd leave her to worry alone in her bloodstained shirt.

A pang of guilt battled through the anger. People lashed out when they were scared, and Lily had every reason to be upset right now. Maybe he should have stayed. Even if only in his truck so he was nearby if she needed something.

Tightening his grip on the steering wheel, he ignored the sudden impulse to head back to the hospital and instead drove under the dirty, white letters announcing he'd arrived at McKay Ranch. He parked next to his brother's old, dusty truck in front of the ancient barn that was now used for storage. Overgrown grass filled the pasture beside the barn, the split-railed fence caging in nothing but dirt and weeds.

Madden blew out a long breath and tried to shut off all thoughts of Lily as he hopped out of the truck and climbed the familiar wooden steps of the wraparound porch. The chipped, white paint matched the two-story farmhouse where he'd been raised. A sprinkling of wildflowers clustered at the base of the house, but the home-made window boxes his mom used to always fill with vibrant blooms were empty.

Since Mama's death years before, no one had the heart to fill them.

His dad, Walter McKay, sat in one of two rocking chairs, baggy overalls covering his slim frame, his ever-present pipe in his hand. "Heard you had one hell of a day."

"One of the worst," he said, settling into the chair beside his dad. The sun hovered above the mountains in the distance and sent bursts of orange through the darkening sky.

He'd spent countless evenings rocking on this porch, staring at the sunset or watching the clouds. Sitting next to his old man, discussing his problems. It'd been a long time since he needed one of those chats, but after the day he'd had, nothing could soothe him like this.

"Dax is inside. He can grab you a beer. Might help calm your nerves."

"Maybe in a bit." Madden removed his cowboy hat and rested it in his lap. "I need a minute."

"How's Kevin doin'?" Walter asked with his gaze fixed on the horizon. "He might not be my favorite person, but he didn't deserve to be shot down in the street like a rabid dog."

"He was still in surgery when I left."

Walter turned hard, gray eyes on him. "What about his girl? You leave her there alone?"

So much for not thinking about Lily any more today.

He rubbed the back of his neck. "She told me to leave."

"And you listened? That's gotta be a first. Hope someone was there with her. No one should be alone when waiting to find out if a loved one will live or die." Walter returned his attention to the cloudless sky.

Madden winced. His father's words had landed like a missile. Lily hadn't called anyone to join her at the hospital, but that wasn't his problem. He'd done more than was expected, and Lily had made it clear his company wasn't wanted.

Hell, if he'd stayed, she probably would have found a way to get him thrown out of the damn hospital.

"Anyway," Walter said, as if sensing Madden's desire to change the subject. "Any ideas who took those shots?"

"Deputy Sanders didn't say much but sounds like there are no suspects. Not even sure if it was a random act of violence or not."

Walter lifted his pipe to his thin lips and puffed. "Not a ton of violence like that in these parts. A few rowdy tourists have caused some trouble in the past year, but nothing on this scale."

His dad might be right, but Madden couldn't be sure if Walter believed his words or just wanted them to be true since his actions were what brought those tourists to town. Guilt was a heavy burden, one Walter carried on shoulders that grew frailer every day.

"Well," Madden said, ignoring the wistful sadness in

his dad's voice, "let's hope they catch whoever did this fast. No one wants a violent criminal roaming the streets."

"I hope for Kevin's daughter's sake this wasn't a targeted attack. They might want to make sure they finish the job."

The knots in Madden's stomach tightened. He'd never thought whoever shot Lily's father could show up and attack him again if he survived the surgery, and he'd left her all alone. With no protection. He should return to the hospital. Stay near just in case.

No. She'd told him to leave. She was a capable woman with plenty of people to call if she needed help.

Besides, even if Lily was in trouble, he was the last person she'd want around.

Chapter 4

Lily couldn't stop her hands from shaking as a doctor stepped through the doors that led back to the part of the hospital she wasn't allowed to enter.

The part where her father lay on an operating table while fighting for his life.

The sight of every scrub-covered employee sent her heart straight to her throat. She hoped and prayed for answers, but hours later, she still had none.

The older man in blue scrubs passed her and headed for a middle-aged couple in the corner of the waiting room.

Disappointment forced the air from her lungs. Hanging her head, she squeezed her eyes shut and willed the stiffness in her neck to go away.

"Lily?"

The tentative voice opened her eyes.

Eve stood in front of her, her expression pinched with worry and hands filled with a brown bag and to-go cup.

Lily blinked up at the other woman. She'd known Eve most her life and considered her a casual friend. But the hours Lily spent working at the ranch didn't leave much time to build strong relationships with anyone other than her father, their ranch hands, and the horses she loved so much.

"How are you holding up? Any word on your dad?" Eve asked.

Lily shrugged and shook her head. "Last I heard, he was still in surgery. I don't understand why it's taking so long. I just want to know that he's okay." She would have cried, but her emotional well was spent.

"Can I sit?" Eve gestured toward the empty chair beside Lily.

"Sure."

"I hope you don't mind, but I brought you some things. A clean shirt, some food and coffee." Eve placed the bag at Lily's feet then handed over the hot cup.

Taken aback by the unexpected kindness, Lily cleared her throat then took a sip of the sweet drink. "So much better than the crap I got earlier from the cafeteria. Thank you. This was really thoughtful."

Eve offered her a sad smile. "You shouldn't be here alone. I found your keys in your truck, and had it dropped off at your ranch, so you don't have to worry about getting back to town. If it's okay, I'll sit with you until you're ready to go home. I'll drive you."

The moisture she thought long dried up pooled in Lily's eyes. "You don't have to do that. I'm fine. Really."

"I'm sure you are, but you'll be better with a friend with you."

"You're right." Lily reached for Eve's hand, then a thought nagged at the back of her brain. "How did you know I was by myself?"

Eve winced. "Madden called me."

Heat slammed against Lily's cheeks, anger flashing brighter than the fluorescent lights in the godforsaken waiting room. "He had no right to do that. I don't know what kind of game he's playing, but I don't want to be a part of it."

"Honey, I know there's no love lost between you two, but Madden's not trying to do anything beyond being a good neighbor. He wanted me to know you were here and would need a ride home. That's all. But none of that matters right now, so put Madden out of your mind and let's just focus all our energy on your dad."

A little of Lily's indignation leaked from her system like air from an old tire. She might not completely trust Madden's motives, but he wasn't worth another one of her thoughts. And regardless of what brought Eve to the hospital waiting room, she was glad to have a friend by her side.

The doors leading to the surgical unit swung open again. An older woman with tired eyes and a white cap covering her head crossed over the shiny, linoleum floor and made a beeline for Lily. "Ms. Tremont?"

Lily rose on shaky legs. "That's me."

Eve stood beside her.

"I'm Dr. Waters. We just finished your father's surgery. He has a long road ahead of him, but I see no reason why he won't make a full recovery. He's a very lucky man."

Lily swallowed a snort. If he was lucky, he wouldn't have been shot to begin with. "Is he awake? Can I see him?"

"He's still heavily sedated and will stay in the ICU for a couple nights at the very least. You may visit for a short time, but he won't be awake and seeing him with so many tubes and machines may be a little upsetting."

"I can handle it. I need to let him know I'm here. Talk to him and tell him I'm all right."

The doctor gave a tiny nod. "I can take you back there now, but we only allow one visitor at a time."

Eve looped an arm around Lily's waist and pulled her

in for a quick side hug before grabbing the cup. "Go. Visit as long as you can. I'll be here waiting."

Gratitude washed over Lily as she followed the doctor down a wide corridor. The smell of disinfectant hung heavy in the air. Nurses buzzed from room to room, caring for patients and speaking with doctors. Lily's nerves stretched tighter with each step. By the time they reached her father's room, anxiety practically oozed from her pores.

Dr. Waters stopped at room 104. "Try to keep your visit brief. He needs rest."

Lily walked past the doctor and entered the dimly lit room. She ignored the lone chair pressed against the far wall and approached the bed. White rails caged her dad in place. Machines beeped and hummed beside him, broadcasting numbers and stats that might as well be in another language.

Tears clogged her throat and strangled her as she approached her dad. Tubes ran out of his mouth, connecting him to a machine to help him breathe. IVs connected bags of fluid that hung from hooks beside him. "Daddy?"

She held her breath, wishing he'd open his eyes and grin. That he'd shed the medical equipment that kept him alive and tell her it was all a big joke. That he was fine, and they could go home and share a nightcap on the porch.

But he didn't move. Didn't speak. Didn't do a damn thing to take her out of the nightmare she'd endured for the past few hours.

She coughed, clearing the emotion from her throat, and forced herself to be strong. She placed her hand over his and cringed at the cool, lifeless feel of it. "It's me, Lily. I talked to the doctor. She said you'll be right as rain in no time. You've just got to rest and take care of yourself. Let the doctors and nurses do their jobs, okay? I know lying around and doing nothing is hard for you. But now it's time to let other people take care of you for once. Then we'll get you home where you belong."

Minutes ticked by, the sound of the machines her constant companion, until she couldn't stomach the sight of her father looking so small, so vulnerable.

So close to death.

She raised his hand and pressed her lips to the thin skin on his knuckles before placing his arm gently at his side. "I'll be back, Dad. I love you."

Thirty minutes later, Lily gathered what was left of her energy as she prepared to peel herself from Eve's car. Blood still stained her shirt since she hadn't found a need to change on the way out of the hospital, but she'd forced down the sandwich Eve had brought.

"You can drop me off at the white barn," Lily said.

Eve maneuvered the car over the gravel drive, past the large cabin, and parked in front of the old structure that housed her horses. "Why the barn?"

"Horses don't care if I'm tired. They still need to be fed." As much as she wanted nothing more than to stand in the shower for an hour and wash away this horrible day, she couldn't shrug off her responsibilities. Not even for one night.

"Would you like help?" Eve asked. "I might not know my way around a ranch, but I'm pretty good at taking direction. We can get those pesky chores finished in half the time."

"You've already done so much. I couldn't ask you for more."

"Then it's a good thing you didn't ask, and I offered." Eve turned off the engine and hopped out of the car before Lily could refuse.

Because as much as she didn't want to put Eve out anymore, the thought of getting into the shower even faster was just the push Lily needed to climb out of the vehicle and into the warm night air. Her body yearned for the comfort of her home, but a peacefulness washed over her as she pushed open the barn door and breathed in the scent of hay and horse.

This was her sanctuary.

She led Eve to the storage room at the back of the barn and showed her where the horse's food was held and how to access water for the buckets inside their stalls. "If you can feed and water the horses, I can muck the stalls."

Eve went right to work while Lily grabbed a shovel and wheelbarrow. By the time she got to the last stall, sweat dripped down the back of her neck and her muscles ached. She was tired as hell, but a good tired. The kind of exhaustion that only came after hard work, and would help her mind shut off when she crawled into bed at night.

Queenie, her golden American quarter horse, whinnied then butted her long nose against Lily's shoulder.

"I see you, lady." Lily rested her forehead against Queenie's soft muzzle and sighed.

She'd always loved her mother's horse, and their bond had grown after her mom passed away. As though the two needed each other in a way no one else understood.

And now, she needed the unconditional love of this animal who meant so much to her.

The clearing of a throat shifted her head so her cheek pressed against Queenie.

Eve wiped the back of her wrist across her forehead, smearing dirt on her skin. "Everyone's fed and watered."

"Thank you. Really. You can't understand how much this means to me. I owe you big time."

Eve ran a palm along the strong muscles at Queenie's neck. "Are you kidding me? I was like a kid in a candy store with all these horses. Just wish it was a different situation that brought me out here."

"Me too. How about I buy you a round of drinks soon? A girl's night out."

"You mean at the bar I own?" Eve asked, grinning.

Shrugging, Lily chuckled. "I'll figure something out. But for now, why don't you head home? It's getting late."

"You sure?"

"Yeah. Positive. Thanks again."

Once Eve left, Lily spent a few more minutes with her favorite horse and let Queenie work her magic. By the time Lily walked up the porch steps, her anxiety had dropped a few notches. Warm, hot water spraying down on her would untangle the rest of her worries—well, maybe not all of them but hopefully enough to let her get some sleep.

Stepping into the home she shared with her father, unease crawled over her skin. She flipped on the lights in the entryway to chase away the darkness. Quickening her pace, she bypassed the living room and kitchen and hurried to the hallway, turning on more lights as she went until the housed blazed like midday. Slips of paper on the burgundy rug caught her attention, and she plucked them off the floor.

Inventory lists stared back at here. What the heck?

Apprehension settled in the pit of her stomach as she ducked her head into her father's office. Moonbeams streamed in through the large windows, highlighting the papers spilling out of the filing cabinet and overturned furniture.

Someone had been inside. Were they still there? Waiting for her?

Not wanting to stick around to find out, she ran outside,

jumping into her truck and locking the door. Her heart raced as she found her phone and placed a call to the sheriff's department.

"Hello, Cloud Valley Sheriff's Department." The female voice was smooth and stern.

"This is Lily Tremont. Someone broke into my house." Her voice shook as badly as her hands.

"Are they still inside? Are you safe?"

"I'm outside, sitting in my vehicle. I didn't check the rest of the home."

"I'm sending deputies out right now."

"Thank you." Lily disconnected. She studied the area, hoping no one would jump out of the bushes or emerge from the side of the cabin. Each second passed slower than the last. She felt like a sitting duck, alone and waiting for the other shoe to drop.

She could call Eve. Ask her to head back to the ranch. But if danger lurked, she didn't want to put Eve in the middle of a bad situation.

She could call Madden.

The idea struck her like a bolt of lightning. She didn't trust him. Hell, she didn't even like him.

Memories of his gentle touch and kind eyes floated back to her. He'd stayed by her side for hours today, even if his intentions were annoying. Not to mention he could get here a whole lot faster than a deputy coming from town since he was right next door.

Swallowing her pride, she found the business card he'd thrust at her before he'd left the hospital and quickly made the call before she lost her nerve.

"Hello?" His voice was low and raspy like he'd gargled a handful of rocks.

"Madden, it's Lily. Can you come over to the ranch? Someone was in my home, and I'm scared."

A beat of silence pulsed on the line, and she held her breath. Hating the anxiety ping-ponging in her gut.

"I'll be there in five minutes."

Disconnecting, she kept a firm grip on her phone, her eyes on her house, and ignored the tiny pulse of excitement about seeing Madden McKay.

Chapter 5

Even if Madden was grateful to cut his tense evening with his dad and brother short, he hated the reason.

Lily must be terrified if she called him for help.

The thought circled his brain as he pulled into the long driveway that wound around Tremont Ranch.

A wave of nostalgia tightened his grip on the steering wheel. It'd been years since he'd stepped foot on the neighboring ranch—years since he'd been welcomed. As kids, he and Dax would often tag along with their mom while she visited Mrs. Tremont. The two women had been friends for years, grabbing a cup of coffee or a sip of wine when possible. Probably discussing the struggle of being married to stubborn ranchers.

Back then, Lily had been a tomboy who'd climb trees and roped calves, proudly showing the McKay boys the differences between their two ranches. One, a working cattle farm filled with hardened ranch hands and smelly cows, the other bustling with fun activities and polished in a way that made Madden feel like he'd stepped into an alternate universe.

But those days had ended with the death of Lily's mother.

Now, as he drove toward the large cabin at the center of the property, the polish he remembered from his youth had faded. Even with only outdoor lighting on the barns and moonlight, he could see the years had taken a toll on the property.

Property that had been hit hard lately with the new hotel stealing tourists who normally would stay at Tremont Dude Ranch.

The glow of headlights from Lily's truck snapped him back to the present. The past didn't matter right now. Not when Lily's father had been shot and she waited for him because someone had broken into her house.

Parking in the spot beside her, he shut off his vehicle and jumped out.

Lily climbed down from her truck and met him before he could open her door.

He struggled not to wince at the sight of the dried blood on her shirt and the shadows under her red eyes. "Are you hurt? What happened?"

Wrapping her arms around her waist, she averted her gaze as if second-guessing the decision to call him. "Just shaken up. I went in and noticed papers in the hallway. Someone was in my dad's office. I didn't stick around to see if anything was taken or if anyone was still inside. Just called the police and got the hell out of there."

"Good. That was smart. Do you want me to look inside for you?"

"That's why I called you over here, isn't it?" she snapped. "I hope you didn't think I was just scared and wanted your lovely company."

Her brisk attitude rocked him back on the heels of his cowboy boots and he held up his palms as if speaking to a spooked horse. "No. Definitely didn't think that."

She squeezed her eyes shut for a beat, and when she opened them again, she finally met his stare head-on. "I'm sorry. That was uncalled for. I'm exhausted. It's been a long day, and the last thing I expected was to come home to more stress. I didn't know what else to do after I called the authorities. I figured..." A hint of desperation clung to her voice as it trailed off.

"You figured you'd call someone close by who owns a security company who might be able to help." He finished the sentence for her in a way that wouldn't ding her pride. Wouldn't let her know he understood she'd been desperate enough to reach out to him.

"Exactly."

"Have you noticed anything else unusual? Any noises that could have been another vehicle or even a four-wheeler? Someone coming this far out of town would need a way to get here. I can't be positive until I go inside, but chances are whoever was here isn't any longer if their means of getting away isn't around."

Lily's mouth dropped open. "Huh. Never thought of that, but no. No other vehicles except Eve's when she brought me home. Thank you for calling her, by the way."

"No problem," he said, then quickly got back to the matter at hand. "I'll step inside and clear the house. You can wait out here until the deputies arrive. Shouldn't be much longer."

"Nope. Not gonna happen. No way I'm standing out here alone, even if you think whoever broke in is long gone." She lifted her chin and pressed her lips in a straight line.

He'd seen that expression more times than he cared to count. Nothing he said would change her mind. No reason to waste time arguing. "All right then. Stay close. Be on alert. And I know this part will be difficult but listen to me. If I tell you to run, run. If I tell you to stay, stay. Not trying to be an ass, just want to keep you safe."

She rolled her eyes and marched forward.

He couldn't help but grin. She could be a royal pain in the ass, but it was nice to see some of her spunk return. Especially after the day she'd had. Keeping his amusement to himself, he quickened his pace to get a step ahead of her before she reached the front door.

"Ready?" he asked, glancing over his shoulder.

She nodded, eyes wide and filled with apprehension.

He stepped into the entryway. Lights blazed like fire from the giant chandelier overhead. The open concept gave him a good perspective of the area, which seemed clear of any intruders, but he searched every corner to be certain. He noted the French doors off the kitchen appeared compromised.

"Did you lock this door before you left today?"

"I didn't check," she said. "Usually we lock everything up, just to be safe. But I can't be positive."

He made a mental note to tell the deputies his suspicions then went down the hall. The mess in the office spiked his blood pressure. Instinct urged him to tidy the clutter and put the room back in place, but the sound of sirens told him the deputies were here. They needed to see the damage for themselves.

Lily stood just inside the doorway. "Why would someone do this? Break in and throw things around the room like confetti? We haven't seen the rest of the house, but so far, it doesn't appear as though anything was taken."

"Honestly, it looks like someone was searching for something. I don't want to speculate, but if the intruder had a specific thing to find, they'd come in and do exactly what was done. Go through the targeted area as quickly as possible, not caring about the mess. Grabbing what they needed and leaving before getting caught. If we find that no other room was raided, it will be telling of the intruder's intentions."

Lily furrowed her brow. "Sorry, my brain is mush. I'm not following."

"If the office was the only place someone searched, they were probably looking for something related to the business."

A doorbell rang, confirming law enforcement had arrived. "I can keep clearing the house if you want to answer that."

She hesitated, her gaze lingering on his for a beat before dropping to the floor.

Either she was too tired to hide it, or she hadn't changed as much as he'd thought over the years, but he could read her like a damn book. "Or I can stay with you. The deputies will search anyway. No reason for us both to go through your home."

A glimpse of a smile poked through. "Good point."

She led the way back to the front of the house and welcomed the deputies. He recognized both, though didn't know either of them well.

The woman, not much older than him, offered a hand to Lily. "Ms. Tremont, I'm Deputy Silver. This is my partner, Deputy Hill."

The younger of the two removed his hat, revealing dark hair and blue eyes. "Evening. Sorry about your troubles. May we come in?"

Lily stepped back, allowing them access to the house. "I called Madden McKay." She waved a hand in his direction, and he gave a nod. "He owns Sunrise Security."

Madden offered a hand to each of the deputies. "I searched the main living areas and office before you arrived. The rest of the house needs to be cleared, but figured you'd want to handle that yourselves. The doors off the kitchen appeared to be tampered with. Might be where an intruder gained entrance."

"Thanks," Deputy Silver said. "We'll take a look, as well as go through the rest of the residence, but first we have some bad news for Ms. Tremont."

A soft gasp echoed off the high ceiling, and Lily's body swayed as if about to crumble. "Is my dad okay?"

The crack in her voice moved Madden to her side. He secured an arm around her waist and held her upright.

Deputy Hill frowned. "We received word from the hospital on our way here. Someone snuck into his room and attacked him in his bed. He's stable for now, but it's unclear if he'll stay that way."

A strangled sob shook Lily's shoulder.

She collapsed against Madden's chest, and he held her close as she cried.

An eternity passed by the time Lily and Madden stepped back into her home, and she was ready to fall asleep on the spot. After speaking with the authorities and a return trip to the hospital to see her dad, she was convinced one more step might be the death of her.

"Do you mind if we head downstairs? That's where my living space is." Never in a million years did she imagine she'd invite Madden McKay to her bedroom, but the wall of windows in the living room made her feel exposed. As if whoever had put this nightmare into motion watched her every move.

"Sure. Wherever you're most comfortable. Give me one second." Madden made a lap to double-check the house was locked then met her at the staircase leading to the basement.

She hated how safe he made her feel. He'd stuck by her

side while the deputies cleared the rest of the house then asked her questions about her father. Each insinuation that her father had involved himself in something that had put a target on his back had landed like a missile. Her dad might not be a saint, but he wasn't a criminal.

Madden hadn't said a word. Just offered her support and comfort and protection.

And now, as the clock ticked into a new day, he was still there.

Once downstairs, she flipped on the light, highlighting the stone wall that matched the one directly above it, the fireplace a smaller version than the one upstairs. The couch and love seat centered around it were a lighter beige and softer than the dark, firm leather her father preferred. The low ceiling wouldn't allow wooden beams to be stretched across it, but the white tile and marble countertops in the connected kitchen mirrored the place she shared most her meals with her father.

Leaving her childhood home wouldn't have been wise since she spent most of her hours working at the ranch or visiting her dad, but she'd wanted her own space.

Space that gave her all the qualities she loved about her home but with a little more privacy.

Madden whistled. "Wow. Not what I expected."

She couldn't help but laugh. "Let me guess, you thought it'd be dark and gloomy. A lonely, desperate cellar for the lonely, desperate woman?"

"I'd never call you desperate."

The somber tone of his voice turned her to face him. She braced her hands on the back of the sofa. "Only lonely?"

He shrugged. "Wouldn't know that. Don't know too much about your personal life."

His remark reminded her that the reason he was here

wasn't personal. At least not in the "let's sit and chat and get to know one another" way. Madden might be a means to an end, but he was still the main reason her ranch was failing.

He was still the enemy.

"Never mind. That doesn't matter. I want to thank you, officially, for everything you did for me today. You've spent a lot of your time helping me. I want to pay you for that time."

Irritation pinched his mouth. "I didn't help you so you'd give me money. I did it because it was the right thing."

"You can think that if you want, but I don't want any charity. Not from you or anyone else in this town. Having you close has made me feel safe. I didn't understand how important that was, and I don't want to give that up until I know for certain whoever is after my father won't set their sights on me."

Anxiety danced up her spine. She straightened the moss green throw on the back of the couch, as if smoothing the soft fabric would sooth her nerves.

"That's smart. Sunrise Security can offer you protection until it's no longer needed."

She lifted her chin. "I don't just want protection. I want to figure out who is after my father and why. Can you help with that?"

Shifting his weight from his left leg to the right, he scratched the back of his neck and sighed. "I'm not an investigator, Lily. I've never worked with law enforcement. But I have experience with tracking down criminals. With solving problems and I tend to know how to ask the right questions. I can't promise you I'll figure out this mess, but if you want me to try, I will."

Relief blossomed in her chest. "I'd be grateful if you started now. If you could stay close for the duration. I'm not sure how much sleep I'd get if I was here alone. There's only one bedroom down here, but the couch pulls out to a bed. I can sleep on that if you want my room."

"Not necessary. I'll sleep upstairs and stay on the sofa in the living room. I want to be able to keep a closer eye on things."

A pinch of disappointment shocked her, but she wouldn't let him see it. Besides, she was only scared, and why wouldn't she be? Her father had been attacked twice and someone had violated her home. Anyone would have the same reaction. "Sounds good. We can discuss the payment for your services in the morning."

A vein ticked at the side of his head, but he nodded. "Sounds like a plan. Have a good night. Grab me if you need anything."

Turning on her heel, she headed for the short hallway that led to her bedroom. As she readied herself for sleep, she couldn't help but wonder if she'd just made a deal with the devil.

Chapter 6

The morning sun streamed through the wall of windows in the living room, baking Madden on the sofa. He kicked off the thin blanket and rolled his neck from side to side. His muscles screamed. Damn, he should have slept on the pullout couch in the basement and not the tough leather sofa that hadn't even been big enough for his long legs.

Sitting, he snagged his T-shirt from the floor and yanked it over his head. He'd considered slipping out of his jeans, but the idea of Lily catching him in his boxers kept the stiff material in place all damn night.

Just another obstacle preventing him from getting much shut-eye.

The gurgle of a coffeepot chugging to life set him on his feet. He hadn't heard anyone come into the kitchen, but he wasn't exactly on his game. Not with the emotional hangover from dealing with Lily the day before and a crappy night's sleep.

The kitchen was empty. He followed his nose to the machine on the counter and sent a silent prayer to whoever had set it to go off this morning. Needing caffeine more than he needed to respect boundaries, he opened cabinet doors until he found a colorful array of mugs.

"Can I help you find something?"

The amusement in Lily's voice extinguished his initial impulse to apologize for snooping around her space. He took his time, picking out a bright red mug with a black X over a bull with the words *Steer Clear of Bull* written in white letters. Turning, he hoisted the mug in the air and grinned. "Nope. Found what I needed. Nice taste."

She struggled around a growing smile of her own. "I got that for my dad. Don't judge me."

"Never. I might get one for myself. Want coffee?"

"Yes, please."

He opted for a more dignified white porcelain mug for her, filling them both before handing hers over. "How'd you sleep?" If the dark circles under her eyes were any indication, her night had been as restless as his.

"Not great." She padded across the kitchen floor in her bare feet and rummaged in the refrigerator, pulling out sweet cream. "Want some?"

He shook his head and took a sip of the strong, black brew before settling onto the stool tucked under the large island.

She doctored her coffee then replaced the creamer. Her long hair tumbled down her back, stopping right above her waist. A waist that short cotton shorts and a fitted strappy tank top accentuated.

She bent over to find something else in the fridge, and his mouth went dry. Hell, he may have spent the last handful of years annoyed by Lily's superior attitude, but he was a man after all. And no amount of animosity could erase the way her warm-from-the-bed body tied him up inside.

An image of being tied up in her bed flashed in his mind, causing spikes of lust to burst through his system like a shooting star. Christ, he needed to get a grip.

Clearing his throat, he grabbed his mug and twisted

away from the tempting vision Lily presented first thing in the morning. He stared out the window where mountains loomed in the distance, the same peaks he saw from his old room at his dad's ranch. He swallowed the urge to comment on their beauty. If he was going to survive this assignment, things had to be kept as professional as possible.

The sound of sizzling bacon confirmed it was safe to shift back around. "You don't need to make breakfast. I'm fine with coffee."

"Who said it's for you?"

He snorted out a laugh. "Fair point. I guess I can just sit here and watch you stuff your face. Don't worry about my growling stomach."

"I thought you didn't need breakfast?" Lily buzzed around the kitchen until scrambled eggs cooked in a second pan and bread popped from the toaster.

Amused, he watched her flip the bacon and stir the eggs before buttering the toast she piled on a plate. No way she was making all that food for only her, but he kept any more comments to himself. Just sat and enjoyed his coffee and the view of the beautiful woman cooking.

Lily reached in a cabinet and her shorts inched up a little higher on her toned legs.

He couldn't hold back a small groan.

"Fine, fine. You can eat." She set a plate in front of him then filled her own with food. "Don't expect me to wait on you, though."

"Wouldn't think of it." Chuckling, he slid off the stool and bit back a second groan at the scents of fresh bacon and cheesy eggs. He scooped some on his plate and returned to his seat, Lily now beside him.

"What's the plan for the day?" Lily shoved the eggs around her plate with a fork before taking a tiny bite.

"First of all, I need a change of clothes."

She winced. "Sorry. I didn't think about you not having any of your things here last night."

"No problem," he said, shrugging. "Just don't get too close. My breath isn't the greatest."

Her wince deepened. "No worries there. After we eat, I'll dress quickly, and we can head out. Then what? What's the best way to figure out who's after my dad?"

He bit into a salty piece of bacon and considered how to appease Lily while also keeping her away from danger. "I'd like to take a look at your property. All of it. There's a lot of land and buildings to check. The police did a full sweep of the house and surrounding area, but there are guest cabins and other barns we should search. Make sure nothing else was tampered with."

"I also want to take a closer look at the office," Lily told him. "It didn't appear as though anything was missing, but I could have overlooked something. I wasn't exactly in the right state of mind." She dropped her fork and stared at her plate. "I should go see my dad. I hate the thought of him alone but seeing him in that bed with all those tubes and machines is so dang hard. Brings back too many horrible memories."

The sadness in her voice fisted his heart. He understood where her mind was—where his own mind went every time he was in that damn hospital. As many differences as he and Lily had, they'd both lost their mothers. Both understood the pain of that loss, of living with that grief.

"Your dad knows you love him whether you're sitting by his side or not. We'll visit whenever you want, but there are some other things to do first. Search your property, get me clothes and I need to stop by the office."

She blew out a shaky breath and nodded along with his

words. "Yes, I need to sign a contract or whatever it is to make this official."

"Sure. A contract." He sipped his coffee, not looking forward to the conversation that loomed with Reid. Sunrise Security was supposed keep people and their property safe, not solve crimes. Reid might not be on board with extending their services, even if only for one job.

But for Madden, the decision was already made. He'd made a promise to Lily and couldn't turn his back on her even if he wanted. Besides, if the last day had proven anything, it was that Lily Tremont could get under his skin in a way he never thought possible.

And the only way to wash his hands of her was to do what she paid him to do then get the hell out of her life before she drove him crazy.

Lily got ready in record time. She'd thrown on jeans and a fitted T-shirt, opting for a high ponytail and minimal makeup. Madden was the last person she needed to impress, but she also didn't want to look like a slob.

She'd been surprised that he'd cleaned the kitchen while she dressed and was grateful for the couple of ranch hands her father still employed who'd showed up to tend the property. She still had her own chores to see to, but at least the morning work would get done while she went into town with Madden.

Madden sat behind the steering wheel and studied the two men. "Those guys work for you and your dad for long?"

She flicked her wrist toward the man entering the horse barn. "That's Charlie. He started working here right after my mom died, so close to fifteen years. Daniel not quite as long, but probably eight, nine years."

"Do they have access to the house?"

"Not that I'm aware of. Dad's always kept the ranch hands separate from the main house. Wanted clear boundaries for the men he employed and his young daughter." She couldn't help but grin at the memories of trying to sneak the cute summer help inside, only getting away with it once.

"Any more staff?"

Her grin vanished. "Not full time. When we have visitors, we hire people to come and help with cleaning the cabins and cooking meals. Try to give our guests the full dude ranch experience. We don't have the need to keep many people on payroll. At least not until we figure out how to turn things around."

Madden grunted and headed away from the ranch toward town. "Any of your employees—current or past—hold a grudge? Would want to hurt your father?"

The idea made her sick. They loved the people who worked at the ranch like family. The main reason for ire over the ranch's struggles was the people they'd had to let go. People whose paychecks were taken away because of the lack of work. But she couldn't imagine anyone blaming her father, hating him enough to try and kill him.

Everyone understood the real reason for fewer tourists at Tremont Ranch was because of the McKays.

"No. No one who works for us would want to hurt me or my dad. I'd bet my own life."

"I'd still like to talk with them. Maybe someone noticed something off or saw someone sneaking around the property recently. You never know what little detail could lead to answers."

"I'm sure Charlie and Daniel would be more than willing to tell you anything they may know. They were upset when I told them what had happened to my dad last night. Both promised to be on the lookout for anything useful."

Not wanting to continue the conversation, she stared out the window. Blue skies and the bright sunshine predicted another beautiful day ahead, but nothing could chase the dark clouds above her. Every aspect of her and her father's lives would be picked apart in the next couple of days, and she'd gladly expose her very soul if it meant tracking down whoever was responsible for hurting her dad, but she wasn't looking forward to the scrutiny.

After driving into town, Madden parked his truck on Main Street, in front of Sunrise Security.

Frowning, she stepped out of the truck and met him on the sidewalk. "I thought you wanted to clean up and grab some things at your place before heading into work."

"I do," he said, unlocking the front door and ushering her inside. "I keep the loft above the office. Dax is at the farmhouse to help Pops. I wanted a little more privacy, and the loft made sense."

"Why does Dax need to help your dad? It's not like there's much of a ranch left to run." She cringed at the bite of her words and held up a hand before Madden could say anything. "Sorry. I can't say I'm happy, or even understand, why your family sold so much of your land to developers. But while we're working together, I'll try to keep those opinions to myself."

Madden didn't speak, but the tense set of his shoulders broadcasted his irritation.

She sighed and followed him through the dark office space to a stairwell that went upstairs. She couldn't say Madden was a friend now, but he'd been a lifesaver last night. He didn't need to be rewarded with her sharp tongue. She couldn't forgive him and his family for the hole they'd put her and her father into, but she could at least be civil.

Inside his apartment, he flipped on lights and waited for

her to enter before closing the door behind her. "I won't be long. Make yourself comfortable."

He took a step away, and she grabbed his arm to keep him in place. He locked eyes with her, and the pain that flashed in them had her regretting her remarks even more. "Listen. I really am sorry. I shouldn't have said anything. I don't want there to be tension between us. Not after everything you've done for me."

Something shifted in his expression. He dropped his gaze to her hand for a beat before bringing it back to her face. "Really, it's not a big deal. I'm used to the comments from everyone in town. Sometimes I feel like no matter how hard I try, nothing will erase the stain of selling our land. But I can't change the choices we made, and honestly, I wouldn't if I could."

The sadness in his words tugged at her heart and pulled her closer to him. He was so big, so strong.

So unlike the man she'd assumed him to be since he'd returned to Cloud Valley.

Tilting her head to the side, she studied his downturned mouth and his drooping shoulders. "Why not? I remember you as a boy. You and Dax. You both loved that ranch. Loved helping your dad. I even remember your mama telling mine all sorts of stories about the trouble you'd get into. Stories that made them both laugh and talk about how the lessons you were learning would make you one hell of a rancher one day. What changed?"

He winced and pulled away from her touch. "Doesn't matter. Especially now when I have a job to do. Give me a few minutes then we'll head downstairs."

She watched him march to the bathroom and she jumped when he slammed the door. She'd struck a nerve. Something she didn't think possible with Madden. He always appeared so carefree. Happy and oblivious to the trouble his choices had caused others.

Maybe she'd been wrong. Maybe there was more behind his easygoing smile and the reasons for his actions. But at the end of the day, he was right. What was done couldn't be erased, no matter the intentions.

Besides, she had enough to worry about. Madden had dug his own grave, and she didn't have the energy to care if he got out of it or not. She only needed him to keep her safe and help her find a criminal, then he could continue his crusade to clear his family's name.

Chapter 7

By the time Madden dressed, brushed his teeth and led Lily back down to the office, Reid and Peggy had arrived for the day. He wanted a private word with Reid before having Lily sign on the dotted line to make his job official.

He led Lily into the front of the office. "Do you mind sitting in the waiting room while I speak with my business partner?"

Before she could answer, Peggy shot to her feet and hurried to wrap her arms around Lily. "How are you doing, honey? How's your dad? I can't believe what happened yesterday. It's just so horrible."

Lily rested her head on Peggy's shoulder and leaned into the hug. "Thanks, Peg. Dad's in critical condition but stable, and I'm figuring out what I need to do next. Luckily, I have Madden helping me with that."

Peggy shifted to face Madden while keeping one arm hooked snuggly around Lily's shoulders. Her gray eyebrows rose high. "Oh really? I'm so glad to hear that."

Madden ignored his receptionist's unspoken curiosity. "I'll be right out, Lily. Peggy can make sure you have anything you might need."

Peggy gave Lily a little squeeze. "Sure will, dear. Let's

have a seat and I'll grab you some water or coffee or anything you'd like." Peggy steered Lily toward the seating area.

Knowing she was in safe hands, Madden walked back to Reid's office and dropped into the seat across from his partner's desk.

"You look rough," Reid said, leaning back in his chair. "Tough night?"

"You can say that again."

"Didn't expect to see you coming down from your apartment with Lily Tremont first thing in the morning."

Madden rolled his eyes. Gossip in a small town was as natural as the spring water trickling through the mountains, but that didn't mean he wanted to be at the center of it. "We were up there for all of ten minutes. I stayed at her place last night."

"Excuse me?" Mischief sparked in Reid's brown eyes.

Pinching the bridge of his nose, Madden evened his temper before he said something he'd regret.

Like Lily had.

She appeared remorseful for her comments about his family, but that hadn't lessened the impact. Especially after seeing firsthand the toll the years had taken on her land.

"She called when she realized someone had broken into her house."

Reid sat up straight. "Was she hurt?"

Madden shook his head. "The intruder was gone by the time she got there. When I arrived, deputies showed up and told her that her father had been attacked again in the hospital. He's in critical condition with a guard outside his door. She was scared and wanted to hire Sunrise Security."

"Wow. Sorry to hear all that happened to her, but glad for her business. We can keep her safe while the authorities figure out who's after her father. Set up some cameras on her property, if she agrees to that. Switch who's staking out her house. If she's really nervous, we can even take turns being with her. Make sure she's never alone."

The thought of Reid spending time alone with Lily in her home—of her making him breakfast in her short shorts and fitted tank top—fisted Madden's hands. "She wants more than that."

"How much more can we do?" Reid asked, frowning.

"She asked me to help her find the person who's after her father."

Reid barked out a laugh. "What? She knows we're a security company and not private investigators, right?"

Madden shifted in his seat. Reid had been his best friend and partner in crime since they'd met in boot camp twelve years before. Reid had stuck by his side through more than one storm, always believing in Madden even when he didn't believe in himself.

But what he was about to suggest was different. It was changing the entire business model they'd agreed to, that Reid had invested his time and money into.

"But what if we were?"

The amusement fled from Reid's expression, leaving him slack-jawed. "We have no experience with that. Hell, we hardly have experience as a security company because no one in this damn town will hire us."

Madden winced but pressed on. "I know. You're right. But we could be good at this. We tracked down terrorists overseas. We understand how to get information and put pieces together until we get a clear picture. Business sucks right now, but offering something more might be the ticket. Might be what turns things around for us."

Reid picked at his thumbnail, a habit he had when he thought things through.

"Listen, I want to do this for Lily. It's not like Wyoming requires us to have a PI license or anything. I'll handle her case. Stay with her until it's over and help figure out what the hell her dad got himself tangled in. Once this is over, if we don't think it's worth it to explore the investigative side of things, we stick with security. No harm, no foul."

"And you want to stay with her for the duration? By yourself?" Reid's eyes narrowed to slits, as if trying to read exactly what was happening in Madden's head. "I thought you two couldn't stand each other?"

Unsure how to answer, Madden shrugged. Complicated didn't even begin to explain his feelings for Lily right now. Was she a pain in the ass? Yes. Could she spit out venom on a whim? Absolutely. Did a part of him feel as though he owed her something?

Maybe.

Yes, that was it and nothing else. The decision his family made to protect themselves had hurt her and her father. Tremont Ranch getting caught in the crosshairs hadn't been intentional, but that didn't make it any less damaging.

"We're not friends, that's for damn sure, but there's a certain kind of trust there. We've known each other since we were kids, and even if she hates me, she knows me. Knows I'll do whatever I can to help her."

"And that's all this is? Not wanting to spend time with a beautiful woman who wouldn't even look your way the day before yesterday?"

Madden's jaw tightened, but a tiny prick of awareness told him Reid might have a point. "Are you suggesting I'd act inappropriately with a vulnerable woman in a desperate situation?"

Reid lifted his palms. "Nope. Not saying that at all. Just want to make sure we're all on the same page."

"Absolutely. Now that we've got this hashed out, I'll have Lily come back so we can hammer out all the details."

Reid nodded. "Sounds good."

Standing, Madden made his way to the waiting room to grab Lily so she could officially become Sunrise Security's newest client.

After Lily dotted all the i's and crossed all the t's, Madden drove them back to the ranch.

A weird tension had followed them from the office to his truck and refused to leave. His silence shouldn't bother Lily. Hell, she'd spent years hating when he'd open his mouth to say something he thought was charming or sarcastic.

But as much as she hated to admit it, something had shifted inside her. She'd witnessed a softer side of Madden, and even if her animosity never fully thawed, she didn't want to go back to despising the man who'd been her rock when she'd needed one most.

As they drove up the lane, she spotted Charlie beside the fence around the pasture, watching the horses meander along the field.

"Looks like Charlie's taking a break," she said, nodding toward the older man. "Would be a good time to talk to him. I should help with the horses, anyway."

Madden parked close to the barn.

She hopped out and waited for him to walk to her side before making her way to Charlie. She lifted her hand and waved. "Hey, Charlie. How are things?"

Charlie sighed. "Okay, Ms. Tremont. Got most of the chores done. Just wanted to give the horses some time in the pasture before taking them back into the barn. How are you holding up?"

A million responses whirred through her mind, but she simply said, "I've been better. This is Madden McKay."

Charlie grunted. "I know who he is. Why's he here?"

Madden stiffened but didn't respond.

"Here's here to help."

Charlie wiped a large, wrinkled hand over his heavy jowls. "You've got to be kidding me. Your dad would throw a fit if he knew the McKay boy was standing on his property, pretending to be *helping*. What's your game, son?"

"No game, sir."

She had to hand it to him. He took Charlie's attitude in stride, but she noticed the vein beside his temple throb just before he placed his cowboy hat on his head. "Charlie, Madden's been by my side since Dad was shot. Not because I asked him to, but because he was being a good neighbor. When I called later, he came without hesitation. I need his help now to get to the bottom of whatever the hell's going on, and I need you to be on board."

Charlie's big, brown eyes widened. He shook his head as if she'd asked him to kick a dog. "Be on board with a McKay? Have you lost your mind?"

"No, but I almost lost my father last night, and I'll do whatever it takes to make sure that doesn't happen again." Irritation made her words snap out sharper than a whip. "You've been a part of this family for a long time, and I expect you to help us. So get over whatever grudge you're holding on to, at least for the time being, and give Madden the respect he deserves."

She kept her focus on the weathered ranch hand, but she couldn't help noticing the curve of Madden's lips from the corner of her eye.

"I'm sorry, Ms. Tremont." Charlie swept his dirty hat off his head. "You're right. Right now, keeping everyone safe is the only thing that matters. If Madden can help make that happen, I'll do whatever I can to assist him."

Lily crossed over the green blades of grass and gave Charlie a quick squeeze. "Thank you." She pulled away but looped an arm through his. Letting him know that no matter what, they were in this together. She met Madden's gaze with her own, giving a tiny dip of her head.

"Lily tells me you've worked for the Tremonts for a long time," Madden began. "Have you ever come across anyone who wished Mr. Tremont or his daughter harm?"

"Never," Charlie said, puffing out his chest as though he found the question insulting.

"What about staff who've been let go? Anyone hold a grudge?"

"Not against the Tremonts."

The meaning behind Charlie's comment was clear as the blue sky above. Lily jabbed his side with her elbow. "Be nice."

"Sorry," Charlie said. "No one wants to hurt Kevin or Lily. Both are wonderful employers who treat us with kindness and respect. Even with layoffs, people understood. No one saw a need to complain about the reasons they were let go. At least not as far as Mr. and Ms. Tremont are concerned."

Madden ignored the second, subtler jab. "How late did you and Daniel work last night?"

"Well, let's see." Charlie scratched his chin. "I was home in time for dinner, so I would have left here no later than 5:30. Daniel was still here, but we were mostly finished for the day. He wanted to do as much extra as he could so

Ms. Tremont didn't have to worry much about anything besides her dad."

"I appreciate that," she said. "All I had to do was feed the horses and clean out the stalls, which you know is more therapeutic for me than work." She glanced around, spotting only Charlie's old truck. "Where's Daniel now?"

"Said he wasn't feeling well and had to head home. I told him it was all right. Hope that's okay."

"Of course," she said, making a mental note to call later to check on him. Her hands may be full at the moment, but she couldn't afford to let anything at the ranch fall through the cracks.

"Do you or Daniel have access to the main house?" Madden asked.

Charlie shook his head.

"What about the other buildings on the property?"

"We've both got keys to the bunkhouse, although we don't stay there much anymore. We use that mostly when there are guests and there's more work. But we each have a key, and a bed inside. The guest cabins are off-limits to us, unless we're asked to help with something special. The barns and outbuildings aren't locked." Frowning, Charlie cocked his head to the side and studied Madden. "Why?"

Madden kept his mouth closed.

Charlie glanced down at Lily. "Is there something I don't know?"

"Someone broke into the house last night." She cringed, hating the way Charlie's face dropped at the news.

"And you think me or Daniel had something to do with it?" Anger turned his cheeks red, and he jabbed a finger in the air, directly at Madden's chest. "Mind yourself and your damn questions, boy. I'm as loyal as the night is black. That's not a quality you and yours know much about, and

I won't have you insinuating I've done anything to hurt this family."

Lily flattened her palm on Charlie's arm, gaining his attention. "I know you wouldn't hurt us, and so does Madden. He's not asking anything the sheriff's department isn't probably planning to ask. We're just making sure no one was around to see anything suspicious happen last night."

His shoulders dropped and he closed his eyes for a beat. When he opened them again, tears misted in the corners. "I didn't see anything unusual. I'd tell you if I did. I'll keep an ear out. If anything gets said or done that can possibly be connected to what happened, I'll tell you."

"I know you will. Thanks, Charlie. Why don't you head home? I can tend to the horses."

"You sure?"

"Yep. Besides, I've got Madden around to help."

A tight smile settled on Madden's lips that she didn't quite understand.

"All right then. Call if you need anything." Charlie gently cupped her biceps then aimed a steely glare at Madden before turning away.

She watched Charlie walk back to his truck, his head down and a defeated air swarming him.

"Well, that was interesting," Madden said. "Has a bit of a temper."

She bristled, unwilling to hear any negative comments about a man she'd known and respected most of her life. "He's a good guy. He wouldn't hurt my dad."

"What about Daniel? He stayed later last night and skipped out of work early today. Could mean something." Madden leaned his arms on the split-railed fence and stared at the horses.

"Or could mean nothing." She wouldn't make assumptions. But even as she clung to the hope that nothing was happening under her nose that had brought danger to her home, one simple truth remained.

Someone wanted her father dead, and there had to be a reason why.

Chapter 8

Madden followed Lily into the barn. The musty scent of hay and animal feed spiked his pulse. It'd been years since he'd done farm chores.

Years since his body worked the way he needed it to in order to do his part to keep McKay Ranch afloat.

"All right, McKay. Time to do some chores." Lily handed him a pitchfork. "Throw down some fresh bedding while I clean out the stalls. The hay's up in the loft. Toss it there," she said, pointing to a spot on the ground. "Once I'm done, you can help me lay it out."

He swallowed his apprehension. No way he wanted Lily to witness his weakness. He could chuck hay down from the loft. He just needed to take it slow and not overwork his shoulder. Hopefully she'd be too busy with her own assignment to notice his struggle.

Before he could think too much, he climbed the ladder and scooped a pitchfork full of fresh hay. A stabbing pain in his shoulder gritted his teeth. The tool twisted in his faltering grip, spilling the contents on the wooden planks of the loft.

Shame climbed the back of his neck, heating him more than the muggy air trapped at the top of the barn. He should just plop on the hay bale and admit defeat. Confess to Lily that he wasn't capable of doing the damn chores, even something as simple as helping her lay new bedding for her horses.

A gentle humming caught his attention, and he peeked down the wide aisle. Lily chugged along with a soft smile on her face and sweat beading on her forehead. She wheeled the dirty straw to the far end of the aisle and dumped it in a giant barrel before heading to the next stall.

Admiration pressed against his lungs. He'd thought of her as a spoiled, entitled brat for years. Imagined her lounging around the big cabin while others ran her ranch. He'd never pictured her getting her hands dirty, hauling shit around a hot-ass barn.

She was hands-on, cared about the people who worked for her and the land she tended. It was in her blood, in her heart.

A familiar ache made it hard to breathe. He understood her. Understood the love of a place that held so many memories.

As if sensing him watching her, Lily glanced up, fisted a hand on her hip and smirked. "Come on, cowboy. You're not going to make little ole me do all the work, are you?"

Her humor was infectious, and damn it, he'd never seen a more beautiful woman. "Just enjoying the view for a minute."

She scrunched her nose. "Are you feeling all right? Not enough oxygen up there or something?"

He laughed. "Yeah, that's it. Lack of oxygen."

Lily rolled her eyes and disappeared down the aisle, the sweet melody of her hum reaching him once more.

Madden blew out a long breath and steeled his resolve. A simple chore might take him three times as long as it should, but he'd do it. He *needed* to do it.

With a firm grip on the handle, he scooped a smaller pile of hay and let it rain to the spot Lily had requested. Little by little, the pile on the ground grew. Sweat poured down his face. His muscles throbbed, and no doubt he'd need to ice his shoulder tonight, but pride puffed his chest in a way it hadn't in years.

Unable to stand the suffocating heat, he stripped off his T-shirt and wiped the damp material across his brow. Good thing he'd brought a bag full of fresh clothing. He'd need a shower and an entire gallon of water once he finished.

"All right, cowboy. That's plenty. I've got most of the bedding laid. You can head down, then we'll see to the horses."

He peered over the side of the loft, and his heart puttered like a stalling tractor.

Lily stood by the now dwindling pile and leaned on her pitchfork. Strands of wheat-colored hair had slipped out of her ponytail, and was plastered to the side of her face with sweat. Streaks of dirt slid over her cheek. And a look of peace softened her features in a way he'd never seen.

She sent him a tiny salute, filled her wheelbarrow and disappeared into a stall at the end of the aisle.

"I'll be right there." He grabbed his stuff and tossed it on the barn's floor then descended the ladder. He concentrated on each rung, not wanting to slip and give away that his shoulder was like jelly. With his feet firmly on the floor, he stretched his aching muscles and turned to find Lily staring at him, mouth open and eyes wide.

He grinned. "Feeling all right?"

Clearing her throat, she snapped her mouth closed and glanced up from his exposed abdomen. "Fine. Just trying to finish so we can get on with our day. Lots to do."

"I can put my shirt back on. Didn't mean to fluster you.

It was just hot as hell in the loft." The skin of his shoulder tingled, and he couldn't help but wonder if she noticed the ugly scar. But he didn't want to give her the satisfaction of covering himself.

She scowled and heaped hay into her wheelbarrow. "Don't flatter yourself. If you'd rather stand around watching me while your head inflates, go for it. I can understand how this type of work doesn't come naturally to you anymore."

The comment raised his hackles, and he shoved his T-shirt over his head. Her sharp tongue was exactly what he needed. A punch in the gut to remind him Lily Tremont might be a beautiful woman, but his attraction to her was only skin-deep.

"You wouldn't know a damn thing about what comes naturally to me because you've never bothered to ask. You, your father and everyone else in this town think they know everything. Think they've put together some mysterious puzzle to explain the McKay corruption and sinful decisions. But no one knows what we've been through or why we did what we did. Now if you'll excuse me, I could use a glass of water."

He stormed out of the barn and lifted his face to the hot sun. Closing his eyes, he focused on the warm rays on his skin and slowing his heart rate. He had to shut down his emotions—to draw on every freaking experience that taught him patience. He couldn't let her quick jabs get to him, or he'd never survive the assignment that might be his company's saving grace.

Lily stayed a step behind Madden as they walked through the guest cabin in search of anything out of place. For the second time today, she wanted to smack herself upside the head. The awkward silence lingering between her and Madden was 100 percent her fault. When she'd spied him with his shirt off, his muscles hard and glistening with sweat, she'd almost swallowed her tongue.

And when he'd teased her, she fell back on a smart-ass comment instead of taking his remarks on the chin, or even admitting she liked what she saw.

"You notice anything amiss in here?" Madden peeked into the bathroom then stalked the perimeter of the studio-style cabin.

The layout was simple. An inviting king-size bed in one corner, a small kitchen with a table big enough for two and a living area anchored by a cozy fireplace. Clearly a space meant for a couple. A place to unwind with a loved one, a glass of wine and a beautiful view of the mountains. They had bigger cabins for families, but this one always reminded her of what she lacked in her life.

Pushing that aside, she forced a smile. "Everything looks the way it should. Just like all the others."

He nodded and led the way outside where two horses waited. Slipping his foot in the stirrup, he swung himself onto the back of a young Thoroughbred.

Lily climbed on top of Queenie and patted the side of her strong neck. Another apology sat at the tip of her tongue, but she held it back. What was the point? Her words didn't mean anything if she continued to use him as target practice for her insults. She'd need to be better at keeping her mouth shut and showing Madden she could play nice.

"Let's ride along the perimeter of the property," Madden said, lightly squeezing the sides of Ace to guide him into a slow trot. "I have a few places in mind to put some cameras, but I don't want to leave any stones unturned."

They rode in silence a few minutes longer until Lily

couldn't stand it. "Do you remember when we rode like this as kids? Seems like another lifetime ago."

Madden grunted. "Back then, Queenie was your mom's ride."

"This horse was like her second child." A wave of nostalgia washed over her. She blew out a long breath as memories of her mom filled her mind. "She loved this ranch. I can't help but feel like I'm failing her."

"What do you mean?"

She shrugged and kept her eyes on the horizon. The blistering sun was high in the sky. The gurgle of a nearby stream combined with the songs of birds nesting in the pine trees, creating the soundtrack of her life. And the ever-present mountains in the distance promised that some things never changed.

Unfortunately, that wasn't true of most things. Days flew by, bringing new challenges with no end in sight. No solution to the problems heaped at her feet.

"My mom loved this ranch with her entire being. Nothing brought her more joy than watching people experience all the things she thought was special about this town, this place. If she was here today and saw how badly we're struggling to make ends meet, she'd be devastated." An ache blossomed in Lily's chest. An ache of longing and sadness and desperation.

"You're right. This land was in your mom's bones, but she didn't care about it as much as she cared about you. She knows you're trying your best to put things on the right track." He cleared his throat. "I have to believe both our moms are watching out for us. Making sure we're doing the right thing."

She wanted to ask what he meant, but he wouldn't welcome an inquisition. Not by her. "I wish mine would tell me what I'm supposed to do. I always hated her endless opinions and suggestions when I was a teenager. I'd give anything for her to whisper the answer to all my problems in my ear."

"You're a lot like her," Madden said, bringing Ace to a stop beside an old shed at the edge of the property. "At least from what I remember. You're strong and brave. Smart as hell. There has to be a way to fix things you haven't considered. Something you could try."

She circled Queenie to the other side of Ace so she faced the wide meadow filled with plush green trees and gentle slopes covered in colorful wildflowers. "How? We offer the same experience the new hotel does, but we have a heavier price tag. We've slashed our prices as much as we can, but it hasn't helped. I'm not sure how to compete with that."

"Then offer something different."

The matter-of-fact response twisted her toward Madden. "What do you mean?"

He slid off Ace's back and ran a large, strong hand along the animal's shoulder. "You're right, you can't expect tourists to travel here and pay more for the same experience they can get right next door. But what if you didn't cater to tourists at all?"

She frowned. "But this is a dude ranch. No one in Cloud Valley is going to pay money to do the same things they're doing at their own ranches."

He grinned. "Probably not, but what will they pay for?"

She squeezed her eyes shut for a beat and prayed for patience. "You're talking in riddles, McKay."

"Sorry," he said, chuckling. "I'm no business expert. Hell, I'm still figuring out how to keep my office doors open. But what I have learned is you have to be willing to shift, to change, to look at things from a different perspective. You have a lot to offer people, and not just tourists. How can you use it?"

She thought back to the cozy cabin they'd just left. The handful of other cabins sitting empty, waiting to be used. "I did have one idea, but my dad brushed it aside."

"Tell me."

She scrunched her lips, unsure about opening up to him. But no one else in her life had actually listened to her ideas or made her feel she was capable of anything more than tending horses.

"Come on," he said. "You've told me worse things than an idea or two."

She winced. "Good point. Okay, I think we should offer our ranch as a wedding venue. That would appeal to people in town, the surrounding area and maybe even from other states. We have the cabins for the wedding party or out-of-town guests. The scenery is beautiful." She swept her hand to the side to indicate the magnificent views all around them.

A slow smile spread on Madden's face, barely visible beneath the shadow of his cowboy hat. "Sounds brilliant."

Two simple words hacked at all the self-doubt clogging her mind. "You really think so?"

"I do. Makes perfect sense to me."

"I wish my dad felt the same way. He won't hear my ideas." Guilt washed away all positive sentiments. "I'm horrible. The last thing I should be doing is complaining about my dad. Not when he's fighting for his life in the hospital."

"You're not complaining. You're discussing options that could help your family while showing me the property I need to protect. Now, this appears to be the last structure to search, right?"

She nodded, grateful for his knack of putting things into

perspective and shifting her focus on what was important. "Yeah, we don't really use this shed anymore. We stored things guests might need if they were out on the trails. Water, food, supplies for taking care of the horses. Now it's probably full of dust."

"Which will make it a quick search. Then I'll see about setting up some cameras before we tackle the office."

"Sounds good." The shed was small, the siding worn from lack of maintenance and rough weather. She'd been inside a few times, but wasn't in a rush to squeeze into the tight, probably dirty space with Madden. "I'll wait out here. No reason for us both to go in there."

The hinges to the rusty door squeaked as Madden stepped inside. "Holy hell, it's hot in here. Will you keep the door open for me, so I don't suffocate?"

She held the edge of the flimsy wood. "A couple days ago I would have jumped at the chance to nail this thing shut with you inside."

His husky chuckle made her grin. Good. The tension from earlier had dissipated enough for him to find humor in her sarcasm again.

A few minutes ticked by. The old floorboards shifted under Madden's footsteps until he marched to stand in front of her. "You need to see this."

"What is it?" She followed him inside the stuffy space, the door slamming shut behind her. Beams of muted light filtered in through a dirty window.

Madden pointed to a shelf shoved against the far wall.

She leaned forward for a closer look and spied a clear bag with what looked like small, white crystals. "What is that?"

"You might not have been out here for a while, but someone's using the shed. To store their drugs."

Chapter 9

Anger heated Lily's blood. She stormed passed Madden and forced her way out of the shed. Fresh air hit her face and she took two deep breaths through her nose, trying to calm her racing heart.

But her heart refused to slow.

Madden stepped out behind her.

She whirled around to face him. "I can't believe someone is storing their drugs in our shed. And it's not like it was a couple of kids sneaking out here for a joint or some booze. That was…well, to be totally honest I don't know what it was, but it looked scary as hell to me."

"Methamphetamines." He swept his cowboy hat off his head and wiped his forearm over his brow. "Serious drugs. Any idea who it belongs to?"

Her jaw dropped. "Are you kidding me? Does it look like I expected to find that?"

He shook his head and replaced his hat. "No, but you know who spends time out here. Who might have put the drugs inside the shed."

"No one who works here is doing meth. Or selling it. Or storing it." Even as the words came out of her mouth, she cringed. Someone had to put the drugs there. "It has to be someone from town."

"Maybe. Maybe not."

She anchored her fists on her hips. "What's that supposed to mean?"

"All possibilities need exploring, that's all. Even if they make you uncomfortable."

The hesitant look in his eyes turned her stomach. "What are you implying?" she asked, bracing herself for his answer.

Scrunching his nose, he dropped his gaze to the ground. "Someone wants your dad dead. Could the reason be drug related?"

Anger morphed into outrage, but she counted to ten before snapping out the first thought that came to her mind. "My dad would never have anything to do with drugs." Her voice was as slow and steady as the stream gurgling on the other side of the meadow, though the viciousness of unseen rapids brewed underneath.

"I'm not saying he does," Madden said, lifting his palms. "But there could be a different connection. Unfortunately, we can't ask him about it. Maybe there's something in the house that could tell us more."

"Or before I invade my father's privacy, we ask Charlie and Daniel. Maybe they know something."

"We could," he said, drawing out each syllable in a way that told her that he didn't like her suggestion. "But if one of them is involved with whatever the hell is going on, it might be wise to keep them in the dark a little. Leave the drugs where they are so as not to raise suspicions to whoever put them there."

"What about the police? Should we tell them what we found?"

He scratched his chin. "Probably. I'll get ahold of the sheriff's department. See what they say. But until then we can be proactive and see if there's anything else in the house."

His logic made her shove aside the emotional turmoil fighting to make her decisions. "Okay. Let's head back."

Hopping onto Queenie's back, she urged the horse into a canter and took off for the house. The wind cooled her skin. Strands of long hair whipped across her face. Fleeting trickles of joy waded through the muck weighing her down. For a few minutes, she gave into the joy, gave into the flight on top of Queenie's back until the cabin came into view.

She slowed the horse and walked her back to the barn. By the time Madden led Ace into his stall, she had Queenie settled and was ready to tackle her assignment. No matter how difficult.

"I want to be alone while going through Dad's things," she said. "Pawing through his personal items doesn't feel right, but having someone else watching while I do it is a whole other level of violation. I'll be quick, and I promise to tell you if I find anything suspicious."

Nodding, he unbuckled the cinch strap and slid the brown leather saddle and saddle pad off Ace's back. "Understandable. I'd like to at least be close by, just in case."

She almost asked in case of what, but she understood the direction his mind took. "I'll get started while you finish cooling down Ace. Shouldn't take me long."

His clenched jaw told her that he didn't like her plan, but she didn't need his permission. Yes, she wanted him to keep her safe and help solve this case. She hadn't signed up for a babysitter to stand guard twenty-four hours a day.

Besides, he'd gotten under her skin in a way she'd never anticipated in a short amount of time. A little space from Madden was what she needed to help get her head on straight.

Determined to get her unsavory task over with as soon as possible, she hurried inside and went straight to her father's bedroom. She flipped on the light and sadness pressed against her lungs. The king-size bed was neatly made. Not even a single wrinkle marred the deep blue comforter that matched the walls. The book he'd been reading lay opened on his nightstand with his reading glasses beside it. A half-filled glass of water waited to be either used or taken to the kitchen.

Would he ever make it home? Would he finish the mystery that had captured his attention or wear the glasses again—the round ones with the thick black frames she always teased him about?

No, she couldn't stand there and think the worst. Hell, she couldn't think about her father's health at all right now. Not if she was going to snoop through his things then get the hell out of there.

Ignoring the sinking feeling in her gut, she started with the tall dresser in the corner. She took great care as she methodically searched each drawer until she was certain nothing was hidden inside. She moved robotically through the rest of the room, next tackling the closet and nightstands. Searching under the bed and scouring every inch of the en suite bathroom.

A soft knock on the door frame brought her back into the bedroom. Madden stood in the hallway, his thumb tucked into the front pocket of his jeans and his ever-present cowboy hat in his free hand. "You doing okay?"

"Not really, but I haven't found anything out of the ordinary." And for that she was grateful. Each new spot she searched brought fear of not only discovering something tying her father to drug use, but a whole host of other horrors a daughter might uncover about her father she had no use knowing. She sighed, rounding the bed to run her fingertip along the cover of his book. "It's weird being in here without him. Seeing his things and not knowing if he'll ever be back in this room."

"I'm sure he'll be back in no time." Madden walked to her side and stared down at the nightstand. "He's a reader?"

She grinned. "Kind of. My mom was the one who always had a book in her hand. He used to tell her to get her nose out of the pages and enjoy the real world. The last year or so he's started reading more. I'd like to think it makes him feel closer to my mom." She picked up the book, and a piece of paper fluttered from the pages and onto the floor.

"You better not lose his place." Madden scooped the paper and frowned.

"What is it?" she asked, glancing at the makeshift bookmark.

He lifted the sheet for her to see. "Looks like he was taking notes that had nothing to do with the book. Mostly numbers. Big numbers. But that's not all."

She read the scribbled words written in her father's familiar hand and gasped.

Need to pay or else.

Madden disconnected his call with Reid and stared down at Lily, who sat in the middle of the floor of her father's office. A pile of papers surrounded her, and a pronounced frown pulled down her pouty lips.

He hated that look. Hated the aura of sadness and desperation that clung to her like a second skin. He wanted the Lily he'd seen while she rode Queenie. Carefree and laughing. Hair blowing all around her and no thought to anything beyond the simple pleasure of riding her horse.

Glancing up, she hoisted her hands filled with paperwork

in the air. "This is going to take forever. There's so much information in these pages. I need to file everything back in its place, but I can't leave one sheet unturned. Who knows what kind of information might be on it?" She tossed the paper back on the floor and sighed. "How was your call?"

"Reid's on his way. He'll install the cameras so I can help you." He waded through the mess and perched on the edge of the desk. "Talked to dispatch at the sheriff's department. They're sending out a deputy to look at the shed."

"Did you tell them what we found in his book?"

He nodded.

"Nothing makes sense anymore. This is all so over-whelming." She dropped her chin, and a defeated air wrapped around her like a cloak.

He clapped his hands, the sound loud and a bit abrasive in the confined room, then rubbed his palms together. "Let's see how we can lighten the load a little."

She offered him a small, sad smile. "I don't see how that's even possible."

"We'll take things one task at a time, starting here." He reached for her with an outstretched arm. She nestled her palm in his, and an intense heat shot up his arm and settled in his core. Tingles of excitement battled against the voice of logic telling him to keep his distance.

Clearing his throat, he tugged her to her feet and sev-ered the connection. Time to focus solely on the problems at hand and not the way his body reacted to her simplest touch. "You're right. We do want to look at everything in the office, but we don't have to read every single printout right away."

Her eyes were wide as she stared at him, her lips slightly parted, and all he could wonder was what she would taste like.

"But we might miss something," she said, snapping him

back to the moment. "Hell, you saw how close I was to missing the message my dad left in his book."

"True, but someone already went through all this." He flicked his wrist to indicate the mess waiting for them on the floor. "If the person who broke into your house found anything useful, they probably would have taken it with them. Not left it on the floor. We can glance at everything as we replace it, but no need to scrutinize it too closely. If we miss something, we can always comb back through."

"That's actually brilliant."

He grinned. "I have my moments."

She rolled her eyes. "Even a broken clock's right twice a day."

Now it was his turn to roll his eyes. "All right, Grandma. Where do you want everything?"

"Most of this needs to be filed in the cabinet. Each drawer is labeled, so it shouldn't be too difficult to find the right spot. I'll sift through the paperwork and put it in piles, then you can find the right folder. Sound good?"

"Absolutely."

He stayed glued to his spot on the desk as she shuffled through the mess, making orderly piles.

Concentration made a tiny crease between her eyebrows. She scanned every item before finding the right place for it. "Nothing of interest so far."

"Not surprised. My guess is we'll find more information on the computer. It's a good thing your father still has such an old one. The burglar probably expected a laptop, something smaller they could take with them. A giant monitor and tower from the 1980s probably weren't expected."

She snorted out a laugh. "It's not *that* old. But I guess I should be grateful my dad clings to his ways and has refused to upgrade the technology around here."

"Do you have the passwords to get into this thing?" He sank onto the leather chair in front of the monitor and wiggled the mouse on the black pad to bring the screen to life.

Rounding the corner of the desk, Lily slid into the tiny space between Madden and the desk to study the screen. "No, but it can't be that hard to figure out. Most likely someone's birthday or something simple like 1, 2, 3, 4."

"Man, our fathers might be more alike than either one of them ever realized."

She shot him a grin that melted his bones. "You're probably right. Two stubborn old men who always think they're right. Just like their children."

She had to lean across him to reach the keyboard. Her fingers flew across the keys, but the password she'd guessed wasn't correct.

She tried again, and he prayed she was wrong. As much as they needed to get into the computer, her body so close to his spiked his blood pressure. He breathed in her scent, the hay and subtle smell of the horses still on her skin, but the floral notes from her shampoo remained.

"Got it. Mom's birthday." She spun around, and excitement danced in her eyes. She raised her fists in exaggerated celebration then braced her forearm on the side of the chair.

She was close. So close. The air around them buzzed with electricity. Charged by some unknown force he couldn't stop. He should move. Jump out of the chair and put some distance between them.

But he couldn't.

Her gaze locked on his and her eyes widened for a beat.

He swallowed hard. His mouth dry. He wet his lips with his tongue, and the flick of her gaze to his mouth was like throwing gasoline on a fire.

Instinct took over. He touched his mouth to hers. Slowly. Softly.

She moaned and moved her lips against his.

The need to touch her had him cupping her jaw with his palm, his other hand dipping along her side. Her skin was so soft, her lips so tender. Desire flared to life inside him, so hot and raw it was almost blinding.

The doorbell rang, breaking the magic of the moment, and Lily pulled away. She brought her fingertips to her mouth and straightened. "I...we shouldn't..."

The bell rang again.

He cleared his throat and shot to his feet. "Sorry. I shouldn't have done that. I'll get the door. It's probably Reid. I'll let him know where to place the cameras."

He didn't wait to hear any more of her regrets before storming out of the office. He didn't want to listen to all the reasons she wanted him not to kiss her. Hell, they were probably the same reasons swimming around his head.

Because as attractive as Lily was, she was his client and a woman he'd agreed to protect. The last thing she needed was to add more confusion to her already precarious situation. Things between them may have gone from stormy to a light drizzle, but she'd made it clear what she thought of him.

He might be okay with constantly proving himself to the townspeople to build his business, but he wouldn't grovel to a woman who'd made him feel like crap the last couple of years. Even if she'd just given him the best damn kiss of his life.

Chapter 10

Madden stalked toward the front door with the taste of Lily still on his lips and yanked it open. "What the hell did you bring?"

Reid stood on the porch carrying two large brown bags. "Eve sent me with food. Where do you want me to put it?"

He glanced at his watch, shocked to discover the time. Somehow late afternoon had crept in without so much as a thought to eating lunch. "Set it on the island in the kitchen. I'll grab something once we're done with the cameras."

While Reid crossed through the living room to unburden his load, Madden padded down the hallway and poked his head into the office. "Reid brought food from Tilly's. It's in the kitchen if you're hungry. I'm going to help him outside."

Glancing up from the computer, her eyes locked on his and she gave a small nod. "Tell Reid thanks."

"Will do." He left her to find his partner. He couldn't handle another second sharing such close quarters with her. He needed fresh air. A task to focus on that would take his mind away from his own stupidity.

Reid stood in the kitchen and shoved french fries in his mouth. "You really should eat these now. They won't be as good if you have to warm them up."

"I thought you said the food was for me and Lily?" He followed the savory scents of grease and salt.

"Trust me. She won't mind. Want me to find you a plate or just eat from the containers? There's burgers and a big ass salad. Fries and onion rings. Eve even threw in some of her homemade apple pie."

Madden reached in the bag for a fat onion ring and took a bite, closing his eyes as he savored the crispy coating. A part of him wanted to dig in and fill his empty stomach, but he didn't want his presence to deter Lily from coming into the kitchen to eat.

"We have work to do. I'll eat when we're done."

Reid's eyebrows shot up. "I thought I was supposed to put up the cameras so you can keep an eye on Lily?"

"We won't be far." He stomped past Reid and out of the house.

"Everything okay, boss?" Reid asked, following.

"Dude, I told you. Stop calling me that."

Reid grinned. "She's really getting to ya, huh?"

Madden fisted his hands at his sides so he wouldn't smack the amusement off his friend's face. "I don't know what you're talking about. Now, where are the cameras?"

"In my truck." Reid climbed down the porch steps to his truck and pulled a duffel from the passenger seat. "Did you already figure out where we should place them?"

Madden pointed out the spots he'd already picked. "I want some floodlights, too. One by the front and back doors. Maybe by some of the barns."

"I brought two lights. We can cover the house, but I'll need to head back to the office to grab more. Can you get the rest of what we'll need from the back?"

"Sure." Madden found the red, rusted toolbox and ladder. He lifted them from the cab and placed them on the ground.

He rummaged around inside to get to the tools they'd need and carried them to the starting place for the first camera.

The sun beat down and sweat dripped between Madden's shoulder blades. His stomach growled. Hunger hadn't been on his mind until Reid had shown up with food. Now he just wanted to get the cameras installed so he could grab a meal and a shower and settle his nerves. Nerves that were a tangled mess after his dumb decision to kiss Lily.

They didn't say another word as they worked quickly and efficiently until the areas outside the house were properly outfitted.

Climbing down the ladder, Madden plopped on the grass and leaned against the side of the barn. The muscles in his injured shoulder screamed but being active settled him.

"We done in this area?" Reid asked, and sat beside him in the shade.

"Yeah. We found drugs in a shed at the edge of the property. I want to set something up there. See if anyone comes snooping around. The rest of this place is too damn big to patrol, but as long as we know Lily's safe, that's the main objective."

Reid let out a long, low whistle. "Drugs, huh? You think that's connected to her dad?"

Madden shrugged. "Seems like a hell of a coincidence if it's not, but I can't jump to conclusions. I want to talk to my dad. See if we've had any issues with trespassing or he's heard about a drug problem. He doesn't leave home much these days, but he gets an earful every week when his buddies stop by. He might have heard things that could prove useful."

"And how's Lily? She holding up? All of this has to be a huge shock to her system."

At the sound of her name, he swore he could taste her

again. Feel her. "She's fine." The words squeaked out, his throat tight.

"Damn, you've got it bad."

He growled, low and menacing. "Watch yourself. Lily's a client, one who drives me crazy most of the time. Nothing more."

Reid turned and studied him, eyes narrowed. "Tell yourself whatever you need to, but I know you. Something's going on in your head. If you don't want to talk about it, that's no skin off my back. But if you do, I'm here."

Sighing, Madden scrubbed a palm over his face. Talking about his complicated feelings for Lily was the last thing he wanted to do, but if he didn't get them out, he'd choke on them. "I don't know, man. Lily's exactly who I thought she was but also so different. The minute I have her figured out, something new comes out of her mouth that has me rethinking everything."

"Do you need a break? I can take over. I can think of worse ways to spend my day than hanging out with a beautiful woman on a gorgeous piece of land. Just say the word and I'll take that burden off your shoulders for a little while."

The urge to punch the smirk off his best friend's face was enough to have Madden considering the offer. He was in way too deep with Lily, but he couldn't back off now. And he definitely couldn't stomach the idea of her spending time alone with Reid.

"I can handle her. I just need to keep things professional and do the work. Same as any other assignment."

As if reading his mind, Reid snorted. "Sure thing, boss."

Grumbling, he rose to his feet. Leaving the coolness of the shade was the last thing Madden wanted to do, but he had a job to finish. "Come on. We have one more camera to install by the shed."

Then he had to prepare for spending the rest of the night with Lily. He'd dive into the details of this case and keep his lips to himself, even if it killed him.

An intrinsic need for comfort food had Lily reaching for the double cheeseburger over the sensible salad. She debated eating while standing in the kitchen but decided to retreat to the office. Madden might have changed his plans to help Reid with the equipment, but she wouldn't tempt fate. Better to keep looking through her father's computer while also staying as far away from Madden as she could get.

The memory of their too-quick kiss flashed in her mind, and she pressed her fingertips to her lips. The earth hadn't just shaken when he'd kissed her, it'd been shoved off its axis. She might not have a ton of experience with men, but she wasn't a prude, and never had a man made her insides melt with a simple kiss before.

Settling back in her father's desk chair, she took a giant bite of her burger. Better to stuff her face with food than get lost in silly fantasies that would never come true. Hell, she wasn't even sure she wanted them to. Finding Madden attractive and interesting was one thing, taking things between them a step further was another.

When her father healed and was released from the hospital, she didn't need to send him right back to the emergency room. Which was exactly what would happen after he suffered a heart attack because she'd fallen for a McKay.

With the burger halfway finished and nothing of note so far on the computer, her mind drifted to Madden. She needed to get a grip before he returned. She couldn't spend the rest of the evening with him if heat flooded her body every time she thought of him.

Especially since he'd made it clear he regretted the kiss and had fled the room as soon as the opportunity arose.

Needing to dissect her feelings with someone other than herself, she picked up her phone and called Eve.

"Hey, Lily. Did you get the food?" Eve asked when she answered on the second ring.

"Yes, thank you. You've already done so much and now you're feeding me more. The burger was amazing."

"Burger? Can't remember the last time you came into Tilly's and didn't have a salad. I made sure to put your favorite in there."

Eve's confusion coaxed a smile from Lily. No matter how the next few days played out, she had to make more of an effort to connect with such a caring person. "Comfort food won out today. It's been one for the books. I'm not sure how things keep getting worse, but they do."

"I'm sorry to hear that." A beat of silence pulsed on the line. "How's it been spending time with Madden? You two are like oil and water."

Lily snorted out a short laugh. "You have no idea. The more time I spend with him the more he gets under my skin. But I'm also confused. He's not exactly the man I thought he was."

"I know you two have had your differences, and I won't pretend like I completely understand either side, but he's a good guy. Always has been. I'm glad you're seeing a different side of him."

"I'm not sure it's a good thing," Lily said, rolling her eyes to the ceiling.

"Far be it for me to pry, but now I'm really curious about what you guys have been up to out there all alone."

Lily winced at the amusement in Eve's voice. She considered dodging her interest, but the whole reason she called Eve was to get everything off her chest. "He kissed me." The words shot out of her mouth before she could change her mind.

"What?" Eve's question came out in a shriek of excitement. "How the heck did that even happen? I mean, you and Madden hated each other, and after just twenty-four hours you're kissing?"

Groaning, Lily dropped her head in her hand, elbow propped on the desk. "Not *kissing*. Kissed. Singular. One time. And you are not to tell a soul because I'm sure it won't happen again."

"Okay," Eve said, drawing out the word. "Do you not want it to happen again?"

She shrugged, even though no one could see her. "I don't know. It was one hell of a kiss, but it's Madden. No matter how nice and helpful he's been, I can't ever get past what his decision to sell his land has done to my family."

"Have you talked to him about that?" Eve asked. "I mean, really talked to him. Open and honestly with no jabs or mean comments."

She winced then clicked a new file on the computer. "Not really. I mean, we haven't exactly been having heart-to-heart chats."

"Maybe you should. You might never have a better time to really get to the bottom of a problem. Sometimes people make choices because they're shoved in a corner that no one else sees. I understand Madden and his dad made a decision that can't be undone, but understanding their thinking might at least help you let go of some of your anger."

A spreadsheet filled with numbers littered the computer screen. The ranch's dwindling bank account reminded her of why she was so angry. But Eve had a point. Life was too short to hold on to hostility that wasn't helping anyone. Especially if Eve was right and there was a deeper reason the McKays hadn't shared.

She pulled up a different spreadsheet and sighed. "Having one less problem in my life would be nice."

"And then if you happen to kiss again…"

Lily couldn't help but laugh imagining Eve wiggling her eyebrows and smirking. "Not a good idea. Besides, he jumped up like he'd been bit by a rattlesnake and ran out of the room. I didn't even get a chance to talk to him about it before Reid showed up and Madden decided to get out of Dodge."

"Men. I swear they're always making things worse by being idiots. So you didn't get a chance to say anything about the kiss?"

She brought back the moment, replayed it in her head for the hundredth time. She'd been so flustered, she couldn't remember the words that had poured from her mouth. "I… said something but can't recall exactly what."

Eve chuckled. "Sounds like you two have a lot to talk about. I may not be the best person to offer advice on relationships, but the one thing I learned from my parents is don't gloss over a conversation just because it might be uncomfortable. Those are usually the most important ones."

"That's good advice, even if I'm cringing on the inside just thinking about it."

The sound of the front door opening followed by heavy footsteps reached her ears. She hated the fear that hitched high in her throat.

"Hey, Lily," Madden called out. "It's me and Reid. We'll be in the kitchen."

Her muscles instantly relaxed. "He's back. Guess I better work up the nerve to have a fun talk. Thanks for listening."

"Anytime."

Lily disconnected and placed her phone beside the keyboard. The paper she'd discovered sat on the other side. She picked it up and read through the numbers then flicked her glance at the computer screen.

Her pulse quickened. The spreadsheet on the screen consisted of dates, months and years, followed by a number that corresponded with ones listed on the page from her father's book. Maybe the other figures her father had written down were dates, not just random amounts.

Holding the paper up to the monitor, she gasped. She added one more thing to discuss with Madden. Even though she needed to address the elephant in the room, their kiss had just dropped to the bottom of her list.

Chapter 11

Numbers ran on repeat in Madden's brain twenty minutes later as he and Lily rode four-wheelers back out to the shed on the edge of her property. After he and Reid popped inside for a quick drink of water, Lily had called him into the office to show him what she'd found. He might not have figured out exactly what Kevin Tremont was tracking, but it couldn't be good.

Lily swung off her ride and removed the dark blue helmet. Dust and wind had created a beautiful mess of her hair and face. "What's the plan?"

He averted his gaze and bit back a groan. Just when he thought she couldn't get sexier, she had to do something so simple and natural that made her look like she'd walked off a movie set. He wanted nothing more than to comb his fingers through those long, tangled tresses and finish what they'd started earlier.

No, it couldn't happen. Her reaction after they'd kissed had made her feelings clear. The word *shouldn't* from her mouth had been like a bucket of icy water. He'd never pursue a woman after she'd told him no. No matter how badly his body craved her.

Hopping down, he shrugged the backpack off his shoulders and dug inside. "I just need to install a camera on the shed. Somewhere a little hidden."

After working off his initial burst of irritation and confusion, he'd changed his mind about coming so far out on the property without Lily. He'd sent Reid back to the office to grab more floodlights and investigate any drug-related crimes in the area then he'd asked Lily to help him with the equipment.

He didn't really need the help, but she'd agreed quickly enough to tell him he'd made the right call.

"Do you think my dad is involved with selling drugs?" She stared at the old shed as if afraid of the secrets the shingles could tell. Thin, white clouds padded the sky, casting her in shadows.

The tortured tone of her voice gutted him. He couldn't say he understood what she was going through, but he had lived with a father who'd kept a big secret. A secret that had changed the trajectory of their entire family.

But he couldn't get caught up in emotions—hers or his own. Doing so before had proven disastrous. Digging into his bag, he grabbed his equipment and scanned the limited nooks and crannies.

"Hard to say. The deposit amounts you found were large and frequent, but we couldn't track down a bank account. If those amounts were tied to selling drugs, there'd have to be a lot more than what we found. The house has been searched, and unless whoever broke in stole his stash, there'd have to either be more drugs somewhere or another place your dad's hiding them. Not to mention a connection to the supplier."

She stayed rooted to the spot, the long blades of grass and weeds brushing against her legs. "I spend too much time with him for something so major to go unnoticed. I mean, this isn't a scene from *Breaking Bad*. This is my life. My dad's life. No way he's sneaking around, dealing drugs. And to what end? If he was using, that would have been evident in his blood work at the hospital. If he was bringing in tons of money, the ranch wouldn't be limping along so badly."

"Could he be spending the money on something else?" Kevin Tremont might not be Madden's favorite person, but he hated the idea that the man could be using drug money for some other purpose than lessening the burden heaped on his daughter's shoulders.

Lily stiffened, her mouth pressed in a hard line and eyes narrowed. "Like what?"

"Honestly, I don't know. I'm just throwing out any and all options right now. I'm sure the sheriff's department has some ideas. We should sit down with Deputy Hill and Deputy Silver. See if they'll offer some insight."

Spotting the best place for the camera, Madden unhooked the stepladder he'd brought along from the back of the four-wheeler and set it on the uneven ground. Thank God he didn't need to reach any higher. Judging by the look on her face, she might shove the ladder out from underneath him.

"Can they do that? I mean, legally, are they supposed to spill secrets to an open case?"

"Your guess is as good as mine. Maybe it'd be better to speak with someone not on the case." He climbed the few steps and drilled the camera into the siding, just above the door frame. The thick casing would hide the small device if anyone came by, but also give a good shot of any unwanted visitors.

The drill buzzed, sending a nearby hawk into the sky. His shoulder screamed at him to stop. After the work spent moving hay, his muscles already ached. He gritted his teeth, determined not to lower his damn arm before the task was finished. If he couldn't handle five freaking minutes with his arm above his head, holding only a lightweight piece of equipment, he should close his business and slink away into the sunset now.

"Is there someone else in the department we could contact who isn't officially on the case who could give us information?" She took a step closer, raising her voice to be heard above the noise.

His mind went blank as he concentrated. Finished, he dropped his arm to the side and closed his eyes for a beat. He lifted his sore shoulder, moving it in a circular motion to lessen the ache.

"Are you okay?" she asked. "Are you hurt?"

His eyes shot open, and she was even closer.

Concern pinched her expression.

"I'm fine. Just a little sore." He hated the briskness of his words, but he didn't want her to know of his limitations. He didn't want her, or anyone else's, pity. "Finished here. If the camera picks up any activities, I'll get a notification on my phone. That will help us keep an eye on things without having to come all the way out here again."

She nodded, but something in her eyes told him she didn't buy his story about simply being a little sore.

"I can call Deputy Sanders," he said, rolling over her worry for him. "He's good friends with my pops. He might be willing to divulge a little more than some of the other deputies. Especially over a game of poker."

She frowned. "We're going to ask Deputy Sanders to come over and play poker?"

He couldn't help but grin at her confusion. "No, we're going to my dad's house. The weekly poker game's tonight.

Sanders will be there, as well as some other old-timers from town. Nothing gets past those guys. If there's any whispering on the street about drug issues, they'll know. And even though they'd never admit it, they cluck about like a flock of old hens over a game of cards. It'll be easier to draw out information."

The corner of Lily's mouth ticked up. "All right. I'll go to your dad's and talk to his friends on one condition."

He was almost afraid to ask. "What?"

"They let us play."

"You want to play poker with a bunch of old men?"

"Could be fun." She lifted a slim shoulder then fit her helmet over her head before straddling the seat of her four-wheeler.

He watched her take off at top speed down the trail. A lot of unknowns weighed him down, but one thing was certain. Lily Tremont was full of surprises.

After they'd returned to the cabin, Lily managed to grab a quick shower and make herself a little more presentable before heading to the McKay Ranch. And if the look of appreciation shining from Madden's smoky eyes was any indication, she'd done a pretty damn good job of putting herself together.

Not that he looked too shabby himself. He'd cleaned up but kept the scruff clinging to his jawline. Worn jeans showcased his long, lean legs, and a fresh button-up shirt shoved up to his elbows had her ogling his strong forearms.

"Ready?" he asked.

She forced a smile, hating the icy tone of his voice. They'd broken through so many walls just for them to keep popping up. The last thing she wanted was for his moment of vulnerability—okay, if she was being honest a moment where a simple kiss had shaken her to the core—to create a chasm between them that couldn't be crossed.

"Sure am. Is your father okay with me coming?"

This time a pure, genuine grin spread on his mouth. "Are you serious? He'll get a kick out of seeing you."

She hoped so because her father would never be so accommodating with Madden.

Madden led the way to his truck, opening her door and waiting for her to climb in before he rounded the hood to the driver's side. Nervous energy had her clutching her hands in her lap. Neither of them spoke as he drove to the ranch she hadn't seen since she'd been a child.

Driving under the archway that boasted the words McKay Ranch was like driving back in time. As a kid, she'd loved coming to visit Madden and his brother. Spending time on a working cattle ranch had been her version of heaven, a way to show off to the boy whose attention she'd always tried to snag.

When had that changed? When had that innocent friendship and adoration shifted to annoyance and anger? She couldn't blame it all on Madden's family selling off part of their land. That had come years after animosity brewed between them.

Remembering Eve's suggestion to lean into the tough conversations, she stared at Madden's profile. Studied the hard lines of his face. "When did we start hating each other?"

His body twitched as if her question caused a physical reaction. He kept quiet and maneuvered his truck to park behind an old sheriff's cruiser. Shutting off the engine, he faced her. "I've never hated you."

She snorted. "Well, you haven't liked me much. Why? Why did we stop being childhood friends? We went from running around in the woods and riding horses to people who couldn't stand one another. I honestly can't remember when things changed."

A beat of silence stretched in the confined space. "It was after my mom died."

She blinked at the rawness in his voice and searched for words, trying to recall how the death of his mother had altered the way their relationship would play out for years to come.

"She was in that car accident, passed away, and you never came back to the ranch. Your mama did a few times. Brought food for us. Made sure my pops was all right. Hell, that first year without Mom she even brought over back to school supplies for me and Dax." He chuckled, low and wistful. "Good thing too or him and I would have shown up without a damn thing."

She couldn't help but smile. "Sounds like her. Always looking out for others."

"She was a good woman. When she'd stop by, Dax and I would drop everything to see her. I always hoped you'd be with her, but you never were." He twisted his lips to the side, his expression pinched. "Why'd you stop coming? I needed my friend. Needed to have every bit of normalcy I could. Even as a kid I understood nothing would ever be normal again, but I craved that stability. That routine. Hell, I'm sure that's why I went into the military once I graduated. Having my mom ripped away wasn't her choice, but you chose not to come back. I guess I held on to that hurt more than I realized."

Tears burned the backs of her eyes. Shame nearly drowned her. She searched her memory for what had caused that little girl to stay home. To not run to her friends and be there for them. "I was afraid."

"Of what?"

She shifted to stare out the windshield. "I don't remember really. I just know something about coming here and seeing you, knowing your mom wouldn't be here, it was too much for me. I wish I could say I'd been some wise child who understood that some things weren't about me. That life hands us situations where we need to rise above our own fears to be there for those we care about. But I was just a terrified, sad kid who couldn't comprehend that the big, brave McKay boys would want me around."

"The big brave McKay boys were eleven and five and heartbroken." He sighed and shook his head. "Hell, we're still heartbroken."

"I am, too. I was gutted when your mother died. Destroyed when my mom passed a few years later. I suppose some of my anger was from watching her slowly slip away while fighting cancer then seeing you always so carefree and happy. Might sound crazy, but it was like some kind of betrayal. Like how could you find your happiness while I was in a living nightmare?"

She swung her gaze toward him again, and the knots in her stomach loosened. "I always wondered why you wouldn't show up when she was in the hospital. How you couldn't put away your anger when you more than anyone would know what I was going through. But why would you when I hadn't been there for you? I'm sorry, Madden."

He blew out a long, shuddering breath. "Man, what a bunch of wasted time. But you really did act stuck up in high school. There was no need for that."

She burst into laughter. A full, belly laugh and damn it, it felt good. "And you walked around that school like you were God's gift to women. I mean, come on. A little humility wouldn't have killed you."

"I guess not, although you were the only one who seemed to mind." His slight smile melted away. "What brought this on?"

Not wanting to admit she'd called Eve earlier to discuss their kiss, she hurried to create another reason that he'd buy at face value. "The last couple of days have had their enjoyable moments. Moments when I've forgotten my disdain and just enjoyed your company. Moments when memories of our youth came back. The ranch's current issues have taken up so much of my life, I often forget how much history we share."

"Maybe we can try and forget the bad parts and remember the good," he said.

She considered his offer, and as logical as it sounded, it wasn't possible. At least not yet. "I don't think I can do that. I still can't wrap my mind around why you and your dad sold your land to developers. I'm not a child anymore who can't see past my own needs. I know the decisions you made are about you and your family, but my family's livelihood is dying as a direct result of your choice. I need to understand why."

His body stiffened, and he fixed his attention on the old farmhouse in front of them. "Things happen in life that we'll never understand, and we have to learn to be okay with it. If not, we'll drive ourselves crazy."

Without another word, he climbed out of the truck and slammed the door behind him. Leaving her with nothing but her spiraling thoughts and a deafening silence.

Chapter 12

Madden paused on the porch to wait for Lily. He drew in a large breath, filling his lungs with the fresh evening air. The conversation with Lily had been unexpected to say the least, and had struck a nerve he hadn't even known existed. He hadn't thought about the days following his mother's death in a long time. Hadn't remembered the bitter disappointment of his friendship with Lily fading into oblivion.

Was that what he wanted now? Lily's friendship? The impact of their kiss had him wanting much more than that, but a relationship with Lily would never happen.

Because no matter how far they'd come, he could never tell her the truth about why his father needed to sell his land. Not when his father had made him promise to keep his secret.

With her head down and arms crossed over her middle, Lily walked up the steps.

Their conversation had been surprisingly constructive, and he'd blown the whole thing to pieces. He'd fix things later, but for now, they needed to focus on getting information from his dad and his pals. "Ready for this?"

"Ready as I'll ever be," she said.

He winced at her hesitation. Gone was her excitement over a pickup game of cards that had thrown him for a loop.

He held the front door of his childhood home open and waited for her to walk inside before following. Rumbles of laughter floated down the hall from the kitchen, meeting them in living room.

His father seldom used this space, opting to leave the delicate furniture and frilly touches his mother had selected long ago in place. Walter preferred to move mainly between the kitchen and den, often sleeping in his recliner in front of the television instead of alone in his bed.

"Damn it, Walter. You stacked the deck you old sonofabitch!"

Lily glanced over her shoulder with wide eyes.

Madden chuckled. "Sounds like Larry was dealt a rough hand. He's always been a poor loser. Don't let them scare you."

"I'm more excited to play than ever now," she said, grinning.

Good. At least the rambunctious old men had brought the light back into her eyes. "You have no idea what you're walking into." He followed her down the hall into the spacious kitchen.

A round poker table sat in the middle of the room. For years, he and Dax would help their father move the kitchen table out of the way and roll out the green felt table his father insisted on using. Recently, moving the furniture had become more trouble than it was worth. His dad ate his meals on a TV tray while watching a ball game, choosing a tablecloth to drape over his poker equipment when guests came, which wasn't often.

Four men sat with cards in their hands and beers in front of them. Two scowled, one laughed, and his dad grinned with a mischievous gleam in his gray eyes.

He had a good hand.

Madden never understood how his dad's old pals couldn't see that look. They'd played poker together every week for over a decade.

Walter glanced up and his grin spread. "Look what the cat dragged in."

"Hey, Pops. How's it going?" He skirted around the edge of the table, slapping a hand on the old men's shoulders as he made his way to his dad and placed a kiss on his wrinkled forehead. "You taking these suckers for everything they're worth yet?"

"He's trying," Larry Blackstock growled. "He's a cheat. Always has been."

Deputy Sanders sat beside his dad. He dipped his chin in greeting then aimed his attention at Lily. "Hey, Lily. How's your dad doing?"

The crowd grew quiet, all eyes turned to Lily.

Walter and Kevin Tremont might have a beef between them, but every man sitting at the table knew Kevin and his daughter. Their town was small, their community tight. And no one liked seeing one of their own hurt.

Lily offered a small smile. "He's hanging in there. I didn't get a chance to see him today, but I spoke with the doctor. We're holding out hope he wakes soon."

"That's good to hear," Larry said, setting his cards face-down on the table. He shook his head and his disheveled silver hair flopped with the movement. Wrinkles cascaded down his face as if gravity insisted on winning the fight. "Still can't believe how everything played out. A damn shame, that's for sure."

Marvin Williamson, his dad's oldest friend who was more like family to Madden, clicked his tongue. His familiar cowboy hat with the burnt red material wrapped around the base of the hat still sat on his head. "This world's goin' to hell and taking us all along for the ride. Things aren't the way they used to be. No reason a man should fear being gunned down in the street. Sheriff better figure this mess out quick. People want answers, and they want them now."

"While that might be true, right now I think Lily just needs a chair, don't ya?" Walter wagged a finger at Madden. "Come on now boy. You know better than to let a lady just stand around waitin' on you. Grab her a seat."

"Yes, sir." Two folding chairs leaned against the wall, probably brought out by Dax after he'd informed his dad he and Lily would be stopping by. He opened one and placed it at the table then repeated the process with the second one.

Pulling a seat out a little for Lily, he waited for her to sit then took the chair beside her.

"You gonna sit before offering our guest a drink?" Walter barked.

Madden shook his head and stared at Lily with raised brows, trying to rein in his patience. "Would you like anything? Food? Water? A time machine to travel back to when you decided to come here?"

She struggled against a laugh. "I'm fine. And thank you, all of you. I know my dad would be touched by your concern."

Marvin, who sat on the other side of Lily, patted her hand. "We're here for you both. For anything you need."

Mumbles of agreement echoed around the table.

Taking that as a perfect opening, Madden cleared his throat. "Have any of you heard of drug problems in town?"

The mumblings stopped. Marvin and Larry fiddled with their cards. Deputy Sanders worked his jaw back and forth. Walter sighed.

"What am I missing?" Madden asked, bouncing his gaze from man to man while Lily stiffened beside him.

Deputy Sanders flicked his attention to Walter before focusing on Madden with a pronounced frown. "The town has had an influx of drug issues recently. With the new resort, dealers have come into town to tap a new market. Nothing too serious has happened, just busted some deals and a few incidents with petty crime."

Madden avoided his dad's forlorn expression, probably uncomfortable with the knowledge a surge of crime in their community came from a situation where he held some responsibility. "What kind of drugs?"

"Marijuana. Meth. Found some cocaine a few weeks back on a tourist in town who busted into the general store."

"What about the suppliers? Any idea where these drugs are coming from?" Madden asked.

"We've found a few cooks. Small-time growers. Nothing major." Deputy Sanders shifted in his seat. "Why do you want to know?"

"Do you think my dad is involved at all?" Lily lifted her chin a tiny fraction, but Madden could see the slight tremor of her hands. She was strong and brave to tackle the issue head-on, but she couldn't hide her fear. At least not from him.

Deputy Sanders's eyes widened. "Kevin? No. I mean, I don't have any knowledge of such things. I heard about what was found on your property—Hill and Silver have been chasing that angle—but I don't see how your dad could be connected."

Tension practically leaked out of Lily, and a tiny smile touched her lips.

"Has Deputy Hill or Deputy Silver said anything else about the case?" Madden asked.

"Not really. They've been out of the station a lot, and I've been picking up more time patrolling the town so they can focus on the case. Not much crossover."

"Makes sense." He wished he could uncover more information, but at least he knew the deputies in charge of finding Kevin Tremont's attacker were doing their due diligence. Hopefully they'd find the truth soon.

The front door squeaked open, followed by slow steady footsteps. Madden took note of the familiar faces around the table. The number of players at his father's weekly poker game had dwindled after they'd sold their land to developers, only the three men in the room choosing to remain loyal to a decades-long friendship. No one else had set foot in their home in years. "Expecting anyone else, Pops?"

Dax walked into the kitchen, his mouth in a hard line and his fitted shirt smeared with dirt. "He's always expecting me, aren't ya Dad? You know, the son who's left behind. Came to grab some grub and maybe sit in on a hand."

Madden bit back a groan. He had enough on his plate right now. His petulant little brother was the last thing he wanted to deal with. While the group welcomed Dax, Madden leaned close to Lily to whisper in her ear. "Do you want to head home?"

She shook her head. "That'd be rude. Besides, I'm in the mood to hustle a roomful of men out of their hard-earned cash."

He couldn't help but laugh. No matter what the situation, Lily was always in her element. Willing to blend in and put her best foot forward. He studied his brother as Dax grabbed a beer from the fridge and popped off the cap.

Maybe it was time he learned a few lessons from Lily.

A weird tension crackled in the air as soon as Dax entered the room. Lily had seen Madden's brother around town, but hadn't really taken note of the man he'd become while she'd been busy keeping her head above water.

As Dax stood at the kitchen counter with a beer in his hand, she couldn't help but notice the hard lines of his face. He had a certain edge that Madden didn't have. Where Madden oozed an almost cockiness that she hated to admit came off as charming, Dax appeared closed off, angry somehow despite his smile as he stalked to the island and dragged a chair to the table.

"Hey, Lil. Shocked to see you here."

"I could never say no to a good game of poker," she joked, trying to lighten the mood.

He snorted. "Sure. How's your dad?"

"Fine. Thanks for asking." She didn't want to go into the details again, and it was clear that Dax only asked so he didn't look like a complete dick.

Dax took a long pull of his beer then set the brown bottle on the table. "Can I keep a stallion in the old barn for a few days, Pops?"

Madden narrowed his eyes, head tilted to the side. "Where'd you get a stallion?"

Dax's smile disappeared, replaced with a scowl that turned his hard edges dangerous. "What does it matter to you? I got to make a living, don't I? You made sure I had to look elsewhere, so that's what I'm doing."

Madden's hands curled into fists at his sides. Irritation radiated from his skin. He blew a long breath out his nose. "Glad you found something. What are you doing?"

"Training horses over at the Williamsons' ranch." He nodded toward Marvin, the proud owner of the cattle ranch across town. "Bought a young stallion old Marv can't break and asked me to help. It'll be easier if I have him here, if Pops is okay with it."

"When did you guys start buying horses?" Madden asked.

Marvin lifted a shoulder. "You know how it is. Life's

always changing. Needed to branch out a little. Dax has always been good with horses so figured I'd ask for his help."

"You can bring him here," Walter interjected. "Got plenty of room."

"Thanks. This guy's a real rascal. Stubborn as hell. He'll need extra attention. I have to figure out the best approach to use with him." Dax scratched the dark whiskers on his chin.

"Lily's good with horses," Madden said. "She might have some suggestions."

Dax raised his eyebrows, amusement shining from his blue eyes. "I'm good. Thanks."

The condescension dripping from his words raised her hackles, but she kept her opinion to herself. Clearly there was some kind of animosity between the brothers, and she didn't want to put herself in the middle. Besides, she had enough problems of her own to deal with.

"I'm around if you change your mind. But for now, let's play cards." She forced a cheerful smile.

"Been a long time since we've had a lady at the table," Walter said, grinning. "You sure you can handle us?"

"Trust me, I can handle anything."

The men chuckled as Larry dealt the cards and Madden placed poker chips in front of each of them.

Studying her hand, excitement stirred in the pit of her stomach. As hard as her life was right now, a confidence she'd never experienced grew inside her, and she finally did believe she could handle whatever was thrown at her. And she couldn't help but wonder if the man who sat beside her had something to do with it.

But in this moment, her victory had nothing to do with Madden. She shoved the pile of chips into the center of the table and grinned. "I'm all in."

Chapter 13

After Lily took all his money, Madden convinced her to call it quits and head back to her place. The other men were happy to see her leave and hold on to what little cash they had left. He was happy to put some space between him and Dax.

The sun had started its descent, casting an orangish glow in the sky. He jumped out of his truck and stared at the open country beyond the fence. His job at Tremont Ranch the past few days wasn't the type of work he once did, but it was nice being outside. Having the opportunity to absorb the land, even if it wasn't his own.

"Beautiful, isn't it?"

The awe in Lily's voice turned him toward her, and his breath caught in his throat. "Yeah. Beautiful." He turned back toward the mountains before she caught him staring.

"Can we take a ride?" she asked, still facing forward. "This is my favorite time of day to take Queenie out. I love how everything has some kind of magical glow around it and the world is just a little bit quieter. It's the best time to focus my mind, and I could really use some focus."

No matter how much he wanted to, he couldn't tell her no. Not when his reason for staying off a horse was tied to the constant throbbing in his shoulder. Better to agree the find a way to make it a quick ride. "Sure."

"Thanks." She led the way to the barn, hauling open the heavy door with little effort. Standing in the wide aisle, she stopped for a moment and closed her eyes. He could practically see the strain melting away, her muscles loosening.

He envied her. Envied her ability to pour her whole heart into what she loved.

"Do you remember where everything is?" she asked, heading toward the tack room.

"Yup. Do you want me to saddle Ace again?"

"If that's okay with you. He's my dad's mount and is used to being ridden daily."

He waited for her to grab what she needed to get Queenie ready then found Ace's saddle, saddle pad and brushes. He carried everything to Ace's stall.

Ace whined and butted his nose against Madden.

"Hey, big guy. Gonna take it easy on me again today?" He worked quickly and efficiently to ready the horse, offering plenty of pets as he went. When everything was situated, he slipped the bridle and reins over the horse's neck, gently placing the bit in Ace's mouth. "All right. Here goes nothing."

Madden guided Ace outside where Lily and Queenie waited. He made some last minute adjustments on the girth then heaved himself on the animal's strong back. "Ready?"

"Always. Let's head a different way tonight. I don't want to go by the shed. For a few minutes, I want to forget all my problems, not come face-to-face with them."

"Lead the way."

Lily maneuvered Queenie away from the barn in the opposite direction of the shed. "There's a meadow behind the house I love. Goes down to a quiet, little stream."

"Sounds nice." He kept Ace at a steady pace, the reins loose in his hands. As long as he didn't have to use his arm too much, he could relax and enjoy an evening stroll on a magnificent creature.

The meadow stretched out in front of him, long blades of grass interrupted by a smattering of colorful wildflowers. Pine trees stood tall in the distance. The faint outline of the stream looked like a single line cutting through the landscape at this distance.

"Your dad was great tonight," Lily said, interrupting his thoughts. "I was nervous to go to his house, but he made me feel nothing but welcomed."

"That's Pops. Wants to be friends with everyone. Never muttering a bad word unless it's about one of his sons or something in jest. He's one of the good ones." A beat of love pulsed through him. He'd been blessed with a wonderful role model, a father who loved his kids without limits. He'd do anything for the old man, even when it made him a pariah in his own town.

"I hate that I've judged him so harshly." Her soft words were almost lost on the subtle breeze.

A lump formed in his throat. "The last couple years have been tough for him."

Lily gave a noncommittal hum. "Dax surprised me. I hate to say I haven't noticed him much lately. In my mind, he's still the kid who followed us around. He's not a kid anymore, that's for sure. He seemed upset."

He huffed out a humorless laugh. "He's always upset."

Lily spared him a glance before returning her focus ahead of her. "Sorry to hear that. I can't say I understand the dynamics between siblings, but I hope you both realize how lucky you are to have one another. Someone who can share the burden of life's troubles."

He swallowed the retort that came to mind. Dax wasn't one to share anything except his complaining. His brother was quick to judge Madden, blaming him for everything, without understanding a damn thing. "Dax is…hell, I can't even say I really know him anymore. So much changed while I was away. And when I returned home, we both expected things to just go back to the way they were. But that wasn't possible. For any of us."

Lily pulled on her reins, halting Queenie. She stared at him with nothing but compassion in her wide eyes.

The wind blew wisps of hair across her face, and his fingers itched to comb it back. To brush away the long strands to show off her long, elegant neck.

As if reading his mind, she tucked her hair behind her ears. "It's funny how one choice, one action, can have a rippling effect on so many people. I hope whatever the issue, you both can find a way past it. I'm learning that life's too short to carry ill will or animosity in our hearts. Well, that, and people tend to surprise you when you open up a little." Her narrowed stare told him exactly who she meant.

He grinned. "Fair points, but this conversation won't do much to help you unwind. I thought that was the reason for this whole ride."

"True. How about a race? We see who can make it to the stream the quickest, then let the horses take a little break and get a drink before heading back to the house so I can call and check in on my dad."

He opened his mouth to refuse, but she kicked her heels into Queenie's sides and shot off like a train barreling down the tracks. He wanted to stay put and watch, just admire her fluid movement on the horse. The two moved as one as they raced toward the gentle slope, the pink and orange swirls of dusk casting Lily in a magical light.

But he had to move or risk her questioning why he wouldn't take the bait to her challenge.

Gritting his teeth, he tightened his grip on the reins and urged Ace forward. "Be gentle with me, boy," he whispered against the horse's ear.

He leaned into the wind and clenched the muscles in his thighs to keep steady in the saddle. Wind smacked against his face. His heart lifted with every stride, and he urged the animal faster. Lily had gotten a head start, and her laughter trailed behind her. He might not catch up completely, but he had to at least give a solid attempt.

Pushing Ace into a gallop, he sprinted forward. He smiled wide, a lightness lifting his spirit in a way he hadn't experienced in years. He forgot the pain in his shoulder, forgot his limitations, and just enjoyed the simple pleasure of racing an old friend on a horse.

Lily glanced over her shoulder and grinned seconds before Queenie leapt over a fallen log. Her saddle slid to the side. Shock registered on her face seconds before she was thrown off the horse and crumpled onto the ground.

Pain ricocheted off every bone in Lily's body. Her eyelids fell shut and she fought against the instinct to curl into a ball among the grass. Her palms stung as if she'd been sliced by razor blades. Ringing in her ears muffled the sound of hooves pounding the earth.

Queenie?

Crap, she needed to open her eyes and find a way to her feet. But even the thought of such a sudden motion seemed as difficult as moving mountains.

Strong hands touched her tender body. The familiar smell of cedarwood and citrus relaxed her muscles and calmed her nerves.

Madden.

"I've got you," Madden said. "Are you hurt? Can you open your eyes?"

She did and winced against the unusually harsh glow of twilight. "Do I have to? My head is killing me."

He grimaced. "We need to get you back to the house and make sure there aren't any serious injuries. Can you stand?"

She took mental stock of her body. Everything hurt, but she didn't think anything was broken. "I think so."

With Madden's palm under her elbow and his arm wrapped around her waist, he helped her to her feet. Worry drew down the corners of his mouth.

Queenie stood near Ace; her saddle lay in a heap on the ground by the fallen log.

"What the hell happened?" She hadn't been knocked off a horse since she was a teenager, and she'd never been neglectful of putting a saddle on properly.

"It was the weirdest thing," Madden said, staying close to her side as she limped toward the hunk of leather. "Queenie jumped and the whole saddle slid off."

Lily patted Queenie's back as she passed, letting the animal know everything was all right, then knelt beside the saddle.

Madden kept his hand on her elbow and crouched beside her. Keeping her steady, he picked up the leather strap hanging off the side of the saddle. "The cinch is severed."

"What? Let me see." She held her hand out for the rough material, and her stomach dropped. "This doesn't make any sense. Everything seemed fine when I tightened it."

"Look here." He ran his finger along the material. "Not a straight cut. Someone must have torn it enough to not make it noticeable when you readied Queenie for a ride but enough that it'd eventually snap. If not tonight, then at some point."

She shook her head, not wanting to believe someone would purposely try to hurt her. If she'd taken Queenie for a ride alone or the jump her trusted pet had taken had been bigger, the result could have been catastrophic. "Did your phone notify you of anyone on the property today?"

"I'll double-check, but I didn't get any notifications."

Frustrated tears stung her eyes. "How is that possible? Someone had to be in that barn. Someone sabotaged my riding gear."

"You're right, but we don't know when it happened. The cameras just went up this afternoon. If the tear was small enough, it might take days to completely come apart. Maybe we should speak with Charlie again, and I still need to track down Daniel. They might know who all had access to the tack room recently."

He didn't say more, but she knew where his mind went. Both Charlie and Daniel had plenty of time to tamper with any of the equipment in the barn.

"We need to get you back home. You have some cuts we should clean, and I still want to make sure nothing more serious is wrong. I'll come back and get your saddle. We'll need to leave it here for now."

Groaning, she leaned against Madden. "Normally I wouldn't hesitate to ride Queenie bareback, but I don't think it's a good idea right now. My head is killing me, my back's sore and I'm not sure how well I'd stay on."

"Will either horse let us ride double?" Madden asked. "If not, I'll help you get on Ace and walk beside you while holding Queenie's lead."

A rush of heat washed over her. Riding double made the most sense and would get them back to the cabin much faster. But the idea of being nestled against Madden with his arms wrapped her would knock her over if he wasn't keeping her upright.

She cleared her throat, forcing her to pay attention on the issue at hand. "Queenie will be fine with both of us, and then we can keep Ace's gear in place. You okay riding bareback?"

His tightened jaw gave away a hint of reluctance, but he nodded. "I'll manage. Let's get you up there first."

Lily pressed a kiss to Queenie's nose. "Sorry about this, girl. I'll give you extra treats once we get home."

Grimacing, she fisted Queenie's coarse mane in her hands while Madden circled her waist in his palms and lifted her off the ground. She swung her leg over the horse's back.

Queenie stood still as a statue.

"Good, girl." Lily patted Queenie's neck, the movement making the cuts on her hands scream.

Madden handed her Ace's reins. "Hold this while I get on."

She took the loop of leather, guiding Ace a little closer.

Blowing out a long breath, Madden pulled himself up behind her and hissed out a groan.

Concerned, she glanced over her shoulder. "You okay?"

"Yeah."

The gruffness in his voice didn't convince her.

"I'll take Ace," he said, hooking one arm around her middle. He caged her in, securing her. Protecting her.

She handed him the reins and melted against him. The heat of his body seeped into her back. His nearness was intoxicating, making her lightheaded. His scent surrounded her, and she fought every instinct in her aching body to turn around and finish the kiss they'd started earlier.

"You ready?"

Oh God, was she ever. She needed to speak, to answer, but desire clogged her throat and stole all coherent thoughts. "Mmm-hmm."

She lightly tapped Queenie's sides and urged her forward, Ace keeping a nice pace beside them. She wrapped her hands in Queenie's mane and swayed with the movement, confident Madden would keep her upright, and way too comfortable in his arms.

Chapter 14

By the time Madden retrieved Lily's vandalized riding gear and helped her settle the horses, darkness had fallen. He followed her into the cabin and steered her into the bathroom.

"Do you have a medical kit in here?" The dried blood on her face and scrapes on her arms spiked his blood pressure, but she'd insisted they see to the animals before tending her injuries.

She slumped onto the edge of the tub. "Should be under the sink."

He found the kit then peeked in the linen closet for a washcloth. "I need to clean your cuts first, okay?"

"Sure." She sighed, the sound filled with exhaustion and a hint of annoyance.

He struggled against his own aches and pains, but he'd deal with that later. He soaked the cloth in warm water and wrung it out before kneeling before her. "The blood's dried so I might have to apply more pressure than I'd like to, but I'll be gentle."

She didn't respond, but her wide eyes relayed her trust, or at least her acceptance that he wouldn't stop badgering her until he made sure she was all right.

Carefully, he dabbed the washcloth over the marks on

her cheeks and forehead. Her face was inches from his. He kept his free hand anchored on the edge of the bathtub to keep from caressing her skin. Blood and dirt came off, revealing shallow scratches.

She hissed out a breath.

He paused. "You good?"

"Just stings a little."

He lowered his arm and studied the cuts. "Nothing too serious, unless you have other wounds I can't see."

"I hope that's not some attempt to get me out of my clothes," she said, smirking.

He lifted his palms. "I'd never be so sneaky. Trust me, if I wanted you to take off your clothes, I'd have more creative ways."

Pink colored her face, and she lowered her gaze. "My hands are a little banged up from when I tried to cushion the fall, but that's it," she said, holding her hands in the air for his inspection.

His stomach muscles clenched. Damn it, flirty banter that led to picturing her naked was not a wise move. Forcing his mind to focus, he pressed the damp cloth against her palms. "I want to put some antiseptic on the cuts to make sure they don't get infected."

"Okay." Her voice was barely above a whisper, her gaze now trained on him.

Space. He needed space. Standing, he unzipped the medical kit and found the ointment as well as a small bottle of over-the-counter pain medicine. "Do you want any ibuprofen? It will help with the soreness. Your body took quite a hit today. Better to stay on top of managing the pain. At least for tonight."

"Thanks."

He unscrewed the top and jiggled out a couple of pills,

making a mental note to take some for his shoulder later. Passing them to her, her warm skin sent a jolt of electricity through his body.

She jerked back. "I can handle the rest. Besides, I'd love a hot shower. I need to get the rest of this dirt and sweat off me."

Thankful for an excuse to leave, he cleaned up his mess then left the bathroom before he did something stupid like suggest they wash up together. He'd already made one monumental mistake by kissing her. She'd rejected him once. He wouldn't make the mistake of kissing her again.

The sound of the doorbell yanked him out of his head. He hurried to the front door, not surprised to find Deputy Hill and Deputy Silver on the porch. "Evening," he said. "You want to talk to Lily about what happened earlier?"

Deputy Hill removed his hat and nodded. "Yes, sir. We'd like to take her statement and look at the saddle in question."

"Come in and have a seat in the living room. I'll let her know you're here." He retraced his steps back to Lily's bathroom down in the basement. He knocked loudly, but she must not have heard him over the heavy spray of the shower.

He opened the door a crack, mindful not to peek inside. Steam rolled out and slid against his face. "Lily, deputies are here for your statement."

"What?"

Christ. He'd rather walk barefoot over lava rock than set foot inside her bathroom right now. He'd had a hard enough time controlling himself before she was naked in the shower. "Deputies are here," he said, practically yelling. "They want to talk to you."

Nothing but the splatter of water drops on tile reached his ears. Gritting his teeth, he opened the door wider and took a tentative step into the room. Steam covered the glass of the shower, but he couldn't miss the peach outline of her body on the other side.

She popped her head out of the now-open glass door, hiding the rest of her delicious body behind the shower stall. Her wheat-blond hair appeared darker when wet. The long strands hung over one shoulder and dripped water on the dark blue rug. Her eyes were hooded, her full lips parted in a small o-shape that had fire shooting from his core. "Madden?"

His name was spoken more like an invitation than a question, but one he couldn't accept. Hell, he was probably hearing things. She was just wondering why he'd interrupted her shower. "Sheriff's deputies are here to talk about what happened earlier. They want your statement."

"Oh, okay. I'll be right there."

He swore he heard a note of disappointment in her voice, but instead of dwelling on what it meant, he got out of there before he forgot law enforcement waited in the living room to discuss a crime.

But the biggest crime in his mind was that there was a beautiful, interesting, naked woman mere feet away and there wasn't a damn thing he could do about it.

The pulse between Lily's legs had her groaning as she shut off the hot water and stepped out of the shower. She'd hoped standing under the hot spray would ease some of the soreness in her muscles. Instead, Madden's unexpected interruption caused a different kind of tension to build in her core.

For one quick, crazy second, she'd thought he'd come to see her for a different reason.

As she patted her skin dry with the cotton towel, she

rolled her eyes. She really needed to talk with him about where they stood. At least then they'd both have a better understanding of each other's expectations.

But that was a problem for another time. Not now as she threw on a pair of red flannel shorts and a T-shirt. She didn't bother to mess with her hair. Hopefully it would dry in nice, beachy waves and not like a chaotic bird's nest.

Slowly making her way upstairs, she found the trio sitting in the living room. "Sorry to keep you waiting."

All three stood.

"No worries," Deputy Silver said, her eyes kind but expression tight with concern. "We won't take up too much of your time. We understand you've had a hard day. We need your statement. We'd also like to see your riding gear."

"Yes, sure. That's fine."

"Why don't you sit?" Madden asked, gesturing toward the spot on the couch next to where he'd sat.

She rounded the coffee table and sank onto the soft cushions. She wished she could close her eyes and sleep the rest of the evening away, but that wasn't an option. At least not right now with law enforcement here to discuss what happened.

Steadying her nerves, she told her story. She started with the decision to take her horse for an evening ride and ended with her saddle sliding off the horse and realizing her cinch had been cut.

Deputy Silver frowned. "How often do you check your gear?"

She shrugged. "A few times a week, but not before every ride. When we have guests, everything is inspected before assigning it. I try to be as diligent as possible. I've never had an issue with mine, or anyone else's equipment."

"Who all has access to the tack room?" Deputy Hill asked. "Is the barn ever locked?"

She swallowed the bitterness creeping up her throat. She hated answering this question but understood the need for full transparency. "My dad and I, obviously, and we have two ranch hands who are still employed full time."

"Charlie Wells and Daniel Winter?" Deputy Hill asked. She nodded.

"We spoke with Charlie earlier this morning regarding the break-in last night. He said he hasn't noticed anyone on the property recently who wasn't supposed to be there, but we'll speak with him again. See if he's noticed any other equipment has been tampered with." Deputy Silver leaned forward in her seat, resting his forearms on her knees. "We haven't had a chance to talk to Daniel Winter yet. Have you spoken with him?"

Unease skittered down Lily's spine. "No, but he was here this morning, though. Madden and I saw him working when we went into town. Charlie mentioned he wasn't feeling well. I've wanted to reach out to make sure he's all right, but things have been a little chaotic."

Madden shifted beside her, and she sensed his discomfort.

She studied the tight lines in his face. He was holding something back, not saying something he thought might be important. "Whatever it is that has you squirming over there, let it out. Now's not the time to hold back."

"Charlie also mentioned Daniel stayed late last night. The night of the break-in," Madden said.

His pained expression told her he hated throwing someone she trusted under the bus, but she understood his reasons.

The two deputies shared a look that had alarms going off in Lily's head. "What is it?"

Deputy Silver scratched the back of her neck, clearly uncomfortable with whatever was on her mind. "Daniel Winter is unaccounted for."

She blinked in surprise, unsure of the deputy's meaning. "What do you mean?"

"We've tried to contact him numerous times to no avail. No one is at his apartment in town, and his truck hasn't been seen since he left your ranch earlier. Because of his connection to the ranch, as well as our inability to track him down, he is currently a person of interest."

The news slammed against her chest like an anvil. "You can't be serious. Daniel has been a trusted member of our work family for years. He'd never hurt my father. He'd never hurt me. I'm sure Charlie told you the same thing, and my father would if he could. Besides, he doesn't own a black truck. That's what you're looking for, right? I mean, the person who shot my father was in a black truck."

Hysteria squeezed her lungs, making it harder and harder to pull in breaths. The lack of oxygen increased the dizziness in her head and increased the pain that had plagued her for hours. Heat crept up the back of her neck and beads of sweat dotted her hairline.

Madden swooped off the couch and knelt in front of her. He clutched her hands in his and settled them in her lap. The coolness of his skin centered her, and she stared into his big, gray eyes.

"You're all right," he whispered. "Just focus on breathing."

She swallowed hard and tried to do what he said—it sounded so simple—but her breaths hitched in her throat and dark spots invaded her vision. "Can't do it. Too hard."

"You *can*. Just look at me, okay?"

She nodded, every muscle in her body rigid.

He tightened his grip on her hands. "Now I want you to tell me five things you see."

The randomness of his request caught her off guard. She narrowed her gaze, focusing on the movement of his mouth as if she could read his lips better than actually hearing him. "Huh?"

A small smile touched his lips. "Tell me five things you see. Trust me."

"You. The couch." The pressure in her chest loosened a fraction, her breathing coming a little easier. She paused, closing her eyes and focusing on evening her breaths and gaining her bearings before opening them again. "The fireplace, Deputy Hill and Deputy Silver."

"Now four things you can touch."

She grazed her finger pads against his rough skin. Her fear eased and her eyesight sharpened. The room stopped spinning. "You."

His smile grew. "Three more things."

She filled her lungs with air. The buzzing in her brain settled. She squeezed his hands, not wanting to let go to touch anything else. She didn't need to, and that thought scared the hell out of her. "I'm okay now. You got me out of my head enough to relax. Thank you."

"You sure?"

She nodded.

Keeping their hands entwined, Madden returned to his spot on the sofa, closer than before.

"Sorry about that," she said, forcing a tight smile. "This is all just so overwhelming. As soon as I think things can't get worse, they do."

"You've been through the gauntlet," Deputy Hill said. "The last thing we want to do is throw more upsetting news your way, but we have to look at every angle to find the person responsible for this mess."

"I appreciate your time and effort," Lily said. "I want you to find whoever wants to hurt my family more than anyone."

Deputy Silver shared a quick glance with her partner then stood. "I think we have everything we need from you. We'd like to take your saddle with us as evidence. I noticed one on the porch. Is that the gear that was tampered with?"

"Yes, and of course, take whatever you need," she said.

"I'd make sure to check everything before you use it," Deputy Hill said. "Just to be on the safe side. If someone was in your tack room and had the knowledge of how to do something so small and unnoticeable that could have potential life-threatening consequences, there's no telling what else they might have done."

A shiver shook her shoulders at the idea of someone pawing through her property, deciding what damage they could do to cause harm. "I'll look at everything in the barn to make sure nothing else is amiss."

Madden rose to his feet, and letting go of his hand was like severing a limb. "I'll walk you guys to the door."

She waited on the couch for him to return, her brain working over her problems.

Madden reclaimed his seat and hooked an arm on the back of the couch, the tips of his fingers casually resting against her shoulder. "What's on your mind?"

Shifting to hike one knee on the couch, she faced him. "Something Deputy Hill said stuck with me. Before I thought we were looking for some dangerous criminal who shoots guns and deals drugs, someone I would never have crossed paths with. But now it's different. Someone had knowledge of my property, of my riding gear. They knew just how far to push things to go unnoticed by me, an experienced rider, and get the outcome they wanted. Madden, I'm afraid the person who's trying to kill my family is someone I already know."

Chapter 15

Madden stared into the freezer, searching for something to help ease the throbbing ache in his shoulder. After the deputies had left, he'd encouraged Lily to turn in early, even if every fiber of his being screamed to keep her awake all night long.

Something had shifted between them, but she'd been through way too much to get to the bottom of it tonight. No, she needed a good night's sleep, and maybe tomorrow they could have a real conversation about their feelings for each other.

For now, he had to find something cold and fight for sleep. He'd opted for the pullout couch in the basement over the too-short leather sofa in the living room. He'd pop a couple ibuprofen, ice his shoulder, then hopefully get some rest. At least tonight he wasn't in his stiff jeans. He wore loose gym shorts instead of his usual boxers in bed and removed his T-shirt to better nurse his injury.

Spotting a bag of peas, he snatched them from the shelf on the freezer door and pressed it against his skin. He groaned, the jolt of intense cold instantly loosening his muscles.

"You know, peas taste better when you cook them. But even then, they aren't exactly what I would call a midnight snack."

He jumped at the sound of Lily's voice, quickly shutting the door and spinning around to face her. He let his arm drop, dangling the frozen vegetables at his side. "I was just…" He trailed off, trying to think of a plausible reason to be rummaging around for frozen vegetables in the middle of the night.

She raised her brows high. "Searching for peas?"

He wrinkled his nose. "I needed something cold."

Flipping on a dim light over the stove, she padded across the tile floor to stand in front of him She stared at his shoulder and frowned. "Are you hurt? You've been so busy fussing over me, I haven't stopped to see if you were okay."

He shrugged, the sudden motion sending another shock of pain through his system. "I'm fine."

Lily rolled her eyes and dropped her gaze to his shoulder.

The heat of her eyes on him burned his skin. He wanted to shift, to move, to step around her so she couldn't see the ugly white scars snaking up his shoulder. But that would only cause more suspicion, spark more questions.

"Doesn't look like you're okay." She gently brushed her fingertips along the puckered skin. "But the scar also doesn't look new. I'm guessing this happened a while ago."

He nodded, unable to speak. Her touch ignited a different kind of heat. One that would morph into a raging fire if he didn't stop her soon.

"Do you want me to go back in my room and leave you alone?" She finally lifted her gaze to meet his.

Words lodged in his throat. He should tell her yes, that he wanted privacy to take care of his injury so he could get some sleep, but the idea of her leaving his side was like a physical blow. So he shook his head, and prayed she wouldn't move her hand.

Without breaking contact, she traced her fingers down

his arm until she grabbed the peas then laid the lumpy package on his shoulder.

He closed his eyes, relishing the coolness on his skin as flames of desire licked higher inside him. Such a dizzying combination.

Just like Lily.

He couldn't figure her out. Couldn't decide if she liked him, hated him, or somewhere in between. And for some reason, what she thought of him mattered.

"Do you want to talk about what happened?"

The tenderness in her voice opened his eyes. A dozen situations flashed in his mind of things they should discuss.

"To your shoulder," she said, clarifying. "I won't press. But I'm realizing it makes things easier when you let others carry a little of your burden. You've done so much to help me. I'd like the opportunity to do something for you."

He debated what to say. He hadn't opened up to anyone about his injury and what it had ripped away. Not even Reid understood the magnitude of what he'd lost.

But Lily would understand.

He wasn't sure if it was his lack of sleep or the fact he wanted a deeper connection with Lily, but a sudden need to unload his emotional trauma pressed on his chest. "I'd like that, but maybe not while standing in the middle of the kitchen."

She glanced around, her attention fixed on the unmade pullout bed in the living room.

"How about the table?" he blurted out before she thought about making herself comfortable on the bed. If that happened, he'd be hard-pressed to control himself. He definitely wouldn't be able to focus on discussing painful memories he'd kept buried for so long.

She gave one long, slow nod. "That's probably for the best."

He took a step away from her, hoping the mounting tension between them would dissipate with a little space. "I'll take those. Thanks." Grabbing the peas, he headed for the two-person table and sank into the hard chair. Maybe he'd made a mistake. If he distracted her, he could forget about ripping open the emotional scab keeping him sane. "You never said what woke you."

She grinned. "The thought of Eve's apple pie. We never dug into it, so I planned to sneak out and take the whole thing into my room. I figured I'd eat as much as I could until I passed out."

"Don't let me stop you."

She rummaged around the kitchen then carried the pie and two forks to the table. "Only if you help me."

"I can never say no to Eve's pie. Especially apple." He drooped the cool bag over his shoulder and took the fork.

Lily uncovered the pie pan and speared a forkful of pie from the center of the tin. She slid the bite into her mouth and moaned. "Dear God in heaven, that woman is magical."

Chuckling, he followed suit. Sweet bursts of cinnamon and apple exploded in his mouth. "All that's missing is vanilla ice cream."

She waved her fork at him. "Tomorrow, if there's any left. Now let's get back to you. What happened to your shoulder?"

The delicious dessert soured in his stomach, and he set down his fork. He sighed, not sure where to start. "As you know, I joined the marines straight out of high school. I love this town, but I wanted a chance to see a little bit of the world before I settled down and took over the ranch. The plan was to spend a few years serving my country, come home and help Pops until it was my turn to take over the ranch. But some plans are never meant to be."

Concern wrinkled the corners of her eyes. She placed her fork on the table and reached for his hand.

Memories assaulted him like shrapnel. The smell of burning flesh and the sound of twisting metal took over his mind. He couldn't let it suck him under, couldn't get caught up in the vortex of fear and regret. He blew out a long breath and focused on the kindness that swam in her blue eyes.

She gave his hand a little squeeze. "You don't have to tell me anything you don't want to."

He steadied his nerves, finally ready to open up. "When I was overseas, I was in a tank on patrol. An IED hit the vehicle. Reid and I were both inside, along with our buddy Ben and one woman—Andrea. The tank rolled and caught fire. I pulled Reid out, but my shoulder was busted bad. Ben tried to save Andrea, but there wasn't enough time."

His throat closed and grief washed over him now just as fresh as the day of the attack. "I vowed to never leave a marine behind. I hate that I couldn't keep that promise."

Tears hovered over her dark lashes. "You did everything you could. It wasn't your fault."

"In my head, I know that. But I'll always blame myself, just like Reid and Ben. We all carry that weight. But even after I left the service, when I hoped to come home and put it all behind me, I never realized I'd be forced to face another war. One I had zero control over."

Understanding softened the planes of her pretty face. "Your shoulder. If one day of chores hurts this bad, I can't imagine what a lifetime on your ranch would do. Is that why you sold your land?"

An internal debate waged inside him. He could tell her

yes and leave it alone. Hell, she might even forgive him and his family based only on the knowledge he had an injury that limited him. Even if it wasn't the entire story.

But the whole truth was hidden behind a secret he'd sworn to keep. A secret that now felt like a lie and was one he was tired of keeping.

The sharp ache inside Lily had nothing to do with her bumps and bruises. She ached for Madden's pain—both physical and emotional. And she ached for the part she played in judging him without stopping and asking questions first. She should have known he had a reason for selling a piece of his family's history, for making a decision that appeared hasty but was really one forced on him and hurt him deeply.

Madden slid his hand from beneath hers and flipped the bag of peas on his shoulder. "Part of the reason, yeah. I move slower. The work is harder. As you can see, even after one day I'm sore as hell. I'm surprised you didn't notice earlier when I helped with chores."

"I thought you were being lazy," she said, winking to make sure he knew she was teasing. "Or just moving at a snail's pace to mess with me."

Humor danced in his eyes, a sure sign they'd moved past their animosity. "Don't get me wrong, annoying you is always fun, but I've struggled to keep up and I didn't want you to think less of me."

"Not possible. For what it's worth, I'm sorry I spent so much time being angry. But I have to ask, what about your dad and Dax? Couldn't they help at the ranch? Was selling really the only option?"

He rubbed the back of his neck, the motion causing the peas to spill to the floor. He didn't make a move to pick them up, just stared at her with a quiet resignation she didn't understand. "Unfortunately, yes. Dax was too young to take over. Hell, he didn't have the same love for the ranch that Pops and I had. Maybe that's because he didn't get the chance, or maybe because he grew up knowing it'd never be his. The plan was also for me to take over one day. If we'd given him an opportunity to step up, things might have been different."

She tried to focus on his words but couldn't make sense of the puzzling explanation. "You couldn't give it some time to see how Dax would handle things?"

A pained expression pinched his face. "We didn't have the luxury of time."

Something in his voice made her stomach drop. She waited for him to say more, the hum of the refrigerator the only sound in the room.

"My dad has Parkinson's."

The news stole her breath. "What? No. That can't be right." She couldn't align the same smiling, teasing man she was with earlier that evening with a person struggling with Parkinson's disease.

Madden sighed and closed his eyes for a beat. When he opened them again, tears glimmered in the corners. "No one knows. Not even Dax."

"But why?"

He let his head fall forward. "Dad was diagnosed right before I came home. When he realized I couldn't handle as much of the workload, he finally broke down and told me he couldn't either. Knowing Dax was too young, he decided to sell. Those developers had been sniffing around for a while, and he knew he could get a good price. He just wanted to be done with it before things took a turn for the worse."

When his voice cracked, she shifted her chair to sit beside him and rested a palm on his arm. "Oh my God, I'm so sorry. I had no idea. I hate the position you both have been in. But why the secrecy? People around here would want to help. Pitch in and lend a hand whenever necessary."

He snorted. "Picture your own father when he gets home from the hospital. Do you think he'll want a bunch of people fussing over him, showing their sympathy for what happened?"

She hated how the word *if* sat on the tip of her tongue when thinking about her dad's return home, but she kept that to herself. "Okay. That sounds like his version of hell."

"Exactly," Madden said. "And that would only be temporary, until he got back on his feet. With my dad, he'll continue to get worse until…" He stopped and cleared his throat before drawing in a long, shuddering breath. "He doesn't want the pity or feeling like he needs a handout. He'd rather have anger and condemnation. I might not agree, but the least I can do is honor his wishes. Give him a sense of a control over a disease that will end up taking everything from him."

Unable to ignore the raw emotion pouring off him, Lily folded him in her arms, mindful of his shoulder.

He stiffened for a second before melting against her. His head falling to the crook of her neck and hands reaching around to grip the material of her T-shirt at the small of her back. "I'm going to lose him, and before that, I'll watch him deteriorate little by little."

She held him tight, wishing she could pour whatever strength or courage she had into him. A hundred clichéd responses flitted through her mind, but none of them would mean anything. Nothing she said would make his situation better or ease the burden he carried. Words didn't mean a damn thing.

Leaning back, she moved one hand to cradle his jaw-line. The rough whiskers tickled her palm. She dipped her chin to stare directly into his sad eyes. "I'm sorry I made an already tough situation tougher. From here on out, what-ever you need, I'm here. For you, your dad and even Dax."

A glimmer of a smile touched his lips. "Not sure there's much you, or anyone else, can do."

"I can listen. I can stand beside you. I can be your friend." A swift desire to show him how much she cared raced through her like a raging river. Before she talked herself out of it, she gently pressed her lips to his. "I can be whatever you need me to be."

His hand came up and gripped her wrist. His gaze, so full of questions, stared at her. "Earlier, you said we shouldn't."

"I was so surprised that I don't remember what I said, only how I felt. And damn it, Madden, I felt good. *You* make me feel good. I'm sorry if I made you think otherwise." She kissed him again as if to put an exclamation mark on her point. "Thank you for confiding in me."

Leaning forward, he rested his forehead on hers and sighed. "I've held this in for so long. Letting it out helps."

"For what it's worth, I think you should tell Dax. He deserves to know the truth, and if there's one thing I've learned the last couple days, it's that secrets hurt others. Even if you're keeping them to protect the ones you love."

He skimmed his knuckles down her sides until he rested his hands on her hips. "You're right. It's past time we told him. But I don't want to think about Dax or my dad any more tonight."

Sensing his need for levity after such a heavy admis-sion, she grinned. "Is it time to finally cook those peas?"

He chuckled, the sound like cashmere against her skin.

"Nah, no more plans for peas. I have something a lot more appetizing in mind."

In one swift movement, he stood and scooped her into his arms. Pain shot up his arm, but no amount of discomfort could stop him. He stalked past the pullout couch and made a beeline for her bedroom, leaving the barely touched apple pie she'd craved behind.

But now, she had a different craving. One that promised her a night she'd never forget.

Chapter 16

A stirring at Madden's side broke into his slumber and tempted him to open his eyes. He didn't want to be roused from sleep. Didn't want to be forced from the bed to tackle the day. Not when he had a warm, beautiful woman next to him.

Last night had taken an unexpected turn. He'd planned to quietly nurse his injury and get some shut-eye. He'd never imagined confessing his secrets to Lily. Then she'd shocked the hell out of him more than once. First with her compassion and kindness, then when she kissed him.

He bit back a groan as the memory made his body burn. He'd have loved nothing more than to strip her naked in her bed and do wicked things to her all night long. But what was happening between him and Lily was new, hell, was special. Instead of rushing and burying himself in her, he'd spent hours learning the curves of her body. Tasting and teasing, leaving them both satisfied but with a promise of so much more to come.

Lily squirmed beside him, as if waging an internal battle against waking.

Needing to touch her, he hooked an arm around her waist and pulled her against him. The oversize T-shirt she fell asleep in bunched at her hips. Her bottom nestled against his groin, reigniting the flames of desire that hadn't been extinguished the night before.

He swept her long, light strands of hair over her shoulder and pressed his lips against the base of her neck. His fingers inched up the soft curve of her side to find the now-hard nipple on her full breast.

She moaned and her ass backed harder into him, as if her entire body urged him for more.

He flicked his thumb against her nipple as his other hand skimmed over her flat stomach and slid into her panties. He glided downward until he dipped his fingers into her wetness.

Gasping, she reached up an arm to cradle the back of his neck.

He trailed kisses to her collarbone as he moved his fingers inside of her. The smell of her sex taunted his senses.

She bucked her hips against him, her breath now short and frantic.

He matched her pace, his heart in his throat. His member throbbing as she bounced against it.

Her muscles tensed and she threaded his hair between her fingers, tugging gently until her body went lax and she sighed and turned to face him. "Well, that was one hell of a way to wake up." Grinning, she sealed her mouth on his.

He held her close, his internal pledge to take things slow evaporating into thin air. No matter the pace they took, he had no doubt what he wanted. Lily was smart and beautiful. Compassionate and sincere. She was nothing like the woman he'd assumed her to be, and he'd kick his own ass for wasting so much time embroiled in some bullshit rivalry neither of them truly understood.

Lily broke their kiss and propped herself up on her elbow. Her lips were swollen, and cheeks flushed. Lust darkened the blue in her eyes. "Last night was amazing," she said. "And this morning's been pretty great already, but I think we can make it even better."

He cradled her jaw in his hand. "Are you sure? I don't want to push you."

Turning his wrist, she pressed a kiss in his palm. "There's a lot of things I'm not sure of, but you aren't one of them."

Something inside of him melted into a pile of mush and happiness. On a growl, he pounced, pinning her beneath him.

Giggling she tucked the tips of her fingers into the front of his gym shorts.

He hissed out a breath, anticipation beating a steady drum in his head.

The blast of the doorbell exploded into the moment, followed by heavy pounding on the door.

Eyes wide, Lily stilled.

"You've got to be kidding me." He fell to the mattress and took a second to compose himself. His entire body screamed to ignore whoever the hell was demanding their attention, but he couldn't. Not with everything else happening outside of this perfect cocoon.

The bell rang again before the pounding continued.

"Something's wrong. It has to be," Lily said, sitting up and scooping her phone from the nightstand. She frowned. "No one called. Who's here so early?"

Jumping to his feet, Madden searched for his own phone, then muttered curses under his breath. With his haste in getting Lily's ass into bed, he'd left his phone plugged into the charger in the living room. "I need to look at the security app. At least the camera we installed should tell us who's up there."

"Okay. I'll get dressed really quick."

He grimaced as she searched through her drawers for clothes, but he couldn't linger. He hurried to the spot where he'd left his device and pulled up the app for the doorbell. Lily's old ranch hand stood on the front porch, his weathered face puckered into a scowl and arms crossed over his chest.

He pressed the button to connect to the sound system on the doorbell. "Charlie, it's Madden. I'll be there in a second."

Charlie's head reared back as if the voice coming through to him came from the heavens. If Madden's nerves weren't stretched so damn tight, he'd laugh.

Lily came out of her room just as he pulled a T-shirt over his head and stepped out of his shorts and into a pair of jeans.

"Did you say Charlie's here?" she asked.

"Yeah. Told him I'd be up in a second. He doesn't look happy. Is it normal for him to stop by and speak with you or your dad first thing in the morning?"

Worry creased her forehead. "Not at all, and I'm going with you."

Before he started up the stairs, he gathered her close and gave her a quick kiss. "I wouldn't expect anything else."

He kept the image of her saucy grin in his mind as he bounded up the stairs, Lily at his heels. He made a bee-line to the door and yanked it open. "Morning, Charlie. What's going on?"

The hard look Charlie gave him made his skin crawl, as if Lily's trusted ranch hand knew exactly what he interrupted and didn't approve. "I need to speak to Ms. Tremont. Now."

Lily stepped around Madden and squinted against the sun. "I'm right here."

"There's something you need to see," Charlie said, frowning.

Lily slipped on a pair of sandals while Madden pulled on his boots.

Charlie waited until they were ready then led them down the porch steps to the big red barn. He didn't speak, which only heightened the tension. He rounded the corner to the back of the large structure then flicked his wrist toward the side.

Lily gasped and covered her mouth with her hand.

Madden stared up and rage heated his blood. Someone had left a message in big, white letters.

YOU'RE NEXT.

Angry tears flooded Lily's eyes. She held them back. She was done letting some asshat swoop in and try to destroy her and her family—tired of the pain and fear.

Now she was mad.

"Does your app show who did this?" she asked Madden as she struggled to keep her voice from shaking.

Madden fiddled with his phone then shoved it in his pocket. The pissed-off expression on his face gave away his answer before he even spoke. "No. I didn't put cameras up on the back side of the barn, and the camera on the front didn't catch anything."

She turned to Charlie with clenched fists anchored on her hips. "Did you see anyone when you got here?"

He shook his head, his scowl broadcasting his own fury. "Not a soul."

Madden moved his jaw back and forth, his narrowed

gaze staring at the ugly message. "How'd you know to come over here?"

Charlie focused all his negative energy on Madden. He glowered, face pinched and red. He stalked toward him, his finger raised and shaking. "I'm sick 'n' tired of you and all your questions. If I had anything to do with this or anything else that's going on around here, would I have woken Ms. Tremont? Would I have run and told her?"

"Not sure," Madden said, tilting his head to the side. His hair stuck up in a disheveled mess. "Maybe you wanted to see her upset? Could be you want to throw suspicion off yourself. There's a whole slew of reasons for bad people to do stupid things. That's usually why they get caught."

"You little son of a bitch!" Charlie lunged forward and grabbed Madden by the front of his shirt. "It's about time someone taught you some manners."

"Stop it!" Lily screamed.

Madden threw his palms in the air, but a sinister glow lit his eyes.

Charlie drew back his fist, and Lily latched on to his elbow. "I said stop. We have enough problems to deal with around here without any more trouble. Charlie, I already told you that Madden's here to help, so stop taking his question so damn personally. And Madden, try to be a little more diplomatic. Charlie's a good man who has my trust and respect. No reason to question him like a criminal."

"Like Daniel?" Madden asked, hands in the air.

Charlie kept a firm grip on Madden's shirt, but his shoulders dropped as his initial anger leaked from his system. "What's Daniel got to do with anything?"

Madden stared around Charlie to lock his gaze with hers. "You want to tell him, or should I?"

Charlie spun toward her. "What's he talking about?"

Dread soured her stomach. As close as she was with the other ranch hand, Charlie was even closer. The two of them had spent countless hours side by side, working the land and helping her family keep their ranch afloat. "We found out last night Daniel's a person of interest. Deputies are looking for him, and he's nowhere to be found."

Charlie stared at her as if her words hadn't registered.

"Have you spoken with him since yesterday?" she asked. Maybe Charlie had information he hadn't provided before because he didn't want to get his friend in trouble. But now, Daniel was knee-deep in this mess whether he meant to be or not. Charlie might have knowledge that could help uncover the truth.

"No," he said, averting his gaze.

Something about his hesitation had her narrowing her gaze. She was tired of secrets. "Charlie, I need you to be honest. If you know where Daniel is, tell me. If he's innocent, then we can clear his name. But withholding anything right now won't do anyone a lick of good."

Blowing out a breath, Charlie raised his eyes to the sky before finally looking her way. "I'm not lying. I didn't talk to him. But I drove by his place after I left here and saw him with a big duffel bag, climbing into his truck. He was gone before I got a chance to flag him down. I know that bag. It's the one he always uses when going away for a few days."

"Do you have any idea where he might have gone?" Madden asked. "Friends or family who'd take him in if he was in trouble?"

Charlie shook his head. "He ain't got many people in his life. He doesn't speak with his brother, and his parents have both passed."

"No friends?" Lily asked, an overwhelming sadness

pressing down on her at the thought of someone she assumed she knew so well being so lonely.

More hesitation.

"Charlie," Madden said, gaining the ranch hand's attention. "Right now, the sheriff's department is only labeling him a person of interest and not a suspect. That could change if we find him and get to the bottom of things. Daniel's name can be cleared, and the deputies can focus on other leads. You'd be helping everyone, not ratting out a friend."

Charlie dropped his head and kicked at the ground with the toe of his boot. "I really don't know where he went, but he's been acting different since his mama passed away last year. Moody and distant. Lost weight. Things you'd expect when grieving a loved one. But then his behavior was more erratic, more unpredictable."

Lily locked eyes with Madden, and it was clear he'd come to the same conclusion. Charlie was right, people often behaved differently when grieving, but what he'd described also pointed to someone with a drug problem. "Did you ever talk to my father about this?"

Charlie nodded. "Brought it up once or twice. Then I minded my own business. I didn't want to bring any more trouble to Daniel's door. He was having a tough time, but it never affected his work. If anything, he worked harder. Was here more than ever before."

"Did he spend a lot of time in the barn alone the last week?" Madden asked.

"Of course," Charlie spat out. "We both do. Not like we babysit each other when we're getting our work done. Why does that matter?"

Lily pressed her hands to her stomach as if the motion

could stop the sinking feeling. "Someone cut the cinch on my saddle."

"What?" Charlie's hound-dog eyes nearly popped from his head. "How'd you know it was cut?"

Madden snorted. "Was pretty easy to put the pieces together when her saddle slid off Queenie. Luckily, she wasn't hurt too bad, but someone's tampering with equipment. Someone who could go in unnoticed and knew how to handle the gear. And now, someone with the ability to vandalize the outside of the barn without detection has come onto the property."

Red crept up Charlie's neck until it engulfed his entire face. "Someone will pay for this, and if it's Daniel, so help me God..."

She rested a reassuring hand on Charlie's arm. "I know."

That's all she could say, because she understood the pain and confusion at suspecting someone she trusted being the one behind so much suffering and betrayal.

"We need to call the sheriff's department," Madden said. "They'll take a look at the scene before we can clean it."

Lily stared up at the threatening message as Madden fished out his phone and made the call. They had better get here soon. Her life was in danger, her world in turmoil and her property destroyed. She might not have control of the first two issues, but she'd scrub the stain off her barn if it killed her.

Chapter 17

After the deputies left Tremont Ranch, giving Lily permission to paint over the threat scrawled across the barn wall, Madden convinced her to head into town for a little breather. Something he needed as much as she did after the chaos of the morning. But instead of a relaxing cup of coffee to calm their nerves, he found himself and Lily at the hardware store, debating over dozens of different shades of the same damn paint color.

"Why are there so many different shades of red?" Lily asked, her mouth in an adorable pout.

He couldn't help but chuckle at her irritation. With everything else going on, finding the right shade of red seemed trivial. But at least it was one thing she could control. Not to mention if she picked the wrong shade, they'd have to paint the whole barn.

Wincing at the thought, he studied the thin strips of glossy paper splashed in color. He plucked one from its place and pointed toward the color on the top. He placed the sample they'd chipped off the barn beside it. "I think this is the closest. We can grab a couple cans of varying shades to make sure, though. We don't need much, and that way we won't have to come back to town to get more paint right away if we're wrong. We can always return the unused cans later."

She nodded. "Good idea. I'll get someone to grab what we need."

He watched her walk away, warmth snaking its way through his chest. He wished they could go back to earlier when their worries were at least on the sidelines, shelved for a tiny moment in time while they lost themselves in more enjoyable activities.

But it was getting lost in those activities that allowed the destruction of her property to go unnoticed. If he'd have been more diligent, spent time patrolling her property instead of being in her bed, he might have caught the bastard tormenting her.

He had to do better. His feelings for Lily weren't going anywhere. And if he slipped up and she was hurt again in the process, he'd never forgive himself.

A few minutes later, Lily rounded the corner with a shopping cart, five gallons of paint and some brushes. "I got what we need. Ready?"

"You betcha."

He walked beside her to the cashier, an older woman who gave them curious glances as she rung up their items. He paid the bill before Lily could grab her wallet from the purse slung across her chest then maneuvered the cart to his truck parked in the nearly empty lot. "You hungry?"

Folding her arms over the edge of his truck bed, she tucked a strand of hair behind her ear and shrugged. "A little. I guess we didn't have a chance to eat anything this morning, did we?"

"Nope, and I'm starving. I also need to go over a few things with Reid. How about we grab some food and take it to my office?" He rounded the back bumper to the passenger door and held it open, waiting for her to climb inside before leaning his forearm on the top of the vehicle. "Do you want Tilly's or something else?"

Hesitation skittered across her face, and she twisted her lips to the side. "I'm not sure I can stomach seeing the spot where my father was shot."

A heavy weight crushed down on his chest. "I'm so sorry. I should have considered that. We can go somewhere else. Or, hell, I can text Reid whatever you want and have him pick it up for us."

She blew out a long breath. "Let's try Tilly's."

"Are you sure?" He dropped his arm and found her hand, squeezing gently.

"Yeah. It'd be nice to see Eve and give her a proper thank you for everything she's done, and I can't avoid this forever. I pass by it most days, and I'd rather have you beside me when I face those memories for the first time."

Her words warmed him down to his toes. Leaning forward, he placed a kiss on her forehead. "I've got you." He smiled then closed the door before climbing behind the wheel.

Silence filled the cab, and a quick glance showed him the nerves displayed on Lily's face—furrowed brow, pinched mouth and hands clasped tightly on her lap. He rested a palm on her knee, wanting her to know he was there.

He opted for the small lot behind the restaurant. Better to ease her into the scene of the crime that had led to her current nightmare. Shutting off the engine, he faced her. "Ready?"

"As ready as I'll ever be."

He hurried around the hood of the truck to meet her then captured her hand. "We can go in the side door first. No need to head right for the sidewalk."

"No," she said, shaking her head. "I want to get this over with."

Matching her step for step, he stayed as close to her side as possible as they turned the corner onto Main Street. Late morning on a weekday meant only a few pedestrians popped in and out of shops or strolled down the sidewalk. He ignored their curious glances, his only focus on being the rock Lily needed right now.

Her steps slowed for a few beats before she stopped at the intersection in front of Tilly's. She locked her gaze on the hard ground, red stains shining in the harsh sunlight. She blinked back tears. "In some ways it seems like it was months ago when I sat there with my dad in my arms. So much has happened since then."

Memories of Lily's piercing scream after shots were fired assaulted him, and he squeezed her hand a little harder. "When I came out that door and saw you covered in blood, I thought you'd been hurt. I've never been so damn scared in my life."

She glanced up at him, her lips curved at the corners. "Really? Even though you hated me?"

"I've never hated you, just didn't understand you. I'm glad we've moved past that."

She turned into him, releasing his hand to wrap her arms around his waist, and buried her face in his chest.

He kissed the top of her head and held her tight. "I've got you," he repeated.

Peering up, she locked her eyes with his. "Thank you." She cut her gaze back to the ugly spot on the sidewalk. "I need to visit my dad today. I hate seeing him looking so small and frail, but I can't stay away because of my feelings. He needs to know I'm there for him."

"Okay. How about we stop by the hospital after we eat?

Then we can head back to your place and clean up the barn. That'll take some time, but we should get most of it done before dinner."

"Does everything revolve around food for you?" she asked, one eyebrow quirking toward the blue sky.

"That and other things." Unable to stop himself, he swept down and pressed his mouth to hers.

The sound of a woman clearing her throat broke into the moment. "Well, well, well. Isn't this an interesting development."

Madden turned to find Eve standing in the doorway of Tilly's.

Her smile was ear to ear, arms crossed over her chest. The subtle wind made her long, auburn hair blow across her face before she tucked it behind her ear. "Looks like we've got a lot to catch up on."

He glanced down at Lily who gave a tiny nod before leading him toward the restaurant. "You have no idea."

An hour later, the salad Lily ate while Madden and Reid went over Sunrise Security's business turned in her stomach. The smell of sickness and industrial strength disinfectant as soon as she stepped into the hospital hallway didn't help.

Madden kept a steady palm on the small of her back.

She stared at the shiny white floors. The bright glare of the fluorescent lights overhead bounced off the linoleum. She trusted him to guide her to her father's room.

The idea tightened her chest.

She trusted Madden. Hell, she not only trusted him with her life, but a larger part of her was opening up to the possibility of trusting him with way more.

"Hey, Duke," Madden said, dipping his chin to acknowledge the deputy standing guard beside the closed door. "How's it going?"

"Been quiet." The young deputy's green eyes were sharp, his stance rigid and on alert under his perfectly pressed uniform. "No one's stopped by to see Mr. Tremont besides medical staff."

Relief loosened the knots in her gut. "I appreciate your diligence. Having him here is difficult, but knowing he's being looked after makes things a little easier."

"Least I can do."

"I can stand guard if you want to take a break," Madden said. "Lily wants some time with her father. I plan to stick close while she's in the room. You can grab a coffee or hit the john if you need to."

"You sure?"

Madden nodded.

"Thanks, man. I won't be long." Duke offered Lily a tight-lipped smile then hustled down the hallway.

Lily hesitated, hating the fear keeping her from turning the doorknob. "You sure you don't want to go in?"

"And chance giving your father a stroke if he happens to wake up and see me standing over him?" He wrinkled his nose and chuckled. "Nah, we'll ease him into the idea of you and me once he's stronger."

His words touched the dark, scary spot inside of her that feared her dad would never make it home.

She shoved those thoughts as far to the back of her mind as she could and forced a brave smile. "Good point. Okay, I'll make it quick."

"Take all the time you need."

Before she could talk herself out of it, she pushed open the cream-colored door and stepped into the sterile room. The sound of beeping machines greeted her along with the painful image of her father lying with his eyes closed in the hospital bed. Her breath hitched. Her pulse sped up, and tears stung the corners of her eyes.

She willed herself to take another step forward then another until she stood at the side of the bed. She rested her hand on top of his, the rough skin on his weathered knuckles familiar and comforting despite its coolness. "Hi, Daddy."

Nothing but the steady beep, beep, beep answered.

A lump lodged in her throat, making it hard to speak, but she wanted him to hear her voice. To have no doubt she was there. "Sorry I didn't come by yesterday, but things have been a bit crazy. I wish you'd wake up and explain everything. I don't understand why someone would try to kill you or why they'd hide drugs on our property or vandalize our barn and my riding equipment. None of this makes sense, and I'm afraid you're the only one who has the answers. You're the only one who can make it stop, but you're stuck in this bed and can't even open your eyes."

She couldn't hold back the tears any longer. Fear and worry and anger swirled together inside her like a dust storm, blinding the way in front of her. Her father was supposed to be her guidepost. He was the one who taught her right from wrong, but right now he'd thrust her into a nightmare she couldn't escape.

Guilt burrowed into her chest. Her father was fighting for his life. She shouldn't be sending out anything except positive energy and love. But damn it, she couldn't help but be a little bit mad at the position she'd been forced into.

A position where her father's actions might have played a role in putting her life in danger.

But what could he have done? What decision could he have made to bring so much turmoil into her world?

She shook her head in an attempt to rid herself of unwanted thoughts. She had to believe the decisions her father made were done with nothing but the best of intentions. If she didn't, she'd crumble.

"No matter what, I will *always* be here for you. You just need to get better, then we'll figure everything out. I know there has to be an explanation, and I promise you, I'll get to the bottom of it." Smoothing back locks of white hair from his forehead, she leaned over and kissed him. "I love you, Dad."

She gave him one more long look then crossed the room to the door where another man she trusted waited. A man she'd doubted for so long and had finally learned the truth. That truth had opened a host of possibilities for her future.

She could only hope whatever truth she uncovered about her dad wouldn't steal the rest of his.

Chapter 18

Sweat dripped from Madden's hairline. The shade from his cowboy hat shielded his face but couldn't do a damn thing to lessen the heat. The sun beat down on him, and the muscles in his shoulder burned. The last thing he should be doing was the repetitive motion of scraping the ugly, white words from the barn. But he couldn't let Lily tackle this project alone.

Taking a break, he glanced down at her. Concentration pinched her face. She dug her scraper against the wooden side as if erasing the threat would erase all the shit taking over her life right now.

If only it could be that simple.

"How about stopping for a drink?"

She kept scraping, kept her singular focus on her task.

"Lily? You want a break?" He rested a hand on her shoulder, and her body jolted as if he'd zapped her with a stun gun.

She pressed her empty palm over her heart and snorted out a short laugh. "I was in some kind of zone. Sorry. I didn't even hear you."

"You set your sights on the barn like you used to on me when you'd chase me down as kids."

She struggled to hide her grin. "I don't remember what you're talking about."

He gave an exaggerated eye roll. "Sure you don't, but we don't need to get into that right now. I asked if you wanted to take a break. We've gotten most of the white paint off, but we'll need a ladder to tackle the top. Then we can paint."

She stared at the barn and wiped her brow with the back of her wrist. "Time flies when you're busting your ass, I guess. I didn't realize we'd been attacking this paint for so long."

Madden glanced at his watch. "Been a couple hours. We could finish the rest of this tomorrow."

"I don't know," she said, tucking her bottom lip between her teeth. "I just want this done. I don't want to wake up in the morning knowing the remnants of what this asshole did is still left behind. This may sound stupid, but fixing this one mess makes me feel like maybe I can fix the rest of them."

Hearing the wistful tone of her voice made it impossible to insist they wait until the next day to paint the barn. Besides, he understood her logic. Her need to get her hands dirty and do something constructive to make things better. Even if it was a smaller, trivial thing compared to the rest of the shit she was wading through.

But he still needed a break.

He waved his fingers in a come-here motion.

She stepper closer and took his hand.

"I promise we will get this done tonight, but my shoulder is killing me, and I need a drink." He hated using his injury as an excuse, but it was the only thing he could think of to get Lily to stop working for a few minutes. "How about we share an ice-cold beer on the porch, catch our breaths, then we'll find the ladder to finish the job."

Worry wrinkled her brow. "Okay. A drink sounds nice, and I could use a break, too."

"I know that's not true, but I appreciate you trying to help me save my manhood." He gave her a wink then tugged her toward the house. He waited until she settled into one of the rocking chairs then hurried inside to grab them each a drink, making the last second decision to find two forks and the leftover pie from the day before as well.

As he returned outside, Lily's smile told him he'd made the right choice.

"Not sure how well beer and apple pie go together, but I'm willing to try." She took her drink and set it on the floorboard then rested the pie tin on her lap.

He snagged a bottle of water from his pocket and waved it in the air. "Thought you might say that, so I brought this in case."

Stabbing the fork into the pie, Lily slid a bite in her mouth and groaned. "Best. Idea. Ever."

Madden swallowed hard. Watching her eat pie was way too sexy. He cleared his throat, needing to stay focused. He'd slipped last night, and someone had snuck onto the property and vandalized Lily's barn. He couldn't let that happen again. Hell, he'd even discussed it earlier with Reid, and they'd agreed to both stand guard throughout the night to make sure nothing else happened to Lily. Until whoever was determined to hurt her was caught, he needed to keep his mind sharp.

Sipping his beer, he stared at the backdrop of mountains in the distance. The lush green peaks with spots of color called to him, grounded him. "It's funny how for years I've sat on the porch with my dad and looked at these exact same mountains. Crazy to think we've seen the same view all this time."

"Dad and I like to sit out here at night after the work's done for the day. Reminds us of why we do what we do, why we work so hard for this place." She placed the fork in the tin. "I'm glad I went to see him today, but it was tough. So many emotions are swirling around inside me, and he's at the center of most of them."

Not wanting to interrupt, he cradled his bottle in his lap and rocked. He hadn't asked about her visit with her father, figured she'd tell him anything she wanted him to know, and he didn't want to say the wrong thing.

She sighed. "I hate being mad at him right now. I should be standing by his side, holding his hand. But even though it cuts my soul to admit this, I *know* he plays a role in everything that's happened, and it pisses me off. I'm angry he's put me in this position. I'm mad he's not awake to clear everything up. I'm terrified he'll die and I'll be left with all this guilt and turmoil, never getting a chance to move on. Leaving me here all alone to pick up the pieces." Her voice broke on the last word, crushing his heart.

"I'm sorry for what you're going through. Hell, I'd take your place if I could. Just know that everything you're feeling is okay to feel. All of it. And no matter what, you'll never be alone. I'll be right here with you, Lily, as long as you want me to be."

She smiled through her tears. "Thank you. I like the sound of that."

"Good, then you should know your dad will pull through and make it home. Because no way he'll let me win your heart without a fight. I'm gonna have to win him over if I stand a chance."

She snorted out a laugh. "Good point. He won't make things easy."

"For you, I'm up for the challenge."

They sat and finished their drinks in comfortable silence. The sound of cawing birds and the squeaking of their matching chairs keeping them company. Once he drained the bottle, he stood. "All right. We better get this done now, or I'll be tempted to head inside and take a nap."

"A dinnertime nap?" Lily asked, eyes wide. "I've never heard of such a thing, but let's get you to the barn before you leave me outside to handle the chores alone."

Standing, he stayed close to her side as she walked to the second, smaller barn that was used for storage.

"We have a few ladders in here. We shouldn't need a super tall one." She pushed open the door, and a subtle creaking raised the hairs on the back of Madden's neck.

He rested a palm on her shoulder to stop her from stepping inside. "Stay right here a second."

"What is it?" she asked, frowning.

"Not sure but something doesn't feel right. Where's the light switch?" The sun wouldn't set for another hour or two, but the storage barn didn't have windows to let in natural light.

"On the wall, to the right."

The sensation of bugs skittering down his spine made him move slowly. He took a step into the stale, musty barn. A wall of heat, along with a continuous groaning met him. Finding the switch, he flipped on the light and dread dropped low in his stomach.

In the center of the ceiling, a lifeless man hung from a thick rope.

"What is it? What's wrong?" Lily barged inside, and bile shot up the back of her throat. She turned away from the morbid scene in front of her, but the sound of the subtle shifting of the rafters as the body dangled would be forever etched in her brain.

Madden wrapped an arm around her shoulders and steered her into the fresh air. "I need to see if I can help him."

"How can you possibly help? He's dead." She squeezed her eyes closed, but when an image of the body slammed against her brain, they flew open again. "Who was that?"

"I don't know, but I'll find out. You stay here and call the police."

Before she could ask any more questions, he took off at lightning speed into the barn. She fumbled for her phone in her pocket and called the authorities as her mind spun. If she believed in such things, she'd think someone had put a giant curse on her and her ranch.

"Nine-one-one, what's your emergency?" The dispatcher chirped out the all-too-familiar line after two rings.

"I need deputies at Tremont Ranch. There's a man hanging from the rafters. I think he's dead." Her voice trembled, and she struggled to keep the bile from coming all the way up.

"Okay. I'll send deputies there right away. Do you know who the victim is?"

"I didn't see his face and stepped out of the barn."

"That's good. Don't touch anything. Just stand tight and help will be there shortly. Would you like me to stay on the line with you?"

Even though she gripped the phone tight like a lifeline, there was no reason to keep the dispatcher on the phone. Madden was right inside, and she didn't believe she was in immediate danger. "No, I'm fine."

She almost laughed at her own words. She was anything but fine.

Clicking off, she tapped her toe against the packed dirt at her feet and bit her thumbnail. She should tell Madden not to touch anything like the dispatcher warned, but she couldn't bring herself to go back inside. She'd assumed witnessing her father being shot was the worst thing she'd ever see. She wasn't so sure now.

A light touch on her shoulder made her jump.

"Sorry," Madden said. "Didn't mean to scare you. Did you get ahold of the sheriff's department?"

Wrapping her arms around her middle, she nodded. Chills raced up and down her body despite the warm air. "They're on the way. Any chance you saved some guy's life?"

He scrubbed a palm down his face. "No. I knew it was a long shot he was still alive, but I had to make sure. Once I verified he was dead, I let him be. I don't want to disturb the death scene. The deputies need to see everything exactly the way we found it."

She swallowed hard, hating the question she had to ask. "Do you know who it is?"

The painful look in his eyes had her bracing herself. "Tell me."

"I think it's Daniel."

"No!" She lunged for the door, needing to see for herself if a man she'd known and trusted for a big part of her life was really dead.

Madden hooked an arm around her waist. "You don't want to see him like that, Lily. He wouldn't want that."

"I don't care," she yelled. "I have to see if it's him. I need to know." She struggled against Madden's hold until she broke free and burst into the barn.

Harsh light beat down from the exposed bulbs overhead. She steeled her nerves and glanced up. Daniel's red and bloated face stared down at her.

Gasping, she covered her mouth with a shaky hand.

Madden stood beside her and coaxed her to lean into him as he held her against his strong body.

Tremors took over her limbs. Tears coated her cheeks. "It's him. It's Daniel."

"I'm sorry, Lily," Madden said, his muscles coiled as if ready to attack anything that came their way. "I know he meant a lot to you and your family. Sometimes people can't outrun their demons. Hopefully now he's free of whatever led him here, and we can find out exactly what he'd gotten himself involved in."

His words were meant to be comforting, but instead raised fury in her blood. Her body stiffened, and she pulled out of his hold. She pointed a finger up at Daniel. "He did not do that."

Madden frowned, doubt rippling his forehead. "Lily."

He said her name as if speaking to a child, which only pissed her off even more. "Don't. Don't say I'm delusional or not seeing the truth. I *know* him. Have known him for a very long time, and what you said was absolutely right. He wouldn't want me to see this. Especially after everything that's been happening around here lately. If he'd wanted to kill himself, he'd have no reason to sneak onto the property, wait for no one to be here and then hang himself in my barn. What's the point?"

Madden shrugged. "Maybe he'd hope someone would be here. Maybe he wanted someone to stop him."

She shook her head. "No. If he'd wanted to end his life, he wouldn't have come here. Hell, why pack his stuff and drive away yesterday if this was his plan? It doesn't make any sense."

Rubbing the back of his neck, Madden flicked a quick glance up at Daniel before returning his gaze to her. "You know him a hell of a lot better than I do, and I trust your gut. So what do you think happened?"

His ability to believe in her despite his initial doubt overshadowed a little of the turmoil chugging her stomach. "I think Daniel was murdered."

Chapter 19

Irritation rolled off Lily in waves. She watched Deputies Silver and Hill drive away, followed by the coroner office's white van, and wanted to scream. Nothing at the scene pointed to a murder, and the two sheriff's deputies all but patted the top of her head and called her pretty when she voiced her theory.

But Madden believed her.

For the first time in her life, Madden made her feel like she could contribute more than what was expected of her. She was smart, capable and, damn it, she was the only one here who knew the man who'd just died.

"I don't care what they say. He didn't kill himself. It doesn't make any sense."

Madden rested a hand on her shoulder and gently kneaded her stiff muscles. "What you said makes a lot of sense, and I think they listened to you. They agreed to look into the death more, even though nothing on the body or in the barn showed evidence of anything happening beyond what it appears."

"How hard will they look? I could see the doubt in their eyes, in the way they exchanged glances when they thought I wasn't paying attention. Not to mention everything else they have on their plate. Proving what they think was a suicide was murder can't be that high on their priority list right now, especially when it helps check boxes in their investigation."

He stopped the motion of his magic fingers along her neck. "What do you mean?"

She shrugged. "He was a person of interest and now he's dead. This makes him look guilty. Like he was sorry for whatever it was that drove him to commit these crimes in the first place. It'd be easy for the deputies to lay all the blame at Daniel's feet and tie it up in a nice tidy bow."

"All their evidence against him is circumstantial," Madden said. "I'd hate to think they'd throw in the towel and take the easy way out because they wouldn't need a conviction anymore. But…"

Her eyes sharpened as he let his voice trail off. "But what?"

"I didn't lie when I said I trust your gut." He lifted his palms as if already in surrender of an argument he anticipated. "But if Daniel is responsible for your father's shooting and everything else that's come along with it, it wouldn't be the worst thing."

"Excuse me?" She fisted her hands on her hips, prepared for a fight. Hell, she half wanted a chance to scream and stomp out her frustration.

The lines of his face softened. "Then you'd be out of danger, and I could stop being terrified someone will take you away from me."

His words pierced her anger like a needle popping a balloon. She shifted to lean against him and sighed. "I get that, I do. And trust me, I want all of this to be over. I want to rest easy knowing I won't wake up to a new emergency. But my bones are telling me I'm right about Daniel. Now I need to prove it."

Madden rested his chin on the top of her head and skimmed his knuckles along the sides of her biceps. "Okay. We can do that. Charlie told us Daniel didn't have any family or close friends. Is there anyone at all you can think of we could talk to for information?"

Shaking her head, shame filled her. She'd meant it when she insisted Charlie and Daniel were trusted like family, but how could she know so little about their personal lives? "Not really. We could go to his place, but I don't have a key. Hopefully the deputies will be diligent enough to at least look in his home."

"I'm sure they will," he said. "What about the bunkhouse?"

"What about it?"

"You mentioned the ranch hands using the bunkhouse when you had a lot of guests and their workload increased. We did a quick glance the other day but didn't look too hard. Do Charlie or Daniel ever keep personal belongings there?"

"I wouldn't know. I respect their space and stay out. I'm not even sure if my dad goes in there."

"Maybe it's time we take a closer look."

A beat of anticipation had her pulling away. There had to be something they'd missed. "Let's go."

She quickened her pace, leading the way to the bunkhouse. Determination set her jaw as she swung open the door and walked inside.

The interior of the structure resembled the guest cabins dotting the property, except wood paneling lined the walls instead of rounded logs. Two sets of bunk beds took up most of the room, with a ratty brown recliner facing the old-fashioned tube TV on a tall stand. A white oven and refrigerator nestled between a short counter and a farmhouse sink.

The cabinets were a dark stained oak. A bathroom could be found behind the lone door at the back of the space.

"Is it always unlocked?" Madden asked, stepping in behind her.

"Not sure. I assume they'd lock it if they were staying here, but there's not really a reason to now."

"Unless there's something inside to hide."

She studied the neat room, searching for anything that appeared out of place. "Guess we'll find out. But I'll ask Charlie. If they usually lock it, we should let the deputies know it wasn't locked today."

"Agreed. Let's start looking."

They went to work in silence. She was grateful that Madden went straight to the bathroom while she peeked inside the TV stand. When nothing but dust greeted her, she flipped up the footstool of the recliner to glance underneath and dipped her hand inside the crevices of the material.

"Men are gross," she muttered, refusing to take a closer look at the crumbs she'd ran her hand over inside the chair.

Madden emerged from the bathroom. "Nothing in there except some toiletries and a man's razor. Some towels."

"All I've got are dust and crumbs."

The side of his mouth hitched up. "Lucky you. I'll check the kitchen."

While he searched the cabinets, she made a beeline for one of the bottom beds. She tossed back the crisp, white bedding then dipped her hand under the mattress. When nothing turned up, she repeated the process with the top bed before searching the bottom of the metal structure.

"Anything?" she asked as she made her way to the second set of bunks.

"Just some canned corn and a box of pancake mix."

Defeat crushed down on her shoulders. She hated the

helplessness of watching tragedy continuing to unfold around her. But she refused to drown in her own sorrow. Instead, she turned to the bed, yanked back the covers and found a handful of brightly covered plastic tags. "What the hell?"

"What is it?" Madden hurried to her side and whistled long and low. "Well, that's interesting."

Her brows snapped together as she tried to make sense of the numbers on the tags. "What are they?"

"Cattle tags."

"We don't have any cattle on our ranch. Why would someone hide cattle tags in the bunkhouse?"

Madden grabbed his phone and snapped a few photos of what she'd found. "Not sure, but I know someone who might be able to help."

"Who?" she asked, jumping to her feet.

"My dad."

The smell of chili and corn bread met Madden at the front door. His stomach growled. Chili was a poker night tradition, the leftovers often heated up the next day in whatever creative way his dad could imagine.

"Hey, Pops," he called out, ushering Lily through the door.

"I'm in the den. Grab a bowl and join me." Walter's voice carried down the hall over the hushed sounds of the television.

Lily hooked an eyebrow. "A bowl of what?"

"Chili. You don't have to eat it if you don't want to, but he won't stop pestering me if I don't take some."

"Sounds good. I'm starving."

He led her to the kitchen where the brown tablecloth once again covered the poker table. A pot sat on the stove with a pan of corn bread beside it. He found two bowls and ladled heaps of hearty soup into them both. He carried the bowls to the living room, where his father sat watching a baseball game while eating his meal.

Walter slurped tomato juice from his spoon before waving to the couch on the side of his recliner. "Well, don't just stand there. Sit and eat."

Madden set the bowls on the coffee table then found two more TV trays. He set them up and motioned Lily to the couch.

"Thank you for the meal," she said, sliding onto the cushion. "Smells delicious."

"Nothing fancy, but it sticks to your ribs. How's your dad?"

She flashed a small smile. "He's as good as can be expected. Still holding out hope for a full recovery."

"Good, good." Walter nodded before dunking a chunk of corn bread in his bowl. "I have a feeling food and chitchat isn't what brought you two over, so spill it."

"We found some cattle tags, and I wanted to get your take on them." Madden pulled up the photos he'd taken on his phone and flashed the screen in front of his dad.

"You know I can't see that damn thing." Walter grumbled and searched for his reading glasses on the cluttered stand beside him. His hand shook slightly as he perched the glasses on his nose then grabbed the phone. "Where'd you find these?"

Setting down her spoon, Lily clasped her hands in her lap. "In the bunkhouse back at my ranch. They were hidden in one of the beds."

Walter frowned. "That's strange. You've never had cattle over there."

"No, sir. Cattle have never been one of our income

streams. Do you have any idea why someone would have the tags?"

"Can't be sure but sounds like someone was up to no good. Especially if they'd hid some other ranch's cattle tags on your property. Why not ask whoever has access to the bunkhouse? They could answer you better than some old man who's been out of the game for a while."

Lily cleared her throat, her nerves on full display.

Madden wrapped her clenched hands in his own. "We spoke with one of the ranch hands on our way here and he claimed to have no knowledge of the tags. The other ranch hand is dead."

Walter studied the screen. "And you think his death is connected to these tags?"

Madden shrugged. "We're not sure."

"One thing I do know is these tags are from different ranches." Walter leaned forward to hand back the phone. "Each ranch has their own specific tag. Use the same color, same shape, same type of lettering. A couple of those tags matched, but most were different."

"How could someone who worked for us get access to tags from other ranches?" Lily asked. "What would be the purpose?"

Madden's gut dipped. There might be a couple of different answers to Lily's question, but in his mind, one was glaringly clear.

And it didn't paint a very pretty picture.

Walter met Madden's gaze as if seeking permission to offer an explanation. He understood how hard it'd be for Lily to hear, but there was no way around it. Madden gave a tiny nod, encouraging his dad to continue.

"Have you ever heard of cattle rustling?" Walter asked.

Lily's eyes grew wide. "You mean like stealing cattle?"

Walter nodded.

"You don't really think that's what was happening, do you?" She bounced her gaze between Madden and Walter, as if willing one of them to offer a different option.

"It's hard to say." Walter scratched the bottom of his chin. "But I don't see any other reason someone would be in possession of so many different tags then hide them. This man who died, did he have any financial problems? Hardships?"

"I don't know," she said.

The heavy sensation in Madden's gut turned hard as a rock. Daniel may or may not have had financial struggles in his life, but Tremont Ranch certainly did. "Any idea how much cattle are sold for these days?"

Walter let out a long, rattling sigh. "Son, it's been years since I've sold cattle. I can't say what the exact rate is these days."

He loved his father's modesty, but he also knew the old man kept a pulse on as much as he could since the day he'd sold his land. He may not be running a cattle ranch any more, but Walter McKay was still a rancher and would be until the day he died.

Shifting the tray to the side, he leaned forward to rest his forearms on his knees—his gaze found his dad's. "I don't need an exact amount. Just a ballpark figure. Hell, even an idea of what you sold one steer for years ago. That might be enough to put this damn puzzle together."

"You're looking at maybe around three dollars a pound, give or take. That fluctuates depending on the economy, as well as the costs associated with taking care of the animals."

Lily's jaw dropped. "How much does a cow weigh?"

If the circumstance wasn't so serious, he'd laugh at Lily's

shock. As a rancher, she'd have an idea of how much it'd cost to keep the steer alive, but she wouldn't be privy to all the money ranchers put in to keep their cattle healthy. "Depends, but at least five hundred pounds and up. If you pass a certain weight, the price can drop a little when selling."

"So that many tags would mean thousands and thousands of dollars' worth of stolen cattle."

"Possibly," Madden said, not wanting to jump to conclusions yet.

"How can we get to the bottom of this?" she asked.

Walter set his empty bowl on the end table and leaned back in his chair. "Match those tags to their ranches. See if they've had cattle go missing lately. Not much chatter 'round here about rustling but doesn't mean it's not happening. Sometimes a missing steer or two is chalked up to a coyote or bear dragging it off. If whoever took these tags was good enough, they'd move around the area. Hell, they'd venture into neighboring states. Stay under the radar as long as possible."

Lily rubbed her fingers in circles along her temple. "Maybe he didn't stay off the radar long enough. But that still doesn't tell us who is behind everything or how that's related to the drugs we found."

Madden didn't want to say it, but odds were high only a few people could be the mastermind behind all the chaos surrounding Tremont Ranch. One of them claimed innocence, one was dead and one lay unconscious in a hospital bed.

Discovering that any one of them was a criminal would break Lily's heart.

Chapter 20

Lily scrubbed the suds-covered dishrag along the inside of the bowl. A hundred thoughts swirled in her mind like the water circling the drain in the kitchen sink. What did potentially stolen cattle, hidden drugs and her father's shooting all have in common?

She didn't really want to know, but she had to get to the bottom of it. No matter where the answers led.

Madden stepped into the kitchen. He leaned against the counter and crossed his ankles. "I think it's clean."

She glanced at the white porcelain and sighed. The red stains were gone but her anxiety remained. No amount of scrubbing could erase the unease tightening her nerves. She ran the bowl under hot water then placed it in the wire rack on the counter.

"My dad's place might not be the most luxurious, but he does have a dishwasher. You could have thrown the bowls in there. Or even left them on the counter. You're a guest here. No need for chores." He plucked a hand towel out of a drawer and began drying the dishes.

The simple act thrilled a secret part of her. A part that'd always wanted a partner to walk with through life. A man who'd cook or clean or talk with her about her day while helping in whatever way he could. Madden kept surprising her, kept checking her boxes.

She plunged her hands back into what remained of the soapy water and found the last of the silverware. "I like washing dishes. It's like meditation. I can keep my hands busy and let my brain rest a little. I haven't been able to do that much lately."

"If I want to let my brain rest, I'd go back in the living room with my dad and watch the ball game."

She snorted out a laugh. "I guess we all have our things. How was your call?"

After they'd finished eating, Madden had stepped out to call Reid about what they'd discussed with his dad. She'd offered to clean despite Walter's protests. She could tell the old man didn't want to feel helpless, but when she'd mentioned how much it'd benefit her to use her hands, he'd relaxed into the idea.

"Reid will start looking into the tags and see if there have been any missing cattle reported while he's keeping an eye on your ranch tonight."

She finished rinsing off the last dish and spun around to face him. "What do you mean while he's watching my ranch?"

"I think it'd be best if you and I stay here for the night. And while we do, Reid will stake out your place."

He spoke so matter-of-factly, as though she was supposed to simply go along with whatever he planned without even consulting her. Sure, she hired him to protect her but that didn't mean she shouldn't have a choice in things. "And why on earth would I agree to stay at your father's house? Where I have no clothes or toothbrush or anything I need for the night?"

"Because last night someone got onto your property right under my nose, and another man died and I didn't even know it until we stumbled across the body." Pinching the bridge of his nose, he shut his eyes for a beat. When he opened them again, angst and regret shimmered inside them. "I don't have enough equipment to properly survey all your property. I can't keep you safe when I don't have eyes on everything. No one will look for you here, and Reid can be on-site if anything happens."

She wanted to argue but not only was his logic flawless, she could sense his urgency. "So what? We're going to sleep in the twin bed in your childhood bedroom?"

He grinned. "You have no idea how many times I dreamed you'd be in that bed."

Grinning, she shook her head. "Regardless if that fulfills your childhood fantasy or not, a night crammed in that tiny bed doesn't sound very tempting. And neither does sleeping together with your father down the hall."

"More like right next door." Madden grimaced. "But that won't be an issue. We'll stay in separate beds. I'll stay in my room, you take the guest room. The bed's bigger, and you'll have your own bathroom. You'll find whatever you need in there."

The idea of being separated from him for the night made her chest ache.

"What is it?" he asked.

Damn, could he read that well? She debated what to say but if she wanted an honest and open relationship, she had to be vulnerable. No matter how much that terrified her. Besides, she had a front row seat to what happened when lies and deceit spun out of control. She didn't want any part of her own life to go down that same path. "Do you not want to sleep with me anymore?"

A coughing fit sounded behind her. She whirled around to find Dax standing in the doorway. Amusement sparked in his blue eyes. "If he doesn't, he's an idiot you shouldn't waste your time on."

Humiliation scorched her cheeks. If it was possible to burrow into the ground, she'd be under the floorboards in five seconds flat. Since that wasn't an option, she lifted her chin and met Dax's stare head-on. "Hello again, Dax. I didn't hear you come in."

A smirk too much like his brother's lifted the side of his mouth. "Clearly. Didn't expect to see you two here again tonight. What brings you around? More poker?"

"Nah. I took enough of your money last night," she said. "Your brother and I had a question for your dad."

All hints of humor fled from Dax's face, replaced by irritation. "What are you bothering him with now?"

Madden worked his tight jaw back and forth. "None of your business."

"Of course." Dax snorted out a humorless laugh. "Nothing between you two is ever my business. If that's the way you want to keep things, maybe you should be the one living here, keeping an eye on things instead of staying in that apartment, pretending to work when you're clearly just getting your kicks in with people paying for your help."

"You son of a bitch," Madden said, storming across the kitchen.

Lily jumped in front of him, placing her palms on his chest to keep him from knocking off his brother's head. "Madden. Stop. Dax is teasing."

Madden's glare melted a fraction. The red drained from his face. "No, he's not, but he should thank you for saving his pathetic life right now."

"Sure, whatever. Thanks, Lil." Sarcasm dripped from every word.

A low growl hummed from Madden's chest, vibrating Lily's hand.

"I'm going to get myself ready for bed. Can I trust you two boys alone or do I need to stay here and play referee like when we were kids?" She glanced between the two men for any signs that the tension between them had dissolved.

A hint of a smile touched Dax's mouth. "At least back then you were on my side."

A glimpse of the boy he used to be warmed her. "I'm still on your side, Dax. Even if you don't see it." She set her sights on Madden and lowered her voice. "Talk to him. He deserves to know the truth."

She kissed Madden's cheek then went in search of the guest room, hoping to find a large bath she could fill with hot water and sink into, soaking until her feet turned to prunes and her problems floated away with the steam.

Madden waited until the padding of Lily's footsteps faded and he was sure she'd found her way to the guest room before he turned all his fury on Dax. "What the hell is your problem?"

"You're my problem, big brother. Have been for a while." Dax strolled past him to the fridge and pulled out a beer. "Want one?"

He wanted a lot more than a beer but accepted the offer anyway. Twisting off the cap, he took a long sip and waited for the alcohol to hit his blood stream and calm him before addressing his brother again. As much as he hated to admit it, Lily was right. Dax deserved to know the truth, and it was past time to tell him why they'd sold their land.

"Want to sit on the porch for a few?" he asked, tilting his head toward the front door. He understood that now was the time to tell Dax everything, but their father might have a different idea. Walter's hearing wasn't what it once was, but the old man had a way of tuning in at the worst times. Better to have this conversation without the threat of being overhead.

Shaking his head, Dax rolled his eyes. "Whatever, man."

Madden counted to ten as he led the way outside and sat in the familiar rocking chair. He needed to keep a calm head to have this conversation.

Dax sat beside him. "You and Lily, huh? Do you want to sleep with her or not?"

"I'll repeat, that's none of your damn business."

Dax chuckled. "Well, you're an idiot if you don't. No matter if her dad hates you. Hell, you couldn't throw a stone around here without finding some girl's daddy who didn't want you around. Might as well go toe-to-toe with Tremont."

"I didn't bring you out here to discuss Lily."

"Didn't think so, but you aren't spitting out what you wanted. Figured I'd talk about something rather than just sit here, drinking a beer and pretending everything's all right between us."

Well, that was as good an opening as any. Madden took another drink then hugged the bottle between his hands. "And why do you think things aren't good between us?"

Dax turned to stare at him. "You're joking, right?"

"No jokes, man. I want to be done with this nonsense."

"Seriously?"

Madden nodded.

"Okay. How could anything be good with us after you stole my dream?"

The anger in Dax's voice hit him like a hailstorm. "I didn't steal anything from you."

"You agreed to sell the ranch," Dax yelled, throwing his arms wide. "This land, this place, it's in our blood. In our bones. I grew up idolizing you and knowing I'd always have a place here. Working this ranch like Pops had. Knowing every night I'd go to bed sore and tired and satisfied. You took all of that away from me."

Anxious energy swirled through Madden. He tapped his toe against the floorboard, needing to get it out of his system before he exploded. "I came home, injured and traumatized, and couldn't do the job anymore. Pops and I didn't have any other option but to get the money we could so he could survive."

"*I* could have done the work. *I* could have kept this legacy going."

"You were just a teenager, Dax. We couldn't put that pressure on you."

Dax shot to his feet and paced. "I'm not a damn kid. Haven't been in a long time. Hell, who do you think took care of this place while you were gone? Who kept an eye on Pops? I did."

A lump lodged in Madden's throat. He hadn't thought about the years he'd been gone. He'd assumed his father had kept a steady hand on running the ranch in his absence while Dax ran around, enjoying his youth.

But none of that was the real reason for selling the property.

"I'm sure you helped Dad a lot while I was gone, but that's different from taking on the responsibility of this whole place. Dad wasn't in a position to help. He needed to off-load things on someone else. It might seem selfish, but he didn't have a choice."

Dax stopped, his broad shoulders drooping. "We always have a choice. You two just chose to leave me out in the cold."

"No, we chose to give you a chance to make your own mark while preserving Dad's dignity."

"What do you mean?" Dax frowned.

"Dad has Parkinson's. He found out right around the time I came home with a bum shoulder. He didn't want to live on a ranch he couldn't run, and I couldn't take over a ranch that was always supposed to be mine. You aren't the only person who had something stolen. We all did. Just in different ways, by different circumstances."

Silence struck Dax, and he sank back in his chair. "Parkinson's? You sure?"

Emotion tightened Madden's chest. His dad had always been larger than life. Picturing what was to come—what had already begun—tore his heart in two. "We're sure."

"I've seen the tremors. I told myself it was normal. It was just an age thing. I never imagined it was something more serious." He scrubbed a hand over his face, and when he dropped it to his lap, tears shone in his eyes. "You should have told me."

"You're right."

Shock registered on Dax's face. "I don't think I've ever heard you say that before."

"Don't get used to it. But you have a point. You haven't been a kid in a long time. I need to stop treating you like one. Should have stopped a long time ago and brought you into decisions that affected your life. I'm sorry I didn't."

Dax rubbed at his eyes. "Appreciate that. Well, damn. Who am I supposed to aim all my pent-up anger at now?"

"Ha!" Madden said, grateful to steer the conversation into less tumultuous territory. "How about using it to whip that stallion into gear. Did you bring him out here?"

"Yeah. I didn't really need to. Just gave me an excuse to be closer to Dad during the day. He gets lonely out here by himself."

Guilt hit Madden like a slap in the face. He'd avoided being out here because he didn't want to run into Dax. Not only had he let their bad feelings color the way he saw his brother, but they'd also kept him away from the place he'd called home most of his life—and the man he'd admired forever.

"I'm sure he likes that."

Nodding, Dax sipped his beer. "So why are you and Lily here? She still in danger?"

"I had a question about cattle tags then figured we should stay the night. It's tough to keep her safe at her place. Too much space, not enough manpower or technology."

"I know a little about cattle tags. I could know something useful." Dax focused on the beer label as he peeled it back with his thumb.

Maybe it was the fact his eyes had been opened to the man Dax had become or maybe it was the shy way his brother casually mentioned helping, but he decided it may be time to take a chance on him.

Something he should have done a long time ago.

He grabbed his phone and found the photo he'd shown his father then passed the device to Dax. "Lily and I found these hidden in her bunkhouse today. Tremont Ranch is bleeding money right now. Finances are a mess. We're wondering if someone turned to cattle rustling to help pay the bills."

Dax slid his fingers along the screen to zoom in on the picture. "I've seen this tag before."

Madden straightened. "When? Where?"

"This is the cattle tag used at the Williamson Ranch. That's where I've been training horses."

Shock reverberated through Madden's system. A single conversation had not only helped build a bridge between him and his brother, but had opened the door to a new lead.

Chapter 21

Lily stepped out of the claw-foot tub and wrapped herself in a large, fluffy towel. Even though she'd rather be in her own home with her own things, at least she could partake in a few indulgences. As much as she hated that Dax had interrupted her and Madden's conversation before he could answer her question, she hoped they'd had an open and honest discussion that would help them both.

And she'd made sure to soak in a hot, relaxing bath long enough to give Madden and his brother plenty of time to talk.

Once dried, she strolled into the charming guest room. A white four-post bed sat in the middle of the room with what she assumed was a handmade quilt on top. Eyelet cases covered the pillows, and a chunky knit throw was tossed over the thicker blanket. A cream-colored dresser stood tall in one corner, pulling double duty as a television stand. A rocking chair finished off the space, making her want to grab the blanket and a book and curl up for the rest of the night.

Crossing over the plush rug covering a large chunk of the hardwood floors, she glanced in the closet for something to wear. Madden's plan to stay at his dad's might make sense for her safety, but he clearly hadn't thought far enough ahead to provide pajamas.

Finding nothing, she checked the dresser draws. "Bingo," she said, pulling out a button-down flannel shirt. She let the soft towel fall to the floor in a puddle and threaded her arms through the shirt's sleeves. She buttoned the front and shoved up the sleeves before gathering the discarded clothing she'd left in the bathroom.

Ding.

The email notification on her phone had her digging in the back pockets of her jeans for her phone. As she pulled up the message, she walked back into the bedroom and placed her folded clothes on top of the chair.

Reading the message, she sucked in a sharp breath and sank onto the soft mattress.

A gentle rap on the door sounded before Madden called, "Can I come in?"

"Of course," she said, her focus still on the phone. A beat of excitement pulsed through her veins, edging out the terror and worry of the last few days.

But a different kind of fear crept in. One based on insecurities and doubts.

"What's wrong?" Madden asked, frowning.

She shook her head, at a loss for words so she simply handed him her phone.

He crossed to her side and sat. A slow smile spread across his handsome face. "This is what most people would call a sign."

"Yeah?" Unsure, she scrunched her nose. "I'm not sure if it's a good idea. Especially now."

Setting the phone down, Madden gripped her shoulders and made her face him. "Someone told you they want to get married at your ranch. They want you to put on a beautiful wedding for their friends and family at a place that means so much to you. You just said this was your dream. Something you imagined doing to keep your land. This is amazing."

The words of the email ran through her mind. "But what about everything that's happened? It's as if the ranch is cursed. Hell, we haven't had a guest in weeks and now the vandalism, drugs and death. I can't host a wedding there."

"You've been dealt a shit hand. Not just the last couple of days, but the last few years. Things happened you had no control over, and the fallout's been tough. But you have a chance to do something different, to create a new dream that could be more fulfilling than you'd ever imagined."

His encouragement gave her something she hadn't had in a long time.

Hope.

"It's hard to wrap my mind around changing the ranch's entire business model, and then there's getting my dad to agree. And I can't forget the fact I don't know anything about throwing a wedding. I mean, really, this idea is crazy."

The more she played it through, the more she doubted her ability to do this. Just because a bride-to-be's venue unexpectedly closed, and she was frantically searching for an outdoor space with majestic views to throw something together, didn't mean Tremont Ranch was the right place.

No, it was too much with too little time. She'd write the woman back and offer a few suggestions in the surrounding area.

"No." She shook her head, and beads of water flew from the ends of her wet hair. "This can't be done."

Madden tucked his thumb and forefinger under her chin and forced her to meet his eyes. "Listen. It can be done.

If that's what *you* want. Sometimes life smacks you in the face and forces you into a corner. But if you open yourself to different possibilities, you'll see that corner is just a starting point for great things. Things that could lead you to wonderful places you never imagined. Hell, lead you to wonderful people you used to avoid."

She grinned and placed a gentle kiss on his lips. "Touché."

"I understand you're overwhelmed right now. Hell, anyone would be. No one would blame you for wanting the dust to settle before making a life changing decision. Just don't shut your mind to anything right now."

She nodded along with his words. "Okay. That makes sense. I'll respond to the message tomorrow. No need to figure everything out in the moment. Now that we've talked me through my issue," she said, pulling in a large breath, "how'd your conversation go with Dax?"

"It was interesting." He squeezed the back of his neck. "Tough at first but necessary. We should have had that conversation a long time ago."

"You told him about your dad?"

"Yeah, then we went in and spoke with Pops. We don't need any secrets between us. Not anymore. Pops and I were trying to protect Dax, but he didn't need protecting. He needed us to trust the man he was becoming. I only hope the choices we made didn't force him into a future he'll hate."

She bumped against him. "A wise man once told me sometimes when we feel we're being forced into something, we see where we should have always been."

"Hmm," he said, scratching his chin. "Sounds like a smart guy."

She grinned, loving their easy banter. "He has his moments."

A comfortable silence stretched between them. The emotions of the day settled on her shoulders, dragging her down. A yawn stretched her mouth, and a quick glance at the clock on the nightstand told her how late the hour had gotten.

"You need to sleep," Madden said.

Staring up at him, her heart galloped as her unanswered question came back. He'd been her rock, her support, her protector but that didn't mean his feelings went deeper than surface level. And as much as she enjoyed the charming guest room, she couldn't help but wonder why he'd chosen to sleep separate. "You never answered me earlier."

He flattened his palm against her jawline, hovering his face inches above hers. "If you think for one second I don't want to sleep with you, you're crazy. I just don't want our first time to be with my dad and brother so close, and I need to keep my head on straight. I can't keep letting things slip through the cracks, and honey, when I'm focused on you the way I want to be, I can't see anything else."

Heat licked up her body, and she swallowed hard. The preview she'd already experienced of what a night with Madden would bring came flooding back, and she agreed. They'd need a house all to themselves. No distractions. No worries. No one to hear the cries of pleasure she didn't want to control.

"I get that," she said. "Do you think you can at least lay with me for a while?"

"Now that I can do. Get under the covers while I shut off the light."

She didn't hesitate and slipped under the colorful quilt.

The light went out and Madden climbed in beside her, gathering her against him.

She sighed and closed her eyes, hoping to always feel as safe as she did in his arms.

As soon as Madden was certain Lily was asleep, he unhooked his arm from her waist and grabbed his phone from off the nightstand. He wanted nothing more than to stay snuggled in bed until he needed his next meal, but he had work to do. He pressed his lips to Lily's forehead then snuck into the hall.

Dax walked out of the bathroom and his brow rose high. "Fancy meeting you here."

"Shut up," Madden said, rolling his eyes. "I have some work to do and don't want to wake Lily. Thought I'd head downstairs and make a pot of coffee."

"Want some company?"

He shrugged. "Sure."

He'd rather sit in a quiet space with his thoughts and make a good plan to share with Reid, but after their chat earlier, refusing Dax didn't seem wise. In the kitchen, he made a beeline for the ancient coffee machine and said a silent prayer as it chugged to life.

Dax sat at the island and folded his hands on top of the wooden butcher block. "So what's going on with you two?"

He and Lily hadn't had this conversation yet. No way he'd talk with his brother about it. "I'm helping her figure out this mess with her dad."

Dax barked out a quick laugh. "Yeah. That's all you're doing."

Madden shot Dax a hard glare before pulling two mugs from the cabinet. "What we're doing isn't any of your business. I thought I'd made that clear earlier."

"Hey, I'm not trying to start anything." Dax held up his hands but couldn't hide his shit-eating grin. "I just thought it was common knowledge you two despised each other. It's been a little jarring seeing you so chummy. Laughing and being all happy around each other like when we were kids."

When the machine stopped spitting out brown liquid, Madden filled both mugs and took the seat by his brother. "Turns out there's a thin line between love and hate."

"Love?" Dax took a long sip of drink. "Wow. Wasn't expecting to hear that word."

Madden scowled into his own mug. He hadn't meant that he was actually *in* love with Lily. It was just a silly expression that hit the mark where the two of them were concerned. But he had to admit he'd felt things the last couple of days for her he hadn't felt in years. If he was being honest with himself, Lily brought things to life inside of him he'd never known existed.

Was that love?

"Mom would be happy," Dax said.

The words caught Madden off guard and a lump formed in his throat. "Excuse me?"

"If you and Lily were an item. Mom loved Lily like a daughter. Loved Mrs. Tremont like a sister. If the two of you made the Tremonts and the McKays officially family, she'd have wanted nothing more."

The realization that Dax was right pressed against his chest, and he struggled against the threat of tears. His mom was never far from his thoughts, but sitting around and talking about her seldom happened. Especially with Dax. That needed to change. Their mother had been a shining light for all of them. That light had dimmed since her death, but they needed to find a way to keep it alive.

He took a sip of the strong, black coffee. "Lily and I've

talked about our past a lot the last couple of days. It's been nice reliving those memories. In doing so, we figured out when things went sour for us. I'll regret the time I missed out on with her, but I won't make that mistake again. And I think you're right. Mom's smiling down on us. Hell, she's probably the one who pushed us together in the first place."

Dax snorted. "Sounds like something she'd do. I miss her."

Madden slapped a hand on his brother's shoulder, feeling closer to him than he had in years—determined to continue to fix the rift that had separated them. Yet another misunderstanding. Another casualty of poor communication. "So do I."

"Anyway," Dax said, blowing out a shaky breath, "enough of this sentimental bullshit. What got your ass out of that comfy bed with a beautiful woman? Any way I can help?"

Grateful for an opportunity to change the subject, Madden laid out every issue he and Lily had encountered since the morning her father was shot.

Dax sat quietly, sipping his coffee and listening without interruption.

"Reid's parked at Tremont Ranch right now," Madden said, finishing the rundown. "He's looking into the cattle tags. Searching for the rest of the ranches to see how much money they lost from the stolen cattle. I want to see if those amounts match the information Lily and I found in her dad's office."

"Good plan." Dax circled his palms around his mug and frowned. "But I agree with Lily. How does that tie into the drugs?"

Madden ran his hands through his hair. Frustration tempted him to rip the strands out at the roots. No matter how much information they uncovered, the big picture was still blurry. "I don't know, man. Maybe it's not connected. Maybe some kids were messing around and needed a place to hide their stash."

"I don't know much about drugs, but my guess is most people who use crystal meth aren't just leaving it around town untouched. That shit's serious. And it's getting to be a bigger and bigger problem around here."

"What do you mean?"

Dax sighed and stared into his now-empty mug. "The new hotel brings in a lot of tourists, which brings in a lot of money to Cloud Valley. Some people love it, some hate it. Like most things, there's good and bad. The bad is all those tourists attract attention from people looking to make a quick buck."

"Which for some means selling drugs."

"Exactly. Tourists who want a different kind of adventure. Who want to cause a little trouble or who are looking for a different high than what they can find staring at the mountains. Folks around here have always dabbled. Hell, ranching is a tough life and some people need an escape. It's a tale as old as Goldilocks and those damn bears. But now there's more money around, which means higher profits."

"Leading to more expensive drugs."

"Add that Tremont Ranch is in the backyard of that new hotel, it doesn't seem far-fetched to think something fishy could be going on."

Madden pressed his lips together, thinking it over. "All good points, but still doesn't explain where any of the profits are going. Even if Lily's dad is selling drugs and stealing cattle, where's the money going? It's definitely not being poured back into the ranch."

"Don't know. Not my job to figure that out, bud." Dax winked then walked his coffee mug to the sink.

"Maybe not, but if you ever get tired of training horses, and Sunrise Security ever needs to expand, you might be a good fit."

Leaning against the counter, Dax chuckled. "You've always been my bossy big brother. No need to make it official with you signing my checks. But now I need to get some sleep. Good night."

"Good night," Madden echoed as he sipped his coffee and unlocked his phone. He'd put the idea of Dax working for him in the back of his mind. Right now, he needed to speak with Reid. They had a criminal to catch, and a ton of strings to unravel before time ran out and another travesty fell into Lily's lap.

Chapter 22

Lily woke to an empty bed and in an unfamiliar room. Blinking, she adjusted to the light filtering through the lace curtains and forced herself to sit and take stock of her surroundings.

Homemade quilt, four-post bed, yesterday's clothes folded on a rocking chair in the corner.

Awareness trickled through the fatigue clouding her senses. She'd slept at Madden's childhood home, in the guest room without him.

Disappointment pulled her back down on the mattress. She'd fallen asleep wrapped around Madden. She'd hoped he'd changed his mind and she'd wake beside him like the day before.

Turning to bury her head in the pillow, she groaned. What was wrong with her? She'd never been one to depend on a man, to yearn for constant companionship and comfort. Maybe the stress had caught up with her and morphed her into some needy woman. Hell, maybe all the feelings Madden stirred inside her weren't even real.

She forced herself to her feet and padded into the bathroom. Just like the wedding venue issue, she didn't need to figure everything out right away. For now, she had to focus on fixing the mess her life had become. The rest would fall into place.

Including the clarity about her feelings for Madden.

After making herself presentable and donning yesterday's clothes, she searched for the McKay men downstairs. The kitchen was empty, but the coffee was hot, so she poured herself a cup and savored the first sip while appreciating the quiet of the house. She hadn't had much of that lately and hadn't realized how much she missed it.

The whinnying of a horse broke into her reverie and piqued her interest. She didn't bother finding her shoes as she strolled down the hallway to the front door and stepped onto the wide porch. The sun had just begun its climb into the sky, but the day already promised to be warm.

Dax stood in the middle of the weed-filled corral with a tan stallion trotting in a circle around him. One hand held the lead, the other used a lunge whip to guide the horse. The beautiful beast bucked and announced his annoyance at being told what to do, but Dax kept his voice firm, his hand steady as he choreographed a graceful ballet with a stubborn dancer.

But it was Madden who stole her attention and her breath. He stood outside the fence, his dark cowboy hat perched on his head and a piece of straw hanging from his mouth. He leaned against the barrier and kept his eyes on his brother. Fitted jeans were molded to his backside, and the T-shirt he wore showed off every muscle.

She wasn't sure who was more magnificent, Madden or the horse, but she'd give just about anything to ride them both.

A hearty chuckle turned her head to the side and humiliation scorched her cheeks. Walter sat in his rocking chair puffing on a pipe with a mischievous twinkle in his gray eyes. If she didn't know better, she'd think she'd voiced her last thought out loud. And if that had happened, she'd go ahead and die on the spot.

Walter lowered his pipe and patted the chair beside him. "Come over and take a seat, Lily."

She crossed the worn wooden planks and settled into the rocker so much like the one on her own porch. The arm was wide enough for her to set her mug on, but she kept her palm curled around its warmth to keep it steady. "Good morning."

"Good indeed. I don't get the pleasure of having so much company most days, and I never see those two getting along so well." Walter dipped his head toward Madden and Dax. "I hear I have you to thank for that."

She stared at the enchanting scene before her. The simple act of one man working with one of God's most magnificent creatures while another watched, the mountains covered with the greenery of life in the distance, made something right in her soul.

Made her happy and content.

These were the moments she loved most. The moments that made living the hard life of a rancher worth all the aches and pains and struggles. The moments where she could sit and appreciate nature and all its abundance while witnessing those she loved do the same...

Her heart stalled. Loved? How had she gone from uncertain if what she felt for Madden was real or not to love?

"You okay?" Walter asked. "Looks like you swallowed a fly."

She sipped her coffee to collect her thoughts before responding. "I'm fine. Just thinking about what you said and happy to see Madden and Dax together. But despite what you may have heard, the praise for that doesn't fall on me.

They had the tough conversation, and they'll need to continue to do the work until they're in a better place."

"True, but you encouraged Madden to talk to his brother. Something he and I both put off for far too long. You might be surprised I'm a stubborn old man, and Madden needed that kick in the ass you gave him. And I needed Madden to force my hand a little. Secrets shouldn't have any place in this family, and I'm relieved to be rid of them."

The mention of family secrets yanked her back to the chaos in her life and tied her stomach in knots. "Secrets always come to light. Sometimes it's as simple as talking things through, other times it comes down to ripping a family apart—taking down everyone else who stands in the way."

Walter rested his wrinkled hand on top of her knuckles and gave a light squeeze. "I'm sorry for your troubles. More than you know. I can't help but feel responsible."

The crack in his voice furrowed her brow. "How in the world would you be responsible? You've been nothing but kind and gracious to me, even though me and my father played a part in dragging your name through the mud."

"I played a part. One decision can cause ripples for years. They grow bigger and bolder with time, engulfing people who get caught in the stream. Your ranch was caught in the crosshairs of my choices. Your father's a good man who was placed in an impossible situation. Who was looking down the barrel of a gun and trying to figure out how to keep his ranch alive. If you find out he had his hands in rustling cattle or even those drugs, know it was something he didn't want to do."

His words caused tears to prick her eyes. Each day brought a weight of guilt and shame. Every fiber of her being screamed her father played a role in everything that had happened. A role that would probably paint him as a villain in his own story.

But he was her father, her rock. She'd idolized him since she was a child, and hearing words of absolution before uncovering how dirty his hands were made her fall hard for another McKay man.

"I'm scared to find out the truth," she said, finally vocalizing her fear.

"You're strong like your mother. No matter how things shake you, you'll find your footing." Walter picked his pipe back up and took a puff, the smell of tobacco rising in the air with the spiraling smoke.

She let her gaze drift back to Madden. Watched him laugh at something Dax said and shake his head. As if sensing her, he shifted, and their eyes met. The side of his mouth hitched up and he waved before making his way toward her.

"I like the way he looks at you," Walter said. "Reminds me of how I used to look at his mother."

She couldn't stop her grin. "I'm sure Madden's looked at plenty of women that way."

"Nah." Clicking his tongue, Walter shook his head. "At least not that I've ever seen. Trust me. Once a McKay man sets his sights on the woman he wants, there's no turning back so I hope you're ready, girl. And I hope he treats you right or him and I will go a few rounds. I might not be as young as I once was, but I can whip that boy into shape if he needs it."

She barked out a laugh and rose to place a kiss on Walter's weathered cheek. "Don't worry, I know how to handle myself."

She left the sound of Walter's amused chuckle behind her as she met Madden at the top of the porch steps.

He grinned up at her, dirt streaking down the side of his face.

She swallowed hard, her heart pounding faster than the stallion's footsteps as he galloped nearby. She hoped she was ready for Madden, because after spending the last few days by his side, she didn't ever want to let him go.

Madden parked his truck beside Reid's newer model and jumped out to open Lily's door. Now that all the anger and animosity toward Dax had been sorted, he felt lighter. Freer. Happier.

Okay, so the happiness might have more to do with what was happening between him and Lily. But getting rid of the ugliness inside him left more room for the bright light Lily had brought into his life.

Lily stepped down onto the driveway and frowned. "Where's Reid?"

"Not sure. Maybe he's surveying the property?" He hoped that's where his partner was. A beat of apprehension ricocheted through his system. Nothing had gone as planned since taking on Lily's assignment. Reid hadn't indicated there was trouble, but that didn't mean trouble hadn't found him.

As if sensing his unease, Lily wrapped her arms around her middle. "Maybe you should call him."

Madden found his phone in his jeans pocket, scrolled to Reid's contact information and called him.

The shrill ringing of a phone cut through the quietness of the morning.

"Sounds like it's coming from behind the barn," Lily said.

Leading the way, Madden stomped over gravel and rounded the side of the red barn, Lily right behind him.

He kept his device pressed to his ear, but spotted Reid before he could answer.

Lily squealed and shot past Madden. "What are you doing?"

Reid glanced over his shoulder and grinned. "Morning. Didn't expect to see you so early."

"Chores wait for no man....or woman," Lily said, eyes wide. "But you didn't answer my question. What are you doing?"

Reid shrugged. "Painting."

Madden shook his head and studied the freshly painted barn. Gone was the chipped off threat and the scarred wood left behind. "You didn't have to do this, man."

"I don't mind." Reid faced the building again and glided his thick brush over the wall, erasing the ugliness that had waited for them to handle. "Staying busy keeps my mind alert, and you two have enough to handle. You did most of the work yesterday. I just saw to the finishing touches. Glad I picked the right color. There was a ton of paint to pick from."

Lily laughed, her hands covering her mouth. "This is amazing. Thank you so much."

"My pleasure. Glad to help." Lowering his arm, he scooped a rag from the ground and used it to wipe the bristles. "I wanted to be done by the time you got here. So close. Now I need to clean up. Is there a sink or something in one of the barns? I don't want to track paint and dirt in the house."

"I'll show you. I need to get the horses watered and fed anyway." Lily stared up at the barn for a few seconds. "It's crazy how twenty-four hours ago this broadcasted a message of hate. Now it's a blank slate. Washed clean of the hate and terror. Seeing this gives me hope that all the other stains around here can be erased as well."

She started off in the direction of the stables.

Madden slapped a hand on Reid's shoulder. "Thanks, man. Seriously. This goes above and beyond your job."

"My job is to protect Lily. This helps protect her mental health as much as she helps yours."

Not wanting to let Lily out of his sight, he hurried after her. "Appreciate that."

Reid fell into step beside him. "That's not all I did last night. Since no one came around, I spent time on the cattle tags. I matched a few more cattle tags with ranches in the area, a couple on the other side of the state and one in Montana. I put in some calls but haven't heard back from anyone yet."

"Good work," Madden said, stepping into the stable.

He breathed in deep, filling his lungs with scents of hay and horses that he'd missed so much. He loved his job, and was proud of the business he was building, but he'd missed being outdoors. Caring for the land and animals. He needed to find a way to stay connected to the things that made him who he was.

"Can you pass me along a list of names?" Madden asked. "Maybe Lily or I know some of the owners."

"I might know who?" Lily popped her head out of the feed room.

"Some of the ranches where the cattle tags are from," Reid said. "Is the sink in there?"

"Yes, please, come in." Lily shifted to make room for him to enter. "And yes. I'd like to see the list, although I'm not sure if it will make things better or worse if I know any of the owners. It's bad enough to think someone from this ranch was stealing. It's worse if they stole from someone they know."

Madden hated the doubt in her voice. She loved her father, and everyone else who worked for her. Suspecting one of them of foul play that put both her and her father's life in danger was a tough pill to swallow. "If nothing else, having a personal connection to one of these people may give us better information."

Reid turned on the faucet. Water sprayed out, and he washed the paint from the brush's bristles. Red oozed from the tool and coated the sink.

"We can look at lists later. For now, we need to water and feed the horses then turn them out in the field for a bit. I told Charlie not to come in today so the work falls on you and me, Madden. You up for it?" She wiggled her eyebrows as if in challenge.

"Honey, I'm up for anything you throw at me."

"Good. Then catch this." She threw a pitchfork his way, and he snatched it from the air. "You can clean the stalls."

He could hear her laugh as she walked down the aisle.

"I can help with that. Just let me finish cleaning up." Reid set the now-clean brush on the side of the sink then pumped soap in his hands before scrubbing them under the water.

"No need. You've got to be exhausted. Go home and get some rest. Besides, Lily and I have found a good rhythm. It's been nice pitching in at a ranch again. Didn't realize how much I missed it."

Shutting off the water, Reid wiped the back of his wrist across his forehead. "Things sure have changed quick around here. You two an item now?"

Madden shrugged. He might know what he wanted from

Lily, but that didn't mean her heart was in the same place. "To be determined, but God, I hope so."

A vibration against his thigh had him plucking his phone from his pocket. "Madden McKay, Sunrise Security."

"Madden, it's Deputy Silver. Are you with Ms. Tremont?"

The urgency in her tone set Madden on edge. "I am, why?"

"I tried to contact her, but her phone goes straight to voicemail. You might want to get her down to the hospital now. The deputy standing guard by Mr. Tremont's room just called and he's taken a turn for the worse. It doesn't look good."

Madden didn't waste another second asking questions. He raced into the corridor. "Lily! We have to go!"

Lily stood in Queenie's stall. She ran a palm down the horse's wide nose. "Go where?"

"We have to go see your dad. Now. Something happened."

All the color drained from her face. Her bottom lip trembled, and tears leaked from her eyes.

He pulled her against him and pressed his lips to her temple. He'd give her all his strength right now if he could. But she was strong and could face whatever waited.

Even if what they found changed her life forever.

Chapter 23

Sniffing back tears, Lily took a step away from Madden and wiped her eyes. "What happened to my dad?"

Madden skimmed his knuckles up and down her arms. "I'm not sure, but I guess they tried to call you and it went to voicemail, so they called me. Deputy Silver said the guard contacted her. Where's your phone?"

She patted her pants pocket until she found it then yanked the cell phone out with a shaking hand. "It's dead. I didn't have my charger last night. And I'm still wearing yesterday's clothes." Panic struck her mute. Her chest tightened and breaths came out in sharp gasps.

No. She couldn't fall apart. Not again.

As if sensing her spiral, Madden flattened his palms against her jawline and turned his gaze on hers. "Everything's going to be all right. We're going to go inside, and you'll get changed. Grab anything you need, and I'll drive you to the hospital."

She nodded along with his words, grateful for his presence. "Okay."

Madden trailed his hand to rest at her back and steered her toward the door. "Reid, we've got to go. Can you handle the horses?"

"Yep. I've got it."

"Does he know how to take care of horses?" She didn't know much about Reid except he wasn't from Cloud Valley, and he'd served in the military with Madden. She couldn't waste time, but also couldn't leave her animals hungry.

"He grew up on a farm in Indiana," Madden said. "Trust me. He knows his way around a barn. Now let's get you ready."

Not needing any more reassurances, she sprinted into the house and got ready in record time. Madden waited for her by the front door as she threw her hair into a ponytail and jogged to his truck. By the time she clicked her seat belt into place, the ranch was in the rearview mirror.

Madden captured her hand and didn't let go until he'd parked in the full lot outside the county hospital.

She was out of the truck before he'd shut off the engine. Time ticked by as if in a strange dimension—excruciatingly slow but also at lightning speed. Her heart was in her throat as she approached the doors to the waiting room. They whooshed open, and she stepped inside. The all too familiar punch of disinfectant smacked her in the face and turned her stomach.

Madden stayed a step behind her, but she couldn't focus on him. She had to get to her dad before it was too late.

Finding his room, she ignored the guard stationed where he'd been the day before and skidded inside, but the room was empty. She spun in a circle, fear hitching high in her throat and stealing her breath. "Where is he?"

"Let's find someone to speak with." Madden clutched his cowboy hat in his hands and glanced into the hallway.

Lily couldn't stand around and wait for a nurse or doctor to pass by. She hurried back the way she'd come and stopped in front of the nurses' station.

A young woman with black-framed glasses, short brown

hair and blue scrubs sat behind the large U-shaped desk. She flashed a smile. "Hello, can I help you?"

"Yes. I'm Lily Tremont. I received word my father, Kevin Tremont, wasn't doing well. I went to his room but he's not there." Her voice cracked as she struggled to hold herself together. The possibility that her father may not survive had lived in the back of her mind since the moment he'd been shot, but now that possibility was more real than ever.

Sympathy pushed down the nurse's full lips. Staring at her computer monitor, she worked her fingers over the keyboard.

Each second that ticked by increased Lily's anxiety. She tapped the tip of her finger against the smooth desk, urging the woman to hurry up with her mind.

Madden stood behind her, near enough to touch her but he kept one hand on his hat and the other shoved in his jeans pocket.

"Okay," the nurse said. "Looks like your father is in surgery. He had some complications. That's as much as I can tell you, but if you take a seat in the waiting room, I'll let his doctors know where to find you as soon as they're available."

Frustration fisted her hands, and she bit back a growl. As much as she wanted to scream and stomp her foot until she got more answers, throwing a tantrum wouldn't do anything except make her look ridiculous. "Thank you."

Madden gently touched her back, prompting her in the direction of the waiting room.

She found a cluster of unoccupied chairs in the corner and sat. God, she hated this place. Hated the memories that attacked her. The smell of burnt coffee and the quiet drone of the news channel from the mounted television added to her increasing anxiety.

"I wish I had more information." She folded her hands in her lap and stroked her thumb over the skin above her knuckles over and over. "I don't even know what they're operating on. It could be his heart, I mean, he's old and the trauma he experienced had to weaken him even more. Or maybe his lungs? That's where they operated before. Maybe something went wrong the first time and they had to fix it. Or, oh God, could he have something wrong with his brain? Maybe an aneurysm or a stroke. Something that's kept him from waking up all this time."

"Nothing I say will stop you from worrying, and I wish to hell I had answers for you. But I can tell you that your father is getting the medical attention he needs, and the doctors and nurses will fight as hard as they can to save him."

"You're right," she said. "I know you're right. But you and I both know that sometimes, no matter how hard the best-trained professionals try, some people can't be saved."

Hooking an arm around her shoulders, Madden held her up. Gave her strength. Sat and waited as people came and went and the hours ticked by. Finally, a doctor stepped into the room and his gaze met hers.

She stood. Her heart all but stopped.

Madden rose to stand beside her.

"Ms. Tremont?" the man asked.

"Yes. How's my father? Is he alive?" She swallowed the bile creeping up the back of her throat. If her father had died alone in a hospital room, her world would crumble at her feet.

The man removed the white cap from his mop of brown hair. "He came through surgery. He had some swelling around his brain that created pressure we needed to relieve. We'll need to keep him sedated but hope this will aid in his finally waking soon."

Relief so swift and fierce rushed through her it almost knocked her down. "Can I see him?"

"Yes. I'll take you back to his room in the ICU. Unfortunately, he can only have one visitor at a time, and it'd be best to keep the visit short. He needs rest."

The stipulations didn't surprise her. The rules had been the same after his first surgery. But last time she'd lashed out at Madden and demanded he leave her alone. Now the idea of being anywhere without him was almost crippling.

As if reading her thoughts, he gave her a little nudge. "I'll walk back with you and stand guard until a new deputy is stationed outside his door, okay?"

She let out a rush of air and nodded, grateful for his reassurance as she followed the doctor down the wide hallway to her father's room. Life had taken a lot of unexpected turns the last few days but one thing had remained a constant—Madden's unwavering support.

In an instant, all her earlier doubts disappeared until one truth remained. She wanted Madden McKay to be a part of her life for a very long time to come. Now she just needed to find time to tell him and pray he felt the same way.

Madden sat in the empty chair situated right outside the closed door to Kevin Tremont's room in the ICU. The combination of lack of sleep from the night before and the gut punch of hearing the news about Lily's dad left him shaken. Leaning his head back against the wall, he closed his eyes and fought for a calm that seemed a world away.

The buzzing of his phone sent him upright, and he grabbed it from his pocket.

"Hey, Reid," he said, answering. "What's up?"

"Haven't heard from you. You still at the hospital?"

"Yeah. Lily's in with her dad. I'm sitting outside his room."

"Can't face him even when he's unconscious, huh?"

Madden grunted. "As long as he pulls through, we'll figure out how to get him to stop hating me. As much as I want his approval—more for Lily's benefit than my own—his attitude toward me won't chase me away."

"Hold on to that sentiment. But I didn't call to talk to you about your girlfriend's dad. I have some information from the ranchers who called me back. I can email you details to go over."

Groaning, he glanced at his phone screen before pressing the device back to his ear. "You can try, but my internet service sucks in here. Not sure if it'll come through. Can it wait?" As much as he wanted to know what Reid had uncovered, he couldn't leave Lily, and asking her to rush her visit with her father didn't seem right.

"You're going to want to see this, but I'll come to you. I'm close. See you in a few."

Madden disconnected the call and glanced up and down the wide hallway. He noticed the deputy from the day before studying the selection from a trio of vending machines. Making sure to keep the door to Mr. Tremont's room in sight, he dashed over to the younger man.

"Hey," he said. "Are you here to guard Kevin Tremont?"

"Yes, sir. Saw you sitting there, waiting on Ms. Tremont, and figured I'd give you some space." He fed quarters into the machine and pressed a button, freeing a bag of chips.

"Appreciate that, but can you take over for a bit? I'll let Lily know I have to step outside for a few minutes, but she and I will both feel better knowing someone's stationed at the door."

"Sure thing."

Madden led the way back to the door then tapped lightly before poking his head in.

Lily sat beside her father's bed with his hand in hers. She spoke softly, a sweet smile on her face as her words floated between them.

He hated interrupting but didn't want her to be surprised if she found him missing. "Lily?"

She glanced over her shoulder and the fatigue in her eyes pulled at his heartstrings. "Do we need to leave?"

"No, take as much time as you'd like. Reid called, and he needs to show me some stuff. He's on his way here. I'm going to step outside. I won't be long."

Her eyes went wide, and she started to stand. "I'll come with you."

He shot out his hands palms down and gestured for her to sit back down. "Don't worry. A sheriff's deputy is sitting outside. You're safe."

Gratitude lifted her lips. "Thank you."

"No problem. I'll let you know when I'm back." The urge to storm across the room and kiss her was so strong, but he held back. He didn't want to intrude even more on this moment she needed with her father.

Hurrying from the room, he sent Reid a text letting him know he'd meet him in the emergency room parking lot. The doors opened, and he settled his hat back on his head. Morning had come and gone, bringing the afternoon heat from the blinding sun. A light breeze stirred the lush leaves in the trees on the far side of the hospital.

Reid's red truck turned into the parking lot, and Madden waved his arm high to gain his attention. Anticipation beat through him. Reid made it sound as if he'd found something of utmost importance.

The truck crawled toward him, stopping near the loading zone kept clear for emergency vehicles.

"Dude, you can't park here." Madden approached the driver's side.

Reid waved away his concern. "I don't plan on staying long. Thought I'd bring you this." He extended a small pile of papers out the window. "I'd printed everything off before I left the office. It'll give you something to look at while you're here."

Madden grabbed the sheets and briefly scanned the numbers on top. "This looks like the spreadsheet we found on Mr. Tremont's computer. Why's it so important I see this now?" A tug of disappointment pulled down his lips. He hoped for something to bring this investigation to an end, not data they already had.

"Flip through the rest. I highlighted amounts I received from ranchers with stolen cattle. Estimated figures of what they would have sold for, what rustlers can get on the black market. That kind of thing. I haven't spoken with all the ranches yet, but enough of them match to paint a pretty damning picture."

Quickly flipping through the pages, Madden's stomach muscles tightened. "Shit."

"Yeah, doesn't look good. And there's more."

A black truck pulled into the lot and searched for a parking spot.

Madden hooked an elbow on the window. "Tell me."

"I found an account connected to Kevin Tremont. Not a lot of money in there, but a lot of movement. Big deposits followed by big withdrawals."

"How in the hell did you find that?"

Reid smirked. "I have my ways."

He should demand to know what those ways were, but

he'd do that later. Now he needed to speak with the sheriff's department and see if they had any of the same information.

Information that could put Kevin Tremont behind bars.

The roar of an engine caught his attention, and Madden shifted just in time to spy the black truck gunning forward. His heart thundered in his ears. "What the hell?"

The truck stopped, the window lowered and the driver fired off three quick gunshots before charging toward the exit.

Madden fell to the ground and covered his head with his hands. Adrenaline coursed through his veins, threatening to explode from his body. Glass rained down on him. With the taillights in sight, he jumped to his feet. Fear slammed against his gut.

Reid slumped against the seat. Eyes wide, and blood trickling down the side of his face.

Chapter 24

"Reid! Holy shit. You're shot." Madden spun toward the now open doors to the emergency room. Two doctors ran out. "Help! My friend needs help. Now."

Reid groaned and pressed the palm of his hand to the side of his head. "I'm not shot, you idiot. The glass from the windshield got me. I'll get it checked later. We need to go after that asshole."

Before Madden could argue, Reid threw open the driver's-side door then hunched onto the passenger seat.

Gritting his teeth, Madden jumped into the truck and slammed the door shut. Reid was a grown-ass man who knew his own limits. If he said he was good enough to wait for medical attention, he trusted Reid's instincts.

The black truck raced out of the parking lot and turned toward town.

Madden slammed on the gas and the vehicle lurched forward. The shooter had a good lead, but a meadow that stretched alongside the straight, two-laned road allowed a perfect view of the truck as it sped forward.

Reid hung his head in his hand. He sat straight, gaze fixed on the distant taillights. A sheen of sweat coated his pale face.

Madden cast him a quick glance. "You sure you're okay?"

"I'm fine," Reid snapped. "Keep your focus on the truck. I'll call the sheriff's department."

Madden didn't respond, but his partner's surly response had him doubting his decision to pursue the shooter instead of insisting Reid get medical attention right away. He tightened his grip on the steering wheel and urged the truck faster, pushing the pedal to the floor.

The sound of Reid's voice as he spoke on his phone filled the space, but Madden focused on the chase. He couldn't let this guy slip through his fingers again.

"Sheriff's department is aware of the situation," Reid said. "They're sending deputies to cut him off from the opposite direction. There aren't any other roads for this jackass to turn off before he hits town. As long as we keep on his tail until they get into place, he won't get away."

Madden chanced another look at his best friend. He swallowed his fear then zeroed in on the truck. He crept closer. Each inch he traveled stretched on like miles. Cool air poured from the vents, but it did nothing to beat back the heat consuming him from the inside out.

Blue and red lights flashed ahead, and the distinct call of a siren loosened the tension bunched at the back of Madden's neck. They had this bastard right where they wanted him.

The black truck stopped in the middle of the road.

"What the hell is he doing?" Madden asked.

"Looks like he's turning around."

He closed in on the vehicle, but the driver made a three-point turn and sped toward them.

"Shit," Madden muttered.

The truck ate up the center of the country road. The space between the two vehicles diminished by the second.

"No matter what, don't let him get past you." Reid's command came out on a choked whisper.

Images of Lily's crumpled body after she'd fallen from her horse and the pain displayed on her beautiful face time and time again flashed in his mind. She'd been hurt too many times, her life turned upside down and inside out. He had to put a stop to it any way he could.

"Hold on, man," he yelled. As the truck closed the final yards, Madden cranked the wheel to fishtail the back end of the truck toward the center lane.

Metal crashed against metal, shoving Reid's vehicle off the road. The back end spun toward the gravel shoulder. Madden braced himself. The force of the collision whipped him forward. His ribs slammed against the steering wheel and his forehead bounced against something hard. He squeezed his eyes shut as his head wobbled with every motion. The sound of shattering glass rang in his ears. The tires lifted on one side, balancing the truck in the air until gravity pulled it back down again.

The vehicle landed with a bone-crushing thud. Madden opened his eyes. "Reid. You all right?" he asked as he unhooked his seat belt and searched out the back window for the shooter.

The black truck rolled into a ditch on the other side of the road.

"Damn, dude. A little heads-up would have been nice." Reid groaned and leaned back against the seat. He lifted a shaking hand and gingerly rested his fingertips on the bloody gash on his cheek then rummaged in the glove box for his Glock. "What are you waiting for? Go get the bastard."

Madden grabbed the gun and jumped out of the vehicle. Sirens grew louder, but he couldn't wait for the deputies to get here before apprehending the driver. He trained the gun in front of him with his finger on the trigger.

The black truck lay on its side on the opposite side of the road, the driver's window pointed toward the sky. Smoke rose from the hood.

Moving slowly, he approached the vehicle. Gravel and broken glass crunched under his boots. "Don't do anything stupid," he yelled. "I've got a gun aimed your way, and sheriff's deputies will be here any second. There's no way out."

No sound came from the truck, no movement.

Madden lifted himself on his toes to see inside the vehicle. A man he didn't recognize slumped over the steering wheel with his eyes sealed shut and blood trickling down his face.

Shit.

He didn't want this asshole to get away but also didn't want him dead. At least not before he told him why he'd gone after Lily and her father.

The hum of engines approaching caught his attention. Two deputy's cruisers came to an abrupt stop at his side, and an ambulance wailed behind him. He kept his gaze fixed on the unmoving driver.

Deputy Silver and Deputy Hill climbed out of one car while Deputy Sanders parked and hurried out of the second. All three carried their weapons and wore matching scowls.

"He alive?" Deputy Hill asked, tilting his head to the wrecked truck.

Madden stayed rooted to the spot. "Not sure. He hasn't moved."

Deputy Silver walked forward with her gun trained in front of her. "We have you surrounded. Put your hands up. No sudden movements."

Deputy Sanders rounded the hood of his cruiser and

walked down the grassy embankment on the side of the road. He moved methodically, weapon in place, and managed a peek inside the broken window. "Eyes closed. Lots of blood on the seat."

"Is he dead?" Madden asked.

"I'm reaching in a hand to check your pulse," Deputy Sanders called out to the unresponsive man. "You have three guns trained on you. Don't do anything stupid."

Madden tightened his grip on his weapon. Anxiety rippled across his skin.

"He's alive, but barely," Deputy Sanders yelled. "He needs medical assistance right away."

Madden's shoulders drooped and he let his arm fall to his side as the emergency responders raced past him.

"Sanders, can you give me and Reid a ride back to the hospital?" Madden asked, turning his attention back to his own truck.

The passenger door squeaked open.

"Yeah, no problem. What's wrong with him?" Deputy Sanders jogged behind Madden to his partner's totaled vehicle.

Reid stumbled out. His face was white as a ghost. Sweat fell from his brow and mixed with his blood.

"Shit," Madden said, racing to Reid's side seconds before he pitched forward. Madden looped an arm around his waist and kept him from smashing his face on the pavement. He absorbed Reid's body weight as Reid's muscles went slack, sticking to him like a burr as they folded onto the ground, his unconscious friend in his arms.

The young deputy guarding Lily's father's room burst inside, eyes wide and hand on the butt of the gun at his hip.

"Get on the floor and cover your head. Gunshots were fired outside of the emergency room."

"What?" Tremors took over Lily's body and she slid off the chair. Her knees hit the floor, and she wasn't sure if she should lie down on the cool tile or stay where she was and pray. This couldn't be happening. Not again.

"You're going to be fine. I'm not going anywhere. No one will get through me. I promise."

She stared at his earnest, blue eyes and wanted to believe him. But too many bad things had upended her life and the only person who'd kept her safe was nowhere in sight.

Terror fisted her throat. Oh God. Madden said he was stepping outside to speak with Reid. She sank lower to the floor and grabbed her father's hand. He might not be awake, but she needed his comfort. "Is the shooter still outside? Is anyone hurt?"

"I'm not sure yet," the deputy said. "Just sit tight. I'll tell you as soon as I have more information."

Time froze even as the minutes ticked by on the clock mounted on the wall. A hundred scenarios with a hundred horrible outcomes played out in her mind. She kept her hand latched on to her father's.

What felt like an eternity passed when the radio attached to the deputy's uniform crackled, but she couldn't understand the torrent of words and codes sputtering through the speaker.

Her guard pressed the button on the side of the communicator. "Copy that."

"What's going on?"

Heavy footsteps pounded down the hallway. Nausea swam in the pit of her stomach, and she pressed a hand to her mouth to keep from getting sick. She stared at the door handle, wanting the door to swing open and Madden to come sweeping inside.

More voices spoke at rapid speed on the radio. Lily held her breath and listened for anything she could understand. Anything to tell her what the hell had happened.

The deputy nodded then crossed to her and extended a palm. "You're safe. You can get up."

Accepting his hand, she rose on shaky legs. "Can you please tell me what happened?" Her question came out as more of a command, but she didn't care if the snap of her words offended him.

"There was a shooting in the parking lot. The shooter fled the scene and civilians gave chase. The shooter and a civilian are being transported to the hospital to be treated for injuries."

Madden.

She squeezed her eyes shut against the crushing certainty that Madden was involved in this new disaster. Needing answers, she found her phone and called him. The line rang in her ear, spiking her blood pressure with each passing second. When his voice message played, she disconnected, and tears leaked from the corners of her eyes. Fear lined her lungs, stealing her breath and smothering her heart.

"Hey, it's okay," the young man she'd all but forgotten about said. "You and your father are fine."

Unable to speak, she shook her head. She wasn't fine. Not without Madden. Not without the hope he brought into her life for a different future filled with beautiful dreams and the promise of love.

She choked out a sob. She loved Madden. She may not understand how it was possible to fall so hard and so fast for a man she'd despised for so long, but she couldn't deny it. Didn't want to. But if she'd lost him before she'd had a chance to tell him where her heart lay, she'd never get over the devastation.

The soul-crushing desire to see Madden set her feet in motion. She ran for the door.

"What are you doing?"

She didn't waste a second to respond and hurried into the chaos of the wide hallway. Doctors and nurses spoke with panicked patients and their loved ones. People in hospital gowns and street clothes huddled on the floor, fear clear on their faces.

Lily maneuvered through the throngs of people toward the waiting room. That's where Madden had gone. Maybe he'd still be there. Hope quickened her pace until she spied the waiting room—upturned chairs scattered around the empty space, the television droned in the corner, and no Madden.

Disappointment crushed her windpipe. An overwhelming sense of hopelessness threatened to take her out at the knees, but she couldn't succumb to her emotions. She had to find Madden. He'd been strong for her countless times. Now she needed to stand strong for him.

The shriek of sirens shifted her toward the emergency room doors. An ambulance screeched to a halt, and she darted outside. Fear tripled her heart rate as the sun hit her in the face.

An emergency responder with her blond hair pulled into a stubby ponytail jumped from the cab and hurried to the back of the ambulance.

"Who's hurt?" Lily asked, her voice distant in her own ears.

A male medical responder hurried from the passenger

side and brushed her aside. "Sorry, ma'am. I can't give you that information. Please stay back."

A doctor emerged from the hospital. "What do you got?"

The woman yanked open the back door and jumped inside. "Large gashes on side of the head as well as injuries from a car accident. Another unit is en route with a second victim. More serious injuries."

Oh God. Each word slammed against Lily like an arrow, sharp and right on target. She moved from side to side, lifting onto her toes to see inside the tall vehicle.

A deputy's cruiser sped into the lot and came to an abrupt halt behind the ambulance. The sound of doors opening and closing penetrated the fog engulfing Lily, but she kept her focus on the gurney being lowered by the medical professions.

A light touch on her shoulder jolted her senses. She spun around and gasped. "Madden!" Joy exploded inside her, and she threw herself into his arms.

Burying his head in the crook of her neck, he held her tight.

She waited a beat before pulling back just enough to see his face. A trickle of blood on his forehead told her he hadn't walked away completely unscathed, but it could have been so much worse. "Are you okay? What happened? I was so scared you were hurt."

He squeezed his eyes shut and swallowed hard. "I'm fine but Reid...he's hurt."

The thump of the gurney hitting the pavement echoed in her ears. She glanced over her shoulder in time to see Reid being wheeled into the hospital, doctors and nurses already at work to save his life.

"He has to be all right." Madden's voice cracked. "I

should have gotten him help first. I shouldn't have taken off before I knew he was okay."

She flattened a palm on his cheek, trying to make sense of his words but not wanting to ask when he was spiraling. "He's strong and stubborn like you. He's going to be fine. I know it."

He leaned into her touch. "I hope you're right."

A second ambulance blared its siren and spend into the lot.

"Who else was hurt?"

Anger flashed through the worry in Madden's eyes. "The man who shot Reid. The one responsible for putting us all through hell and trying to kill you and your father. And if the asshole lives to see another day, I'll make sure he pays."

Chapter 25

Anxiousness crawled over Madden's skin like a pack of red ants. Waiting for word on Reid's condition was agonizing. He wasn't family, so no one would tell him anything, even if Reid was just as close to him as his own brother.

Lily sat beside him, her hand glued to his. She hadn't said a word since they'd taken their spots in the waiting room but had stayed as close as possible since he'd returned to the hospital. The relief in her eyes when she'd seen him spoke volumes. He'd wanted nothing more than to sweep her off her feet and carry her far away from this place.

But Reid needed him now, and Lily instinctively understood.

Deputy Sanders rounded the corner and stalked toward him. The bags under his eyes hung lower than usual and wrinkles lined his uniform.

Madden started to stand, but his father's old friend gestured him to stay seated.

"Don't get up. I'll sit. My feet are killing me." Deputy Sanders sank onto the empty chair on the other side of Madden. He groaned as if he'd just finished an eight second ride on a bucking bronco.

"Have you heard anything about Reid?" Madden could barely get the question through the tightness of his dry throat. Too many memories of another time, another accident, another brush with death sat at the forefront of his mind, transporting him back to the desert.

A place he never wanted to go again.

Deputy Sanders nodded. "Just spoke with the doctor. Figured you'd want an update. He got a few stitches from where the glass cut his face, and he has some fluids and medications being fed to him through an IV. He's awake but lethargic. Nothing too complicated. Nothing life threatening. Shock and loss of blood gave him a double punch. They'll monitor him overnight, but he should be free to return home in the morning."

The vise squeezing his lungs loosened, and Madden leaned forward with his elbows on his knees. He drew in a deep breath, blowing it out slowly.

Lily kneaded his shoulder. "Thank God. I knew he'd be okay. Can we see him?"

"He's in room number 203. Not sure if he can have visitors or not, but worst they can do is ask you to leave."

Now that he knew his friend would be okay, Madden straightened and cleared the emotion from his throat. Reid might have been his priority, but updates regarding his friend's condition wasn't the only thing that needed addressed.

"What about the shooter? Get an identification on him yet?"

Lily's hand tightened on his shoulder.

Sighing, Deputy Sanders rubbed the top of his head. "Guy's name is Jason Simon. Ring a bell for either of you?"

"Not at all. Lily?" He glanced down at her wide eyes and dropped jaw.

She shook her head. "No. Is this the man who shot my dad?"

"We believe so," Deputy Sanders said. "As of now, the department is looking at him and no one else. The truck's registered in his name and is the same one witnessed at your father's shooting. The casings found in the parking lot match the bullets used at the site of your dad's shooting. Forensics will be able to add more weight there, but we're waiting for that report to come through. The way things go around here, it could take a couple days."

"Did he give you any details about why he targeted Mr. Tremont?" Madden asked. Getting the evidence against this asshole was important, but he needed to understand the motive behind terrorizing Lily.

Deputy Sanders frowned. "No, not yet."

Lily inched forward on her seat. "Why not?"

"He hasn't woken up from surgery, and we're not sure if he will."

Lily stiffened beside him.

"Son of a bitch." Madden reined in his temper. He might want answers, but not as badly as Lily. She deserved to know the reasons her life had been turned upside down. "Any idea who this guy is? Where he's from?"

Deputy Sanders cast a hesitant glance at Madden before focusing on Lily. "This won't be easy for you to hear, but sources shared Jason Simon is a big name in the drug world. Surveillance has shown him around the new resort out by your place, and he has a rap sheet a mile long. Drug possession and distribution, aggravated assault, intent with a deadly weapon. He's a bad guy, Lily. If your dad pissed him off, he wouldn't just walk away. He'd make him pay."

Lily let out a shaky breath. "I should be more shocked than I am, but I knew something put a target on my dad's back. He couldn't be an innocent bystander with everything that's happened. I just wish I understood the connection. I'd hoped when we found the shooter everything would come to light. Looks like Dad's still the only one who can tell us what we need to know."

Madden remembered the information Reid had found and grimaced. "Does the sheriff's department know about all of Mr. Tremont's bank accounts?"

Lily turned narrowed eyes his way. "What are you talking about?"

He shoved a hand through his hair, hating that he was springing this on her in front of law enforcement. He should have told her sooner. Given her a chance to digest the information before now. But with all the chaos since Reid had shown up, he'd forgotten the papers now folded in his pocket. "That's why Reid came to the hospital. He brought me account information he'd uncovered that's tied to your father. Large amounts of deposits quickly followed by similar sized withdrawals."

"You think these withdrawals were being paid to some drug lord?" Lily asked, doubt dripping from her words. "But what about the cattle tags? And if he paid this guy, why would he want to kill him?"

Madden pinched the bridge of his nose. "I don't know. I'm not sure how this is all such a mess."

Deputy Sanders slapped his palms to his thighs then stood. "That's for the sheriff's department to figure out. The good news is the shooter can't hurt you anymore, Lily. Or your dad. It sucks we couldn't get more answers from him right now, but that doesn't mean we won't get to the bottom of things. Hopefully when your dad wakes up, we'll sort all the details."

A boulder of reality sank low in Madden's gut as he waved goodbye to the deputy. The reason he was hired to protect Lily was gone. The person responsible for putting her in danger was dead. She didn't need him anymore, but the thought of not seeing her every day sucked the air from his lungs.

Lily rested her head against his shoulder and looped her arm through his. "I thought I'd feel more relieved when we found the shooter, but my stomach's still tied in knots."

So was his, but it had more to do with not knowing where things stood between him and Lily. He pressed a kiss to the side of her head, and her blond hair tickled his nose. "You'll feel better when your dad wakes up. For now, we should get you home. It's been another long day."

"We should see Reid before we leave. Find out if he needs anything and let him know he's not alone."

Her consideration for his friend released a torrent of gratitude so strong, it swallowed everything inside him. "You sure you're up for that? I can always come back after I drop you off."

"I'm sure." She tilted her chin to stare up at him. "After we spend some time with him, will you stay with me?"

"Absolutely. I don't need to take off right away. I can hang around for a while," he said, her request lifting his lips.

"I want you to spend the night. I don't care if the threat is gone and I'm safe. I don't want to be alone. I want you with me."

Her unrelenting stare spoke of a million promises that set his core on fire. He cradled her jawline in the palm of his hand. "Baby, I'll stay with you as long as you want me."

Butterflies attacked Lily's stomach in rapid succession as she unlocked her front door, stepped into the foyer and flipped on the lights. Madden had been inside her home countless times. Hell, he'd already been in her bed. But to-night was different.

Tonight was special. A first step in a new relationship that promised so much happiness she could hardly stand it.

As if sensing her nerves, Madden locked the door then turned to her with a grin. "Dinner was good but how about we finish that pie before heading downstairs?"

She breathed a little easier, steadier now as she led the way to the kitchen. So many words sat at the tip of her tongue, questions about Madden's expectations regarding a relationship and the future ringing in her brain. But there was no need to move too fast. They'd already started off at warp speed. Nagging him about his feelings and where he saw things going would only scare him.

"Sit or stand?" she asked, carrying the pie to the island.

Madden found two forks and crossed the tile floor to stand beside her. "Stand. If that's okay with you. Between our visit with Reid and dinner at Tilly's, I need to stretch my legs."

She hopped onto the counter. "We can do both." She grabbed a fork before digging in for the first bite. She'd barely touched her meal, too consumed with the uncertainty of her future, and the burst of apple and cinnamon was exactly what she needed.

Grinning, he stood in front of her and caged her in place with his strong arms. "You're a problem solver."

She snorted and rolled her eyes. "Hardly. I've had my share of problems lately and still feel like I'm wading through the issues, searching for a solution."

"I'm sorry about that," he said, brow rippling in concern. "But things are getting better. Just like your barn. All it took was a little work to paint over the mess and create a clean slate. So what does your clean slate look like? Have you given any more thought to hosting that wedding?"

Not wanting to admit she'd been too consumed with thoughts of Madden, she shrugged. "It still seems like such a tall order. When I spoke about possibly wanting to use the ranch as a venue option, I figured I had months to iron out logistics. To plan and organize. I don't know if I can pull something like this off all by myself."

"You're not alone. You have an entire village behind you. Look at how people have stepped up to help you lately. From Eve who insists on keeping you fed to Charlie who hurried over tonight to handle the horses as soon as you called. Hell, even Reid picked up some slack and painted your barn. Everyone who loves you wants to help you make this place a success, no matter what you choose to do."

She twisted her lips to the side. He was right. This town was filled with people willing to lend a helping hand. All she had to do was ask.

Indecision battled in the pit of her stomach, and she set down her fork. "This is someone's big day we're talking about. I want to know I can deliver what this couple wants instead of jumping in and hoping I don't land on my face."

"Honey, even when we make all the plans in the world, we can still fall on our faces. Sometimes we have to take a leap of faith."

She wasn't sure if he was still talking about her possible business venture or taking that leap on them, but either way, her mind and heart were set.

She wanted both.

"I want to take the jump. I want to try and give it all I've got." The permanent pit in her stomach dissolved. She'd made up her mind and would go after what she wanted with everything she had. And if she ended up with nothing, at least she'd know she'd done her best.

His grin grew impossibly wider and he scooped her off the counter, whooping with excitement into the empty room. "You're going to kick ass."

Laughing, she wrapped her legs and arms around him and held on tight as he spun her in circles. "Stop it. I'm getting dizzy."

He set her on her feet and captured her mouth in his. "I'm so damn proud of you."

"I haven't done anything yet."

"You made a choice. You're grabbing an opportunity by the horns, and you're going to kill it. We'll start making plans tomorrow, tonight we celebrate." His gaze lingered on her lips.

Her heart burst like a confetti popper. Here was a man who not only supported her but encouraged her to do more than was expected. To step out of her box—out of the shadow of her father—and make a stand for herself and the land she loved.

"Thank you."

He tilted his head to the side, brows raised. "For what?"

"For showing up after I was awful to you. For protecting me and teaching me that things aren't always what they appear to be. Sometimes I get too caught up in my own life and don't stop to consider the issues others might be facing. I don't want to be that person anymore. I don't want to walk through life with my eyes closed. You forced them open, and I see so much more now. I see you."

"You've always seen me, Lily. You just saw me as a pain in the ass."

Chuckling, she slapped a hand to his chest.

He trapped it against him with his own, and all hints of

amusement fled. "I didn't give you or anyone else in this town a chance to look past what I was willing to show them. I'm not happy about what you've gone through, but I'm glad it brought us together. I'll never forget what a gift you are."

"Never, huh? That's a long time to not forget, cowboy." She couldn't stop the breathy quality from taking over her voice, but damn it all, the hint of a promise coated his words.

"There's nothing about you I'll ever forget, Lily. I want to memorize every taste, every touch, every line of your beautiful body."

She sucked in a shuddering breath as her legs threatened to give out. She leaned against him, her muscles putty in his hands. Steeling her nerves, she traced her fingertip along his scruffy jawline then over to rest on his bottom lip. "That's a lot to memorize. You better get started."

Chapter 26

The journey downstairs was filled with playful kisses and a trail of clothing. By the time they made it to Lily's room, she was in her black lace bra and panties. The cool air pouring from the vents wasn't enough to dim the heat consuming her. She needed it all off. Now.

Madden stood in front of her with his chest and feet bare, his jeans hanging low on his hips. Stacked muscles rippled along his torso and on his biceps, making her fingers itch to touch him. He closed her door then turned to her on a low growl.

Her toes curled into the soft rug, and desire burst into flames in her core. She reached for him, but he shook his head and avoided her touch. She jutted her bottom lip, head cocked to the side. Her long locks spilled over her shoulders. "Change your mind?"

A husky laugh rose from his throat. "You kidding me? No way. I just want to look at you. You're so damn beautiful."

She squirmed under his perusal, but not because of embarrassment or self-consciousness. He stared at her like a dying man about to devour his last meal, and she couldn't wait to give him exactly what he craved.

He stalked toward her. Fire lit his eyes, clear as day even

in the darkness of the room. Slowly, he traced his index finger down the side of her face then glided it over the exposed column of her neck until he hooked it under her bra strap. He dragged the strap over her shoulder then pressed a kiss on the shallow dent above her collarbone.

Tremors of excitement rippled along her spine, and she swallowed hard. Her rapidly beating heart was the only sound in the room.

"Should we get rid of this?" he asked, tugging on the thin material.

When she couldn't speak, he took a step back, one dark eyebrow arched high. "Should I stop?"

"No," she said, her voice nothing but a wisp of air.

Smirking, he flattened one palm on her hip and put his other finger back under her strap. He locked his gaze on hers as he trailed his knuckle from down the strap to the top of her bra. He dipped his finger inside the material and traced it along the top of her breast. "Tell me if it's too much. If there's anything you don't like. Tonight's about you, showing you how much you mean to me."

She sucked in a sharp breath as her nipples hardened. He hadn't even touched her there yet, but just the thought of his hands on her—teasing her—set her blood on fire.

His chuckle skimmed across her skin. "I like you like this."

She couldn't help but grin. "You mean practically naked?"

"That doesn't hurt. But I mean waiting." He ducked his head to replace his fingers, pushing the rest of the cup of her bra aside to free her breast. "Your body trembling and your wicked imagination wondering what I plan to do next." His tongue flicked out to trace the hard bud of her nipple as he freed the hook at her back, ridding her of the pesky patch of fabric.

She groaned and squirmed, needing more. Needing him.

He moved to take her other breast in his mouth while his hands slid down her sides to dip into her panties. He dropped to his knees, taking the lace with him to the floor.

His face was so close to her most intimate place, but not close enough. She threaded her hands in his hair and encouraged him to take her in his mouth.

Madden griped her hips in his large hands and swiped his thumb along her sensitive mound, combining it with his warm breath.

A shiver shot through Lily, shaking her knees. Her body trembled, and ragged breaths tore from her chest in quick pants. When his tongue slipped into her wetness, she tightened her grip on his hair and tugged. Her balance teetered as her head spun. She ground her hips against him, bucking and writhing as his fingers thrust inside her. His tongue moved faster. Ripples of pleasure cascaded inside her and pushed her over the edge.

Her muscles seized before her body went lax. "Holy shit, Madden."

Grinning, he stood and scooped her off her feet to carry her to the bed. He laid her gently on the soft comforter and hovered above her. "I've wanted to do that longer than I care to admit."

Lily propped herself on her elbows and flicked her glance toward his jeans. "I think it's about time to do what I've wanted."

"Yes, ma'am."

Not waiting another second, she undid the button and helped him move the thick material down his thighs. She traced the hard muscles on his back as he kicked his pants the rest of the way off then removed his boxers.

Her mouth watered as she watched him find a condom

in the back pocket of his jeans. He knelt on the bed beside her, his manhood jutting in all its glory.

"You sure you're ready for this? We can stop if you need more time."

She stared at him with her heart pounding, happiness building inside her. After everything they'd gone through, everything he'd done for her, this was one of the easiest decisions she'd ever made. "I want to take every step with you, Madden. Come here."

She opened her arms and he lowered himself on top of her, catching her mouth in his as he settled over her. She took the now-open condom from him and slid it over his dick.

He moaned, eyes closed and body still.

She moved her hands around to grip his ass and trailed kisses from the top of his shoulder, up his neck, and lingered on his delicious mouth.

He braced himself on one arm as the other hand cradled her cheek. He stared into her eyes as if he desired to know every secret she had trapped inside her brain. "You're magical, Lily. You always have been."

She smiled and pressed her lips to his palm as he entered her. She gasped, her center stretching to fit him.

He stilled, eyes wide. "You okay?"

She nodded. "Better than okay."

He grinned and began a slow, gentle movement. Each thrust sent spikes of pleasure shooting through her. She shut her eyes, savoring the feel of him. Stars burst behind her closed lids. She'd lived nearly three decades and had never felt so damn good—never felt so loved and cherished.

"Open your eyes," he said, his voice deep and gravelly.

She did as he asked and the look on his face stole her

breath. Her heart raced and ached at the same time, creating a heady combination.

He stroked the hair back from her face. "I need to see you. Watch you. I want to know the exact moment you fall apart in my arms."

She watched him watch her, studied the planes of his face as he moved inside her. Each thrust, each movement, each second joined them as one, brought them closer together in ways she couldn't imagine. Words of love and adoration sat at the tip of her tongue, but she held them back.

Spirals of pleasure rose higher and higher until it crashed into a crescendo of satisfaction. She sealed her mouth on his, licking her tongue into the wet cavern as her body was pushed to the edge for the second time by this man who'd stolen her heart.

Madden broke the kiss, his thrusts growing quicker and more frantic as he began to lose control. Hips pumping. She roamed her hands over his broad back, taking him deeper and deeper until he threw back his head and shouted her name as if she was the answer to all his prayers.

On a huff of breath, Madden collapsed and engulfed her in his arms. He rolled to the side to cradle her against him, tucking her head in the crook of his shoulder. His fingertips traced lazy circles against her biceps, and he pressed his lips to her temple as he struggled to catch his breath. "Christ, Lily. The things you do to me."

She shifted to rest a palm on his chest and stared down at him. "You, sir, are the one doing things to me."

He smiled for a beat before his expression turned serious. "My whole world has shifted in the last few days because of you."

"Is that a good thing?"

"That's a great thing. I'm so relieved you're safe, but I

hate that I don't have an excuse to be with you all the time. I don't want to be without you. Ever. And that scares the hell out of me."

Excitement fluttered in her chest like the wings of a hummingbird. "You don't have to be away from me. At least not tonight."

"I have to leave your side for a couple minutes. I'll be right back." He gave her a quick kiss and scooted off the bed and left the room.

She watched him leave, counting the seconds until he came back with a warm washcloth in his hand.

"I didn't know if you needed to wash off, so I brought this."

Touched by the gesture, of his constant thoughtfulness, she took the cloth, and he turned his back to her. She cleaned herself, tossing the washcloth in the dirty clothes hamper, then scooted under the covers. "Thank you," she said, a yawn interrupting her words.

He slid in beside her and gathered her in his arms. "Sounds like you're too tired for round two."

She snorted out a laugh. "I'll take you up on that in the morning."

"My kind of morning. Even better than coffee."

She snuggled close and listened to his even breaths. His chest rose and fell beneath her cheek until exhaustion pulled her under the dark waves of sleep.

Lily jolted awake. She blinked in rapid succession to adjust to her surroundings. Strong arms held her tight, and light snores rumbled from Madden.

That must have been what woke her. She couldn't help but laugh. Guess there's no such thing as a perfect man.

A quick glance at the clock on her nightstand told her

it was the middle of the night. Plenty of time to close her eyes and catch a few more hours of sleep before she'd be forced to leave the bed. And with any luck, after seeing to the chores on the ranch, she could talk Madden into coming right back to her room for the rest of the day.

The loud sound of a horse's panicked cry sent chills racing down Lily's spine. She jumped out of bed and grabbed her robe from the chair in the corner of the room.

"Wake up," she shouted at Madden. "Something's wrong with the horses."

She didn't wait for him to respond and ran from the room and up the stairs. More whinnies sounded from outside. Fear for the animals she loved so much pushed her out the front door.

"Oh my God." The sight of smoke billowing under the barn door stole her ability to move. She pressed a shaking hand to her mouth, not wanting to believe what was right in front of her. "No, no, no."

Another loud cry shot her forward. She had to get the horses out before they inhaled too much smoke, or the barn caught on fire and collapsed on top of them. Gravel embedded itself into her bare feet, but she barely resisted the pain. Her focus was on one thing.

Save the horses.

Reaching the barn, she yanked open the door and flew inside. Waves of smoke poured from the storage room at the back of the aisle. Horses pranced in their stalls. She covered her mouth with the inside of her elbow and coughed as she raced to the end of the aisle to get Queenie first. "Hey girl. I'm here. You're going to be just fine."

She loosened the bolt of the stall when the door at the front of the barn slammed shut. Smoke burned her lungs and her eyes watered. Terror seized her vocal cords, and she sprinted back the way she had come. She pulled on the door, but it wouldn't budge. The frantic beat of her heart combined with the chaos of the horses.

She fisted her hand and pounded it against the rough wood. "Help! Madden!"

Madden jumped out of bed. Cold air hit his skin and slapped his system awake better than any coffee. Lily had woken him from a dead sleep, yelled something, then flew out of the room like the devil himself was after her. He wasn't exactly sure what she'd said, but it couldn't be anything good to get him out of bed in the middle of the night.

Quickly finding his clothes, he dressed and jogged upstairs. "Lily? Are you up here?"

No answer.

But something in the distance caught his attention. Horses?

Shit.

A sense of urgency rushed him out the door. "Lily!"

The barn door was closed, but plumes of smoke rose from the structure. Cool, night air hit his face as he sprinted down the porch steps. Jolts of adrenaline shot through his system. No flames snaked across the structure, but billows of smoke smothered the dark sky.

Damn it, he should have brought his phone, but he couldn't turn back to grab it now. He had to get the horses out safely and pray Lily had called for help.

"Help me. Please. Let me out!"

Lily!

Her screams registered and his body moved impossibly faster. Horror clawed at his insides, and a desperate need to get Lily to safety pushed aside every other thought in his brain. He lunged for the barn door and yanked but nothing happened. He tried again, pulling as hard as he could. The hinges creaked and groaned, but the door stayed in place.

Moonlight bounced off something silver by his hand. Dread curdled in the pit of his stomach. "What the hell?"

A chain with a padlock was wrapped around the latch.

"Lily, I'm here. I can't open the door. There's a chain and padlock in place."

"What! Oh my God, Madden. Get me out of here! The smoke's getting thicker. It's hard to breathe."

"Stay low to the ground and try to keep your mouth and nose covered. Hold on, baby." He hated leaving her but had to find something to rip off the lock.

He raced to the red barn where ranch tools were kept and found a shovel. Gripping it in his hands, he sprinted back out to the stable. Sweat dotted his hairline and adrenaline zipped through his veins. "I'm back, Lily. I'll get you out of there in no time."

"I don't think you will."

A familiar voice sent a spike of fear through his heart. He twisted around as something slammed against the side of his head, and he fell to the hard ground.

Chapter 27

Seconds ticked by like hours. Lily stayed on the hard concrete floor and leaned against the wooden door. Dust and dirt clung to her skin. She held her breath, both to stop the smoke from entering her lungs and to listen for Madden. He'd been right there. About to free her. Where had he gone?

"Madden?" She yelled as loud as she could, but the smoke swimming in her system stole her voice and zapped her energy. She pounded against the wooden barrier trapping her inside the smoke-filled barn.

A coughing fit took over her body. Her lungs screamed for clean oxygen. She couldn't wait any longer. She had to find a way out.

Staggering to her feet, she crouched low and moved toward the cloud of smoke. The old stable only had one way in and one way out. No windows were inside to offer escape. She was stuck, but that didn't mean she'd sit on her ass and wait to be saved, or worse, wait for death.

Clearing the fog and fear from her mind, realization smacked her over the head. There was a water source in the barn. She needed to find the cause of the smoke and extinguish it before things got worse.

The horses whinnied in panic, stamping their hooves,

as she hurried by them. Their fear pushed her to her limits. She couldn't let them die. She had to figure out how to get them all out of there alive. Her gait was slow, and each breath harder to take than the last, but she forced herself through the wall of soot and dirty fog until she stumbled into the feed room.

Buckets. That's what she needed. Buckets of water.

Summoning all her strength, she found a large black bucket and carried it to the sink. While it filled with water, she surveyed the cloudy room, but couldn't see fire. The smoke had come from the back of the barn, so she struggled to carry the heavy bucket back into the aisle and turned toward Queenie's stall.

The mare pranced and cried, demanding attention as she passed.

"I'm sorry, girl," Lily said. "I'm doing all I can. I promise."

Speaking to the horse calmed her nerves. Made her feel as though she wasn't alone—as though she had more to fight for than just herself. Gritting her teeth, she kept moving. Her throat burned and tears fell from her eyes. She wanted nothing more than to lie down and curl into a ball, but that wasn't an option. She had her entire life ahead of her with a man she loved.

An ache spread across her chest. She should have told Madden she loved him when she had the chance. She shouldn't have let fear hold back the words. And now she might never get the chance to tell him exactly how she felt—how much joy he'd brought into her life.

The sickening sound of wood splintering snapped her back to the moment. Flames erupted on the far wall of the barn and snaked up the side. A burst of heat engulfed her, and she stumbled backward.

"No," she muttered. She couldn't combat the now-raging inferno with one lousy bucket of water at a time. Especially when she barely had the strength to carry the water at all.

The fire spread quickly to the rafters. The beam overhead morphed into a glowing red promise of death. Sparks rained down, and she covered her head with her arm to combat the onslaught of burning embers.

Hopelessness crushed her like the heavy blanket of smoke crushing her lungs. Dizziness made her head swim and pain thumped against her temples. Hours before she'd lain in Madden's arms with a whole world of possibilities stretched out before her.

Now she was moments from death. Scared. Alone. And gutted to have come so close to having everything she'd ever wanted for it all to be ripped away.

Dropping the bucket, water splashed on the concrete and up her legs. Sobs wracked her shoulders and she fell to the ground. This was it. This was how she'd die. She squeezed her eyes shut and willed her mind to take her far away.

Queenie's cry reached her ears, and an overwhelming desire to be with her mother's horse brought her to her hands and knees. Loose stones scratched her shins as she crawled to the stall. She pulled herself to her feet, opened the door and staggered inside.

Smoke and tears blurred her vision. She looped an arm around Queenie's neck and buried her face in the horse's mane.

Queenie stood motionless, her shrieks of terror gone as if she accepted her fate alongside Lily.

Lily sucked in a shuddering breath and hacking coughs tore from her mouth. She ran a palm down Queenie's broad nose. "Thank you for always being there for me, old girl. You've been such a comfort to me. I felt Mama beside me every time we rode through the mountains together or meandered across the meadows. I'm sorry I couldn't do more."

A sense of peace washed over her, as if she could feel the loving arms of her mother wrapped around her. She might not be ready to leave this earth, but at least she'd be reunited with the loved ones who went before her.

She just hoped Madden didn't blame himself. He'd done so much for her. She'd make sure to find a way for him to feel her love in the days and months to come.

Unable to keep her eyes open a second longer, she let them fall shut and brought forth an image of Madden's face. His strong jawline and beautiful eyes. The smirk she used to hate but now couldn't get enough of. The picture of him was the last thing she saw before she slid to the floor and her body finally gave in to the blessed relief of oblivion.

Pain ricocheted through Madden's brain, urging him to keep his eyes sealed shut and stay in the warm cocoon creating a fuzzy feeling around his body. But something nagged at him to shake off the pain and confusion and get to his feet.

A scream broke through his muddled thoughts.

Lily!

Fighting through the agony stabbing into the back of his head, he staggered to his feet and grabbed the shovel laying on the ground. Tingling sensations shot up and down his arms and legs as if he'd been locked in the same position for too long. His motions were slow and jerky, but he had to get to the barn. Had to break open the lock and free Lily and the horses.

"You just don't know when to quit, do you?"

The familiar voice came back to him, hitting him harder than whatever had taken him out moments before. Madden tightened his grip on his shovel and swung it around as he turned toward the voice.

The man chuckled and leapt out of the way. "Nice try. Do us both a favor and walk away. This doesn't concern you."

Madden faced his attacker. His vision blurred, and he narrowed his eyes to get a better look at the man before him. The cloud of smoke parted. A skyful of stars twinkled above and poured out enough light to highlight the man mere feet away. The broad shoulders and bushy, gray beard took shape. The sight of the constant cowboy with the burnt red material around the base of his hat was like a pickax straight though his heart.

"Marvin?" Shock made his voice rise an octave.

Marvin Williamson's ranch took up a large parcel of land on the opposite side of town. The family had been a staple in the community since before he was born. Fellow cattle ranchers had ridden the trails alongside him and his father for years.

Hell, Marvin hadn't missed a poker night for as long as Madden could remember—had been one of the few people in town who hadn't turned his back on Walter and the rest of the McKays. He couldn't be the person responsible for tormenting Lily and her father.

The person who now stood in the way of him saving the woman he loved.

The overwhelming comprehension of the depths of his feelings for Lily stole his breath. He should have told her, should have screamed it from the mountaintops, but now she was trapped in a burning barn. Her life on the line.

He wouldn't lose her. Wouldn't watch her die and forfeit the life he wanted to build with her by his side. He just needed to get past Marvin. Tightening his grip on the wooden handle of the shovel, he prepared to charge.

"Sorry, son. I didn't want you to get caught up in this mess, but I don't see any other way now. Set down that shovel." Marvin lifted a gun and aimed it at Madden's chest.

Saliva pooled in Madden's mouth as terror settled in his gut. Crouching, he laid the shovel on the grass at his feet then rose back to his full height. "You don't have to do this. It's not too late to turn things around and walk away." He hated the thought of Lily trapped in the barn, but he couldn't get to her with a gun pointed at him. If he could get Marvin talking long enough, he could figure out a way to distract him.

Marvin shook his head. "This is the way it has to be. I'm a simple man, Madden. You take what's mine, I take what's yours. Plain and simple."

Madden worked his mind over everything he knew about Marvin as well as what he'd uncovered while searching for the person responsible for hurting Lily and her father.

And then it all clicked into place.

"Mr. Tremont stole your cattle," Madden said, palms high in the night air. "You lost out on revenue, and that's why you had to branch out to training horses. I don't blame you for being pissed."

Marvin worked his jaw back and forth. "You don't steal a man's livelihood. I don't care how bad you're hurtin'. Even you and your pops had the sense to just walk away. You didn't mean to hurt anyone when you sold your land. I always understood that, even if it was a choice I could never make. But this is different. Coming onto my land and taking my cows—stealing food from my table. No, I couldn't stand back and just let it happen. Not anymore."

"I agree. Nobody should take other people down to better themselves. Is that what Mr. Tremont was doing? Using the money to feed his addiction?" He struggled to keep his voice calm as the heat from the barn engulfed him.

Marvin spat on the ground, as if just speaking about the crimes against his ranch was enough to make him sick. "I don't know what the hell he was doing, and I don't care. Don't touch my cattle. Don't steal my money." His last statement came out on a wave of fury.

"I get that, but you don't want to hurt Lily. You don't want to hurt me or Pops. You know this would kill him. You're one of his closest friends."

"Like I said, ain't got a choice anymore. You two wouldn't stop digging, no matter what I did to discourage it. Even when I hung that good for nothing ranch hand from the rafters. I figured a staged suicide made him look guilty and made him pay for stealing my cattle at the same time. But you couldn't leave it alone. I'm sorry, Madden, I really am."

A loud pop sounded behind Marvin. Flames erupted on the far side of the barn. Marvin shifted to glance at the now-burning barn, moving the gun just enough so it pointed beyond Madden into the darkness of the night.

Madden sprang into action. Scooping the shovel off the ground, he swung the tool as hard as he could. The metal connected to the side of the old man's head and vibrated Madden's arms. The sound of crunching bone combined with the crackling of the fire, creating the soundtrack to hell.

Marvin crumpled to the ground. The gun fell from his hand and bounced away from his motionless body.

Nausea bubbled in the pit of Madden's stomach. Marvin Williamson was a man he'd admired and respected, loved like family, for most of his life. He couldn't reconcile the monster who would kill an innocent woman with the man he'd always known, but he didn't have time to try. Not when Lily needed him now more than ever.

With his heart breaking, Madden plucked the gun from the patch of grass, aimed the barrel at the lock, and fired. The blast of the firearm rang in his ears. The padlock sprang loose. He ripped it off, unwound the chain, and flung the door open.

An onslaught of heat greeted him. Smoke poured outside, hitting him in the face and burning his eyes. With the inside of his elbow covering his mouth, he ran inside. "Lily!"

Nothing but the snapping fire and panicked horses answered him.

He suppressed the urge to race through the barn. The roof glowed red, prepared to give way at any moment. He squinted, and his lungs begged for clean air.

"Lily! Where are you?"

Moving quickly, he struggled to see through the dense smoke and falling embers. As he passed each stall, he opened the door. Horse after horse galloped toward the exit. The smoke thickened until he spotted the last stall door, which was open, but the horse stood tall and proud inside.

Queenie!

Gritting his teeth, he shoved aside the pain and fear and suffocating sensation of his lungs struggling to take in air. He followed his instinct. If all was lost, Lily would want to be with the animal she loved like no other.

She'd want to be with her mom.

Racing into the stall, he caught sight of Lily curled in a ball at Queenie's feet. Her eyes closed. Dirt and soot covered her face, her hair a tangled mess. Relief crashed over him like healing water but fear still remained. He scooped her into his arms. "I'm here, baby. I've got you."

Her eyes fluttered open and she gripped the neck of his T-shirt with weak fingers. "Save Queenie."

"You heard her, Queenie. Get going."

The horse whinnied, left the stall and sprinted down the aisle, Madden quickly on her heels. His skin was hot, blistering from the fallen embers. He coughed and sent spikes of pine into his scorched throat. A piece of the loft crashed to the floor, and he jumped back to avoid being crushed by the burning wood.

Lily curled against him and buried her face in his neck.

"I've got you," he said, praying it was true.

He leapt over the spreading flames. Stumbling outside, he drew in large gulps of fresh air. He carried her as far away from the barn as he could until his legs gave out and he settled onto the cool grass.

The sound of sirens screamed in the distance. Flames overtook the barn. The structure shuddered and groaned before collapsing into a giant pile of burning rubble.

Watching the destruction, he cradled Lily on his lap. "We made it, Lily. The horses are safe. You're safe. It's all over."

Her eyes slid shut again, but a flicker of a smile shone through her dirty face. "I love you, Madden."

He kissed her forehead and held her close. "I love you, too. I need you to stay awake, okay? Sounds like help's on the way."

She snuggled against him, and a cough shook her body. "Don't need help. All I need is you."

Chapter 28

Lily sat in the back of a parked ambulance with a blanket wrapped around her shoulders, but nothing could stop her teeth from chattering as she watched the collapsed barn burn.

Not even Madden's body heat helped as he kept his arms firmly around her.

"You've got to keep the oxygen on your mouth and nose." A young paramedic gently placed the mask back on her face then checked her heartbeat. The woman's hair was cut short and pushed away from her round, serious face. "How are you feeling? Any dizziness or nausea?"

Lily drew in a deep breath of the clean oxygen, closing her eyes as it slid into her body and helped push out the toxins. Opening her eyes, words escaped her as she watched the horse barn she'd spent so much time in continue to burn to ash. Firefighters circled the damage and doused the persistent flames with streams of water from their giant hoses. Plumes of smoke covered everything it touched like fog. The eerie glow cracked and popped, sending embers shooting across the night sky like stars.

"Lily?"

Madden's soothing voice brought her back to the question lingering in the confined space. Clearing her dry throat, she slid the mask down despite the EMT's disapproving look. "Sorry. I already told you. I feel okay. Just tired and thirsty. I still can't believe this happened. Are the horses okay?"

"Dax called and said they're all tucked in back at Pop's place. He'll keep an eye on them."

The EMT placed a stethoscope on her back. "Deep breaths in and out. I need to listen to your lungs."

She did as was asked and winced. The burning in her lungs had subsided, but taking the deep breath still took more effort than it should.

"You sound okay." The woman looped the stethoscope around her neck then placed clammy fingers on her wrist to check her pulse. "But smoke inhalation is extremely dangerous, and you both have burns that need to be cleaned and examined. Hang tight for a few. I'm going to grab more oxygen and an extra mask for you," she said, nodding toward Madden. "Excuse me for a second. When I get back, we'll head to the hospital."

Madden picked up a bottle of water beside him and unscrewed the cap. "Drink this."

Lily removed the mask, took the ice-cold bottle with a trembling hand and pressed it to her lips. Cool liquid coated her mouth and glided down her throat. "It's a miracle Dax saw the fire from your dad's and called for help. Thank God he did, or this could have spread so fast. I could have lost so much more."

Madden skimmed his knuckles along her cheekbone. "I could have lost you."

She folded her hand over his and squeezed. "But you didn't."

Tears glittered in his eyes. "It was close. So damn close. I don't want to diminish any of this," he said, flicking his wrist toward the chaos around them. "But barns can be rebuilt. Things replaced. If I'd have lost you… Lily, I wouldn't have survived that."

"You didn't lose me, Madden. You saved me. Without you, I don't want to think about what would have happened tonight." Memories of the terror she experienced in that barn, her fear and sadness, flooded over her. She'd been ready to accept her fate, but that didn't mean her heart hadn't broken at the thought of never seeing Madden again.

"You never have to wonder what would happen without me, Lily. I love you so damn much." Madden replaced the mask and kissed her forehead. "Now do as you're told so we don't get in trouble."

She smiled as the clean air filtered through her nose. There was more she wanted to say to this man, but she could wait. She told him the most important part, and now they had the rest of their lives ahead of them to say everything else.

The screech of a siren sounded as a second ambulance peeled out of the driveway, taking away Marvin Williamson.

Madden tensed beside her.

Before she could ask him anything, the sound of heavy boots clomping on gravel grew closer. Deputy Sanders approached, his expression twisted in a heavy mask of pain and confusion. "Madden. Lily. Glad you're both all right."

Madden gave one, brief nod. "Thanks. It's been one hell of a night."

Deputy Sanders snorted and kicked at the ground.

"Did you have any idea about Marvin?" Madden asked, his voice coated in sadness.

"Not a clue." Deputy Sanders ran a hand over his face. "God, what the hell was he thinking? He should have come to me. Told me what was going on. I would have helped any way that I could. We all would have. Instead, he took matters into his own hands and ruined countless lives including his own. This will devastate Beth."

Lily tried to find sympathy for Mrs. Williamson. It was difficult as she sat in the back of an ambulance after suffering at the hands of the woman's husband. But she understood how it felt to be caught in the crosshairs of someone else's secrets.

She drew in one more breath of oxygen then lowered her mask. "Mrs. Williamson will have a ton of people rallying behind her just like I did."

Madden slid an arm around her waist and kissed her temple before returning his attention to Deputy Sanders. "Is Marvin going to make it?"

Her body tensed as she waited for the answer. As much as she hated the hell Mr. Williamson had put her through, she didn't want his death on Madden's conscience.

"He's hanging in there," Deputy Sanders said. "Not sure if he'll make it, but if he does, he'll spend the rest of his life behind bars, along with Jason Simon who just woke from surgery. I'm so sorry all this happened." Dipping his chin, he walked away, his head bent and shoulders stooped.

Lily let her gaze drift back to the destruction on her property. The flames had died down, and the firefighters were busy packing up their equipment. A weight sat on her chest. "What now?"

"Now we go to the hospital and make sure we're okay then head home and go to bed."

She snorted. "That's not what I meant."

"I know, but it's the next step. Then tomorrow we wake up and we take the next one then the next."

"What if I don't know what that next step should be?"

"You do. Listen to your gut, Lily. Look at the options. You can do anything you set your mind to, and I'll be right here to help."

"As long as I have you, everything else will fall into place. I love you, Madden." Exhaustion hit her like a brick wall, and she rested her head on his shoulder. The future waited for her to make it whatever she wanted, but right now, everything she could ever want was right beside her.

Three days later, anxiety rolled around in Madden's gut. He'd assumed racing into a roaring fire to save the woman he loved would be the most stressful event of his life. But that didn't hold a candle to standing outside the hospital room of his girlfriend's father, waiting to see him.

Dax stood beside him with his arms folded across his chest and way too much amusement on his stupid face. "How ya feeling?"

"Fine," Madden snapped. "I don't know why you're even here."

Despite Madden's reassurances that Dax could care for the horses, Lily had insisted they visit his father's ranch every morning to care for her animals. He'd made her promise to take it easy and was helping Dax himself when the call from the hospital came. Dax had insisted on driving them, even though Madden still didn't understand why.

"Moral support for my brother of course." Grinning, Dax peered through the thin rectangular window on the closed door. "She must be relieved he's awake."

Madden's skin itched, but he couldn't show his little brother his nerves. "She was shocked when the doctor called this morning. Relieved, yeah, but also anxious. There are a lot of questions that still need to be answered. Hearing them won't be easy."

"Sometimes the things we need to hear might not be easy, but they're necessary. They help us grow and be better versions of ourselves."

Madden's jaw dropped. "Where the hell did that bit of wisdom come from?"

Dax shrugged. "Who knows. Don't expect it to happen again."

Madden laughed, suddenly grateful to have his brother with him. "I'm nervous, man. I've promised Lily that what her father thinks about us won't change anything, but what if it's a hurdle we can't overcome?"

"Bullshit," Dax said, scratching his chin.

"Excuse me?"

"I get the nerves. The rest is bullshit. You and Lily have been through more in the last few days than most couples have in a lifetime. You two were made for each other, always have been. Her dad's opinion won't change that."

His brother's no-nonsense response loosened some of the knots in his stomach. "You really think so?"

"You'll find out soon. Here comes Lily."

All his nerves settled in the base of his throat and made it hard to breathe.

The door swung open, and Lily offered a tight smile. "You ready?"

"As I'll ever be."

Not wanting there to be any doubt of his intentions, he linked his hand with Lily's and walked into the room.

Mr. Tremont lay in his bed. The tubes were out of his throat, but an IV still pumped fluids into his veins. The top of the mattress was inclined to help elevate his torso. His wrinkles were more pronounced than before and his hair mussed, but there was no mistaking the spark of interest in his narrowed eyes.

"Good to see you awake, Mr. Tremont." Madden nodded in greeting.

"Good to be awake." The older man hacked out a cough then held out a finger toward the plastic cup of water on his side table.

Lily grabbed the cup and lifted the straw to her father's lips.

He took a long sip then leaned back on his pillow with a sigh. "Thank you, sweetheart." He shifted to stare at Madden. "My daughter's filled me in on a few things. The most important being how you protected her. You saved her life. I'm grateful."

The curt words were nicer than anything Mr. Tremont had ever said to him, but that's not what he wanted. Madden wanted his blessing—or at least a commitment to not disapprove—of their relationship. "I'd give my life for her, sir. I love her with my whole heart."

Mr. Tremont worked his jaw back and forth. A few seconds of excruciating silence lingered in the room. "I love her, too. She's my world. I hate that my actions put her in danger. I got involved with some bad people to try and save my ranch. When I couldn't pay them, I made more bad decisions that put both our lives in danger. I'll never be able to express how sorry I am."

Lily smoothed a palm over her dad's arm. "We all make mistakes. What matters is you're alive."

"Madden, thank you for keeping Lily safe. She's going to need you over the next weeks and months as I continue to pay for my crimes."

"Dad, we don't have to talk about that now," Lily said, sniffing back tears. "Your only job is to focus on getting healthy."

Mr. Tremont patted her hand. "I just want to get everything out in the open while I can. I need to make sure you're taken care off when I'm not around."

Madden slipped an arm around her waist and held Mr. Tremont's stare. "Your daughter is strong. Stronger than me. She doesn't need me to take care of her, but I'll stand beside her as long as she'll let me. I can promise you that."

"Then I can rest easy." He closed his eyes. "Lily, tell the deputies I'm ready to talk to them. It's time."

"I'll be back later, Daddy." Lily kissed his forehead then led the way back out to the hallway where she wiped tears from her cheeks. "Damn that man. I can't believe he ever thought working with a drug dealer was the answer to saving the ranch. No wonder he never let me look at the finances or took any of my suggestions to bring in more revenue. He was busy peddling drugs around town."

"If he was using the drug money to keep the ranch afloat, why did he steal cattle?" He hated making Lily retell the transgressions her father had just admitted to, but curiosity got the better of him.

"Daniel dipped into the profits and Jason Simon was hell-bent on making him pay. Dad got the idea to rustle cattle. He and Daniel worked together to steal from ranchers to make enough money to keep their debtors at bay, but when things got worse, Jason Simon decided to take matters into his own hands. He went after Dad before he could find a different way out of his mess. I guess Mr. Williamson connected the dots when things went south."

Not knowing what to say, he pulled her into his arms and held her tight. "He has a big heart. He just didn't make the best decisions."

She melted against him. "And he'll pay the price. But at least he's alive. The rest, we'll figure out as it comes." She pulled back and stared at him with rounded eyes. "Did you mean what you said? About standing beside me? Even after finding out what my dad has done?"

"Are you kidding me? Love isn't contingent on anything, especially the deeds of our fathers. And thank God for that or you and I would never stand a chance. Pop's been crucified for years, and your dad did a stupid thing to save his ranch. They both had their reasons. But we aren't our parents. We get to make our lives exactly what we want, and for my life, all I want is to be yours."

She grinned through her tears. "And all I want is to be yours."

Dax came around the corner and shook his head. "My God, could you two be any more adorable? Enough of this sappy crap, please. Can we head home? I've got stuff to do."

"How is it possible I can't remember a time you weren't interrupting me and Lily?" Madden asked.

"Just lucky, I guess. Come on. Let's go." Dax didn't wait for a response but started for the exit.

Lily giggled and tugged Madden's hand to fall in step beside her. "Better catch our ride. I'll get ahold of the sheriff's department on the way back to the ranch. Let Dad rest for a little bit before he's forced to go over everything again."

"You're okay leaving?"

"I just want to go home and focus on the good. Besides, we need to figure out what to do with that clean slate. I have a wedding to put on."

Smiling, Madden squeezed her hand. They walked into the sunny morning filled with hope for a future they would build together.

Epilogue

Three months later, the evening sun hovered just above the mountains. Pride swelled Lily's chest as she took in the rewards of all her hard work. Swirls of pink and orange across the dazzling sky mingled with the autumn flowers weaved into the arched branches that stood at the end of the white runner. Rows of empty chairs sat on either side of the makeshift aisle, facing the place where the happy couple had become husband and wife moments before.

Lily stood under the archway and listened to the hum of music that floated her way from the giant white tent. Bistro lights blinked to life, and the wedding guests mingled along the perimeter of the tent watching the bride and groom sway to their first dance.

"Looks like you're a hit." Madden strolled down the aisle with his hands in the pockets of his black dress pants. He'd loosened his blue striped tie and rolled up the sleeves of his white button-up shirt past his elbows. His black cowboy hat pulled the whole look together.

The result was lethal.

"Not too hard to put on a killer wedding when this is your backdrop." She waved her hand overhead, indicating the cascade of wildflowers that danced toward the gurgling stream beyond. Cloud Peak stood tall and proud in the distance.

"Don't sell yourself short. You did a magnificent job."

His praise heated her cheeks. "I couldn't have done it without everyone's help. You were right. People wanted to lend a hand. From Eve catering to Charlie helping to clear the destroyed barn to Reid and Dax being my handymen. Even your dad helped me set up the chairs. It took a wonderful village."

The lazy smile she loved so much lifted one corner of his mouth. "A wonderful village with our fearless leader." He settled his hands on her hips and rested his forehead on hers. "Have I told you how beautiful you look today? I really like this dress."

She smoothed a hand over the dusty pink silk. "I'm glad you like it. I was afraid the neckline was too low."

"No such thing." He scrunched his nose as if even the thought of her covering her cleavage repulsed him. "This whole day has been almost perfect."

She stared up at him through the long wisps of hair blowing across her face. "Almost?"

"I can think of one thing that would push the day over the edge to perfection." He slid his hand into his pocket and pulled out a black ring box before dropping onto one knee.

"What are you doing?" She covered her open mouth with both hands. Excitement dipped low in her stomach.

"Lily Kay Tremont, you've brought more joy into my world than I thought possible. You've helped me build a community. Helped me rebuild my family. Helped me build a life I love and am proud of. You make me a better man, and I want to spend the rest of my life proving to you I'm the best man for you. I love you, Lily. Will you be my wife?"

"Yes!" she squealed. "One hundred percent yes."

He slid a square cut diamond on a rose gold band onto her finger.

She gasped and held it up for a better view. "It's perfect, Madden," she said, throwing herself into his arms. "Just like you. I can't wait to continue this wonderful life with you."

Lifting her in the air, he kissed her long and slow.

Whoops and cheers broke them apart, and he set her on her feet.

Laughing, she noticed their friends and family standing outside the tent.

Madden hoisted her hand high in the air. "She said yes!" He pulled her back into his arms, and they slowly swayed to the music in the distance. "Looks like we have a wedding to plan. Know anyone who can help?"

"I might know someone. Thank you for loving me, Madden."

"Anytime."

She rested her head on his shoulder and sighed. Life would always have its ups and downs, its twists and turns, but as long as she had Madden by her side, they could conquer anything.

* * * * *

Harlequin® Reader Service

Enjoyed your book?

Try the perfect subscription for Romance readers and get more great books like this delivered right to your door.

See why over 10+ million readers have tried Harlequin Reader Service.

Start with a Free Welcome Collection with free books and a gift—valued over $20.

Choose any series in print or ebook. See website for details and order today:

TryReaderService.com/subscriptions